Anna Jacobs was born in Lancashire, but emigrated to Australia. She has worked as a teacher, lecturer and human resources officer. She and her husband have two grown-up daughters. She is the author of over forty novels — including the acclaimed Gibson Family saga, beginning with *Salem Street*.

Anna Jacobs also wrote *Family Connections* and *Kirsty's Vineyard*.

CHESTNUT LANE

When novelist Sophie Carr rescues a man hiding in her garden from a group of paparazzi, she finds that her neighbour is ageing pop star Jez Winter. She's loved his music for years and knows he's had a tough time lately: an intruder having slashed his face, then a car accident putting his ability to play music at risk. Life's not been easy for Sophie either, losing her husband just as she was taking off as a novelist and having difficulties with her control freak son William and her daughter Andi, who is into recreational drugs and has lost her way in life since her father's death. And Sophie also has a secret to hide. One that makes her very wary of getting involved with Jez.

ANNA JACOBS

CHESTNUT LANE

Complete and Unabridged

CHARNWOOD
Leicester

First published in Great Britain in 2008 by
Severn House Publishers Ltd.
Surrey

First Charnwood Edition
published 2009
by arrangement with Severn House Publishers Ltd.
Surrey

The moral right of the author has been asserted

Except where actual historical events and characters
are being described for the storyline of this novel, all
situations in this publication are fictitious and any
resemblance to living persons is purely coincidental.

British Library CIP Data

Jacobs, Anna
    Chestnut Lane.—Large print ed.—
Charnwood library series
1. Women novelists—Fiction 2. Widows—Family
relationships—Fiction 3. Rock musicians—Fiction
4. Love stories 5. Large type books
I. Title
823.9′14 [F]

ISBN 978–1–84782–497–4

Published by
F. A. Thorpe (Publishing)
Anstey, Leicestershire

Set by Words & Graphics Ltd.
Anstey, Leicestershire
Printed and bound in Great Britain by
T. J. International Ltd., Padstow, Cornwall

This book is printed on acid-free paper

1

Sophie was strolling through her garden when she saw a man standing under the huge horse chestnut tree that overhung the wall to mesh branches with a similar tree next door. If he'd been facing her way she'd have run, but he had his back to her and didn't seem at all interested in her house. He was standing on a garden seat, hidden by the mass of leaves, peering over the wall at the house next door.

She stopped dead, wondering what to do. He must have come through the old wooden gate that led next door but it was closed now. Was he hiding from someone or spying on them? Curiosity kept her standing there even though she knew the sensible thing would be to creep quietly back indoors and call for help.

But she wasn't the sensible type, as her son pointed out regularly. William was still furious that she'd wasted her money on such a large house — not necessary for one person, he insisted regularly — but she loved living there. It wasn't for the prestige of a Chestnut Lane address, but because the house had spacious rooms and a larger than average garden and that felt good.

Curious, she hid behind a bush. As she watched, the man rubbed a hand to and fro across his forehead as if he was tired and had a headache. He stiffened suddenly and she too heard something from the direction in which he was gazing — men's lowered voices, meant only for one another to hear. But sounds carried clearly in the still air of an early spring day.

The stranger's fists clenched, then he stepped off the bench and swung round, his eyes scanning the garden as if looking for somewhere to hide. As he began to limp slowly towards her, his face was revealed, showing recent scarring on one side. She gasped in surprise as she realized who he was: *Jez Winter!* No doubt about it.

Why was one of the most famous pop stars of her youth creeping round her garden? He didn't do much performing these days but still had the ability to turn out albums that sold steadily, and when he gave one of his rare concerts, he filled the biggest venues to overflowing. She loved his music and owned all his albums. That hawk-like face was hard to forget and the years hadn't dimmed its appeal to her or to many other women.

Her gasp made him turn sharply in her direction, so she moved out from behind the bush and stood motionless. She hoped that showed him she meant no harm, but she had no idea what to do next.

As he saw her, his lips mouthed, 'Oh, hell!' and he froze, swaying a little, his face so pale it seemed as if his features had been drawn on white paper with a charcoal stick.

From behind the boundary fence one man called, 'I'm *sure* he went that way. Let's go after him. I'm not losing a good story now.' Footsteps began moving towards them again.

That must be the paparazzi, who had been in the news themselves ever since the accident for hounding Winter, trying to get photos of his injuries. Even Sophie, who didn't pay much attention to the doings of celebrities, knew about that.

It was the way her trespasser's shoulders slumped that touched her heart and made up her mind. Placing one forefinger on her lips, she beckoned with the other hand.

He stared at her so numbly she had to repeat the gesture before he mouthed, 'Thanks,' and moved forward.

She led the way back to the house, walking on the grass instead of the paths, trying not to make any noise. As they got near the kitchen door she heard a voice call, 'There's a gate here!'

Unlocking the rear door, she went quickly inside and waited for Jez to join her before locking the door carefully behind them. She'd had a burglar the previous year soon after she moved in, so she never, ever left an outer door or window unlocked, not even if she was only walking round her own garden. That seemed very sad, but she lived in an upmarket area and she'd accepted the fact that it made her more of a target for burglars.

'Come through into my sitting room. It looks out on to an internal courtyard, so you'll be safe from prying eyes there.'

He followed her, limping slightly. 'I'm grateful.'

She gestured to a chair. 'Do sit down. You look exhausted.'

'I am. It's taking longer to recover than I'd expected. I thought I'd covered my tracks today, but those sods seem to be psychic about sussing out where I'm going.' He studied her face and said with a wry smile, 'You recognized me.'

'Hard not to. I enjoy your music, have done for years. And when you had the accident, it headed the TV news for a few days, as have your visits to hospital for plastic surgery. I didn't know they'd let you out of hospital after the latest.'

'They haven't. I let myself out early this morning, couldn't face another day penned up in there. Thank goodness this was the last operation. The gutter press had been baying at the door for days and if I hadn't had a bodyguard outside my room, that fellow presently lurking next door would have got his precious photo of this and earned a fortune at my expense.' His voice was bitter as he jerked a thumb towards the scarred side of his face.

He stared blindly into the distance for a moment or two then said in a voice which grated with frustration, 'I'll pay you well to let me stay here until I can get someone from my security team to pick me up.'

She stiffened. 'Why should I need paying?'

Silence, then his shoulders moved in the tiniest of shrugs. 'People usually do.'

'Well, I'd be ashamed to take money from someone in trouble.'

He looked at her properly then, studying her face as if to peel off the layers of skin and find out what she was really thinking. His expression slowly softened, as if he liked what he saw. 'Then may I please stay here until someone can come and fetch me? I don't intend to go back to that hospital, but my security staff will have to set up a temporary refuge while I house-hunt. I suppose it'll have to be a hotel again because the journos know where my old flat is.' He sighed. 'And anyway, I hate that place. It's where I had the intruder. If I hadn't had the accident shortly afterwards, I'd have found a new home by now.'

She smiled. 'You've had a bad year.'

'Tell me about it. That's why I was looking at the house next door. I lost my last home in the divorce settlement, but that place was more to *her* taste than mine anyway. Well, one big house is much like another, isn't it?'

She didn't comment on his public quarrels and violent break-up with his second wife. That marriage had lasted less than a year. Although his music was beautiful, his private life hadn't been anything to boast about.

Sophie, on the other hand, had loved her husband dearly and been desolate when he died. Her two grown-up children still missed their father, she knew. She'd made a satisfying new life for herself because you had to move on, you couldn't bring them back. And ironically, she was quite well off now, hadn't needed his insurance money, because she was suddenly wildly successful in her own right. 'Yes, of course you can stay here until your friends come for you. Is the house next door for sale? It's been empty for so long, I thought they were going to knock it down and build smaller places. Not many people can afford a huge house with staff quarters these days.'

'It is for sale. They couldn't get planning permission to knock it down because it's a listed building. I thought if I viewed it without the usual circus, if I stayed indoors all the time I was there and only looked out at the gardens, then perhaps no one would notice me and I could get a feel for the place. I got details of houses a day or two ago and sent for some of the keys but told them I'd show myself round.'

Another of those bitter twists to his lips. She ached to see anyone so unhappy, especially someone who'd given her so much pleasure. Best to let him talk it out, she decided.

'They couldn't send the keys over fast enough, knowing who I was. Anyway, this morning I took a taxi and went out without a minder, something I've not done for years. It was no good, though. Those pests must have had people watching the entrance to the hospital delivery area, where I sneaked out, or else someone tipped them off. I didn't even get inside the house. They turned up just after my taxi left. Luckily I saw them before they saw me, but I must have made too much noise getting away from them or left tracks. That garden's badly overgrown.'

He closed his eyes for a moment, muttering, 'I wish to hell they'd leave me alone.'

'It must be hard living in the limelight all the time.'

'You'd think I'd be used to it by now, but as you get older you crave a bit of peace.'

He still looked as wary as a cornered animal,

6

she thought. Well, that's what he was, really. 'Would you like a coffee while you're waiting? I was just going to make some. And I have some home-made cake.'

He looked faintly surprised, then nodded. 'I would, actually. If it's not too much trouble.'

'No trouble at all.'

There was a knock on the front door and he stiffened again.

She got up. 'Better if I answer it, don't you think? It'd look strange not to.' She laid one hand on his shoulder as she passed him, could feel the tension there. 'Don't worry. I won't give you away.'

When she opened the door, she found three men waiting, one with a camera at the ready. 'Can I help you?'

'Did anyone come to your door?'

'No, but I did wonder if I heard a noise down that side of the house a few minutes ago.' She pointed. 'I thought it was a fox after the birds. I have a feeder out there and — '

Two of them ran off in that direction without a word. Only the third one bothered to toss her a quick 'Thanks', before pounding after his colleagues.

Nasty creatures! she thought as she locked the door again. She turned to see her visitor standing in the doorway of her living room.

'I'm grateful.'

'You're welcome. Now, coffee and cake. I'll bring it through.'

When she carried the tray in, he was slumped in a chair, one hand covering his eyes.

'Here you are.'

He mustn't have heard her coming because he jumped in shock, then tried to smile.

'Don't,' she told him gently.

'Don't what?'

'Force a smile. And you needn't chat at all if you don't want to. Just sit there quietly and rest. You can test the cake for me and give me your honest opinion. It's a new skill of mine, baking. I always used to worry about being too big, but now I've given up on trying to look like a stick insect. My genes aren't programmed for it, anyway. I concentrate on enjoying life — though that doesn't mean I eat a ton of junk food.'

'That's the first time I've heard a woman say that.'

She grinned. 'I can't tell you how comfortable it is to eat what you want. And I've not put any weight on. This seems to be my natural size and it's comfortable to live with, even if it doesn't suit the fashionistas.' She poured his coffee, gave him a piece of cake then cut one for herself, looking out at the small water garden in the central courtyard as she ate, not attempting to make conversation.

After a while he put down the mug and empty plate. 'Thank you. That's the first food I've enjoyed for a long time.'

'Good. It's the first almond cake I've ever made. It's hard to find recipes without wheat in them. I'm wheat-intolerant, you see.'

'Coeliac?'

'Worse. I seem to be intolerant of all cereals except rice.'

'Must be a nuisance.'

'Sometimes. But far worse things than that can happen to a person.'

'Well, the cake's delicious, whatever's in it. Um, would you mind if I — ' He broke off. 'No, I shouldn't ask.'

'Go ahead. I can always say no.'

'Could I stay here for a bit longer, please? It's so peaceful. And you're the first person I've met in a long time who doesn't try to fill the silences with babble or pester me with questions about how I'm feeling.'

'I enjoy silence.'

'So do I. Which may sound strange coming from a muso.'

'I don't think so. We all need peaceful times in our lives. I love your music, by the way.' She waved one hand towards her CD collection. 'I have all your albums. Such beautiful melodies. 'Tears May Fall' is my favourite track.'

This time his smile was unforced. 'It's one of mine, too.'

'Stay as long as you like.' She stood up. 'I'll be in my office. When you want some company, come and find me. There's no hurry. I'm at the far end of the corridor. I'm only working on correspondence today, so I can stop and start at will. Oh, and the cloakroom is on the left.'

It was a full hour before she heard movement, first the sound of him limping along the corridor then water flushing in the cloakroom. After that the footsteps came towards her office, so she turned to greet him.

He stood framed in the doorway, still looking

9

utterly exhausted. 'I've just realized I don't even know your name. I do apologize. It was very rude of me not to ask.'

'Sophie.'

'No second name?'

'Sophie Carr.'

He frowned. 'That sounds vaguely familiar.'

She picked up one of her books and handed it to him in silence.

'You're a novelist.'

'Yes.'

'I've not read a novel for ages. I must buy a copy of this. Unless it's full of angst and violence. I couldn't stand that at the moment, I'm afraid, however well written.'

She wasn't surprised. A deranged intruder had broken into his home and held a knife to his throat, then a month later he'd been involved in a car accident, which had badly damaged his left side. 'You're quite safe with my books. I write relationships novels. Women's fiction, they call it sometimes, though men read my stories too and email to tell me they've enjoyed them. And the stories always, always have happy endings, because it's my choice for the hero and heroine to get together.'

His expression was bleak. 'It's a nice fantasy — that relationships can be happy, I mean.'

'My parents were happily married for fifty-nine years. Where's the fantasy in that?'

'Sorry. Didn't mean to sound so negative. But you must admit that's unusual these days.'

'I was happily married too, for twenty-seven years.'

'Was?'

'Bill died a few years ago. If he hadn't, we'd still have been together.'

His voice was gentle. 'I'm sorry.'

'I'm used to it now, but he just dropped dead one day, so it was a dreadful shock. Heart attack.' She wasn't sure her daughter was over it, even now. Andi had been such a daddy's girl. 'Anyway, how about some lunch? It's only leftover chicken and mushroom risotto.'

'Are you sure?'

'Of course I am.'

'I'd love to, but I'd better make a phone call first.'

'To your minders?' When he nodded, she said quietly, 'Do it later. Enjoy the meal first.'

The wary look had returned to his face, so she spoke bluntly. 'I'm not trying to get anything from you. If I can do a good deed — for anyone, anyone at all, doesn't matter whether they're rich or poor — I do it willingly. After I lost Bill, my friends were so kind to me, so tolerant of my grief, and they helped me with — other problems. I vowed to pass on that kindness.' She saw him relax. A smile lifted the corners of his mouth briefly and he put up one hand to brush back his jaw-length hair, a familiar gesture to his fans, something of a trademark. The brown hair was streaked with grey now, but he was still a very attractive man.

'So I'm your good deed for the day?'

She chuckled. 'I suppose so. If I pull the blinds down, you could come and sit in the kitchen while I heat the risotto.'

11

She worked quickly, getting out cheese, rice biscuits and a bottle of sparkling water to finish the meal.

He didn't talk much, but he ate everything she set before him and looked much more relaxed afterwards.

'I'd forgotten how good simple meals can be,' he said as he pushed his cheese plate away. 'That was wonderful. They give me fancy towers of food at the hotel, which look beautiful, but there's not much substance to them and they're awkward to eat.'

She chuckled. 'I know what you mean. They fall all over the plate. Drives me crazy. Shall we take our coffee out into the courtyard? It's sheltered and sunny, and the wall's too high for people to see over.'

'I'd like that. You have a very restful home.'

'Thank you. It's what I was trying for.'

'Did you and your husband live here?'

'No. I felt it better to have a change once I'd sorted out a few problems and was thinking straight again. My books had taken off by then so I could afford to buy a place on Chestnut Lane.'

When he'd finished the coffee, Jez fell asleep between one sentence and the next, the faint frown that had seemed a permanent fixture smoothing from his forehead as his eyes closed.

She tiptoed away and went back into her office. It had been a strange sort of day.

Poor man. Money didn't buy you happiness, did it? Well, she'd found that out herself, though she wasn't in Jez Winter's league money-wise, nowhere near. It was so unfair that she'd done well as a writer only after Bill's death, so the husband who'd supported her through all those years of rejections hadn't reaped the rewards.

A story idea slid into her mind, the way they did sometimes, and she sat very still, letting it flourish and bring other details about the characters with it. Suddenly she knew exactly how she was going to start this new book. Forgetting her guest completely, she created a new computer file and began roughing out the opening scene.

★   ★   ★

When Jez woke up, he couldn't think where he was and jerked upright in the comfortable recliner chair, staring round in panic.

It was a book lying on the table that reminded him of his rescue by — what was she called? Oh, yes, Sophie. An unlikely heroine, softly curved, gently spoken and nothing like the elegant, brittle women he seemed to attract these days.

He stood up, wincing at his stiffness. The left side, which had caught the brunt of the car smash, had been damaged in so many ways. He looked down at his hand. The feeling was nearly back in full now, thank heavens. At first it had seemed as if he'd lost the ability to play guitar or piano properly and no amount of reassurances by his specialist and a top physiotherapist that things would improve had taken away that fear. It had haunted many a sleepless night till the improvement began to show and he was able to make music again, albeit very clumsily at first.

His hand was a little less dexterous than it had been but was still improving, and he could play well enough for his own pleasure, not to mention his needs as a composer. He wasn't a concert pianist or a classical guitarist, after all. Even if he did more gigs — and he wasn't at all sure he wanted to bother — it was writing music he enjoyed most these days, and recording it in his own studio.

He also jammed occasionally with a few old friends, solely for their own pleasure. When these friends, also famous, were in London, they usually managed a get-together, though that didn't happen often enough for him.

Half the guys who'd been his friends in the early days were dead now, though. Just like the cliché, they'd succumbed to sex, drugs and rock and roll. He'd tried all those things, too, but had settled for the music. Unlike drugs, it didn't come back to bite you. And sex was overrated, really. He hadn't felt much need since he and Cheryl had split.

He walked out of the sitting room, past a wide staircase and along to the cloakroom, then on to the office. Sophie was sitting at the computer, her fingers flying across the keyboard, her shoulder-length, honey-coloured hair gleaming in a stray ray of sunshine, showing occasional silver threads. Not dyed, then. What a pretty colour it was!

She seemed to sense his presence and swung round, her smile as gentle and friendly as everything else about her. He wished . . . he didn't know what he wished. But he'd enjoyed her company and her peaceful house so much, he didn't want to leave. It had been like an oasis in a desert.

'Enjoy your sleep?'

'Yes. Very refreshing. But now I really must phone my security staff for help.'

She nodded and turned back to her computer.

In the sitting room he took out his mobile, switching it on, selecting a number, dialing, then watching a bird come to the feeder outside and peck happily away. Someone picked up at the other end before the phone could ring a second time. Kevin. His chief of security and general factotum.

'Where the hell have you been, Jez?'

'I slipped the leash and went to visit that big house in Hampstead.'

'We saw the keys were missing and Craig went there. He found no sign of you.'

'Yeah, well, the press got on to me and I had to escape.'

'Where are you now? Somewhere safe, I hope?'

'I'm next door. I was given refuge by the owner. She's been really kind.'

'Why didn't you ring sooner?'

'I fell asleep. Best sleep I've had for weeks, actually.'

Kevin's voice softened. 'That's good. What number are you at?'

'Damned if I know. Have to go and ask her. It's one of a group of four *desirable modern residences*. Hold on a minute.' Jez strolled back to the office, feeling guilty about interrupting Sophie again. 'What's the number of this house, please?'

She told him, but he could see she was itching to return to her work. 'I'll — um, just . . . '

By the time he reached the door, her fingers were clicking away again. He felt vaguely miffed, then shook his head at himself. *Conceited sod! You can't expect everyone to hang on your words.*

The voice on the mobile squawked at him, reminding him of what he'd gone to find out, so he passed on the number to Kevin.

'I'll ring you back when we've got something arranged. Will she let you stay till then, Jez?'

'I don't think she'll even notice whether I'm here or not.'

'You must be slipping. Or else she's over eighty.'

'She's younger than me, but she's got a life. She's a novelist, Sophie Carr. Have you heard of her?'

'Yeah. She's one of my wife's favourite authors.'

'Get Donna to buy me her books.'

'Which ones? She's written quite a few.'

'All of them. I need something to do while I'm recovering. You can't play a guitar all the time.' And he'd still got a long way to go before he'd be bouncing around the universe again.

He didn't like to disturb his hostess so wandered through the ground-floor rooms, hoping she wouldn't mind. It was a big place for one woman. He found a room set up with a

16

walking machine and a TV, a formal dining room that looked unused, and finally, on the other side of the internal courtyard, was a . . . damned if he knew what that room was for. A shrine was the nearest he could come to defining it.

The room was devoid of furniture, but had a couple of saris in glowing shades of deep rose pink, dull purple and rich blue draped across the two windowless walls, and a two-foot-high Buddha sitting serenely on a low, ornately carved table. A vase in front of it held one perfect flower. There was a stained-glass panel in the window, floor to ceiling, showing lush tropical flowers. It cast jewel-coloured patches of light everywhere. Something as beautiful as that must have cost a fortune. With the saris, the whole room was glowing with colour, not garish, very harmonious.

On the floor was a quilted piece, like no rug he'd ever seen, with curving patterns and different textures in shades of white on white, coloured only by light falling through the stained glass.

He had an inexplicable urge to sit on that rug and close his eyes. But he didn't want to intrude on her private place, so went back to ask her if he could make himself a cup of coffee.

'Go ahead. And have another piece of cake. There's plenty.'

'Do you want a cup?'

'Mmm? No, thanks.'

And she was typing away again.

The phone rang as he was walking back to the kitchen and he heard her answering it, telling someone not to come round today.

He smiled wryly. He'd have liked to find out more about her, but could understand what was driving her. He was just the same when he was writing a song, working out the words and arrangement, impatient of interruptions.

A dark limo arrived an hour later and turned into the drive. Hearing it, Jez lifted the corner of the kitchen blind to peer out. Before the limo had even stopped in front of the house the three journalists came running along the street to the gate.

Craig, his assistant minder, got out and stayed at the gate, arms folded, keeping them at bay, looking mean and powerful. Jez grinned. Craig wouldn't hurt a fly, fought only in self-defence, but no one need know that.

Kevin got out of the limo, by which time Jez had opened the front door. 'Just a minute.' He went back to his hostess. 'Sorry to interrupt you again, but they've come for me.'

Sophie swung round and blinked as if roused from a deep sleep, then smiled. She seemed to smile a lot.

'Sorry. When an idea takes me, I forget about the rest of the world.'

'I'm like that when I'm writing music.'

'You'll forgive me for being a poor hostess, then?'

'You've been a wonderful hostess, given me a few hours of real peace. I can't thank you enough.'

'I'll see you out.' She walked with him to the door. Cameras flashed from the gates and she looked towards them in surprise. 'Are they still here?'

'Ignore them. This is Kevin, my minder, or Chief of Security if you want his posh title.'

She shook hands, giving Kevin another of her lovely smiles, then turned back to Jez. 'Good luck with the house-hunting.'

He held her hand in his for a bit longer than he should have. It was as soft and warm as a plump little bird and he didn't want to let go. 'Thank you for everything.'

'It was my pleasure.'

Again the cameras flashed and he saw her wince. He supposed they'd now have their photo of his ravaged face. And her with him. Damn, he should have thought of that and told her to stay inside. Suddenly, protecting his face didn't seem half as important as protecting her and the haven she'd created here.

He wanted what she had, a peaceful home where you could simply relax. He'd make that his next priority.

He was sorry when the front door shut behind her, sorry to be back in a limo behind tinted glass that made the whole world seem shadowed. There was more flashing of cameras as they drove out of the gates. As he turned to look back at the house, he saw the group of journalists move purposefully up the drive towards it.

'Maybe we should go back and help her?'

'It'll make things worse if we do,' Kevin said. 'Anyway, she won't be stupid enough to open her door to them.'

★ ★ ★

It took a minute or two for the sound to register with Sophie. She looked round in puzzlement. How long had someone been knocking? She glanced at her watch. Only a few minutes since Jez left. He must have forgotten something.

She hurried to answer the door. It didn't take long for it to register that it wasn't him, but the press.

'He's left,' she said and moved to go inside again.

A foot shot past her to jam the door open. As she turned to remonstrate, camera lights flashed. She shoved the foot aside and tried to get back into the house, only now it was a hand that was holding the door open.

She froze for a few seconds, nothing in her experience having taught her how to deal with this sort of thing. While she hesitated, the door was pushed further open and she began to feel frightened. 'Please get out of my house!'

The man holding the door open ignored her request, his expression feral — there was no other word to describe it. It was as if he was the hunter and she the prey.

'Get out of my house and off my property,' she repeated, trying to close the door.

'Just tell us what it's like being Jez Winter's lover,' he demanded. 'Is he good in bed? Is his temper as bad as they say? Has he ever thumped you?'

She gaped at him in shock, unable to believe these were serious questions. The man beside him started shouting at her, his voice a blare of meaningless sound.

The third man, who was her own age, pushed forward. She thought he was going to barge right into her house, but instead he elbowed the intruder away.

'You're out of order, Talbin.' He turned to Sophie. 'Sorry, love. I'm Peter Shane from *In Depth*. If you ever want to do a real interview, without the smut, call me.' He pressed a card into her hand. 'Better close the door now.'

She did so, grateful for his help, leaning against the inside of the door for a moment because her knees felt wobbly. Voices still yammered outside, two men having an argument from the sounds of it. 'Stop being such a wimp!' she told herself and went to telephone the local police station, explaining her dilemma.

In a short time she heard the sound of tyres on the drive. After that an authoritative voice outside told the group of men to leave the premises.

There was a knock on the door and this time she used the spy-hole to check who it was before she opened it, relieved to see the uniformed police officer.

'Are you all right, Ms Carr? Can we come in for a minute?' The man flashed his ID and his companion did the same with hers.

Sophie held the door open. 'Thank you for coming so quickly. I was a bit worried when one of those men wouldn't let me close the door.' Though it was the man's expression that had frightened her most. He'd looked cruel, enjoying a moment of power. Thank heavens for the other fellow, Peter Shane, who had at least been courteous!

21

'Better be careful how you open the door from now on, Ms Carr. Care to explain what this is all about?'

'Yes. Come and sit down.' She explained what had happened that day, shuddering again as she relived the feeling of being hunted and trapped.

'Is Jez Winter likely to be coming back?'

'I shouldn't think so. It was just a chance meeting, because I could help him out. I'd never met him before. I'm doubly glad I did help, now that I've seen what those horrible people can be like.'

'You're quite famous yourself,' the female officer said with a smile.

'Not that sort of fame, and I wouldn't want it, either. It's my books that go out and face the public. I only give talks occasionally, and not to people like that.'

'You should think about getting some automatic gates with an intercom fitted to your drive,' the male officer said. 'Those fellows won't give up for some time if they think you're involved with Winter. Anyway, a famous woman living on her own is always a target. I hope you have a good security system here?'

'Er — no.'

'Might be worth getting one installed.'

When they'd left, Sophie made sure every external door and window was locked and went into her meditation room. She lit a joss stick, set it in front of the statue of the Buddha, inclined her head in a gesture of respect for what he represented, then sat down on the quilt cross-legged.

She sighed in relief as the familiar feeling of peace washed through her. She wasn't a Buddhist, wasn't anything really, but she loved meditating. And she was very fond of this particular statue of the Buddha, which she'd found one bleak day when she had felt there to be no hope in the world. His serene smile had seemed to promise her a brighter future so she'd bought the statue.

It had meant a lot to her to set up this meditation room and its peaceful atmosphere always calmed her down.

Gradually, her body relaxed and she let her mind float, not thinking, not worrying, just being. When she came out of the meditation, she felt in tune with herself again, ready to write for another hour or two, strong enough to ignore outside annoyances.

2

Andi Carr sat on the bus, fuming about the reprimand she'd just received from her boss and worrying about his warning to shape up or ship out. He'd even asked her whether she was using drugs. As if it was any business of his what she did in her spare time.

If she had anywhere else to go, she'd hand in her notice straight away and not wait to be pushed, but her mother refused to let her live in the new house, even though it was plenty big enough for six people, let alone two. Her mother didn't seem to care that she was unhappy. She had tons of money these days, but never thought to toss a few thousand in the direction of her children. Mean, her mother was.

If Andi's father had still been alive — tears came into her eyes at the mere thought of him — *he* would have helped her out and looked after her until she found a halfway decent job where they didn't think they owned you body and soul. Just because she'd been late for work a few times! She'd stayed on at the end of the day to make up for it, hadn't she, dealing with customer complaints and doing any other odd jobs her boss loaded on to her? Work as a general dogsbody wasn't the be-all and end-all of life.

She wasn't sure what was. There didn't seem much point to it, really, which was why she'd not gone on to college. Her father had done everything right and had still died just after fifty. *He* hadn't benefited from his wife's success at all. As for Andi's brother, William was a stick-in-the-mud and his wife was even worse, a real control-freak.

Enjoying each day was the best you could do with your life, Andi reckoned, which meant making the most of your leisure time, and she certainly knew how to party.

She got off the bus at her usual stop then remembered it was her turn to cook tea. Cursing under her breath, she turned round and walked along to the local supermarket. She didn't dare get ready-cooked food again, or even a takeaway pizza. Her flatmates were both into Healthy Eating in a big way. She was sick of hearing those two words, spoken reverently as if they always had capital letters. She bought the bits and pieces she needed, saving the receipt for the housekeeping jar.

Why had she lumbered herself with such picky people to share with? Because she hadn't wanted any more flatmates who skipped out without paying their rent and electricity bills, that's why. She'd thought the original two guys fun at first, but came home one day to find they'd upped sticks and gone, taking her CD player with them. Her mother had had to help out that time, because otherwise the rental agent would have thrown her out of this flat. But her mother had pulled a sour face over it and made Andi feel like a real loser.

After that, she'd chosen two people with good jobs and a sensible attitude to life to share with,

25

pretending she agreed with them. Which she didn't. But dull people were much safer when it came to paying up and they pulled their weight in the house, as well. Her mother had trained her too well. Andi couldn't live in a pigsty, or even a semi-pigsty, had been horrified at how some people lived when she first moved out of home.

Ross was back already. She could see the light under his bedroom door when she went up to change out of her work clothes, and hear his radio going, some boring talk show. What a nerd he was! Hardly ever went out and spent most of his time playing with his computer.

She went into the kitchen and got down the jar of housekeeping money. After counting out what was owed to her, she began to put the meal together. She'd have to ask her mum for some more recipes. Her flatmates were complaining about too much pasta and Bolognese sauce. Well, they'd have to put up with it today. It was all she could think of and it was easy to make. At least she'd bought a lettuce to go with it. You couldn't get much greener than that!

She'd be forced to stay in tonight. Not only was she short of money till payday, but no one had asked her out on a date for ages. Most of her girl friends had started going steady in the past few months. They were fools. They'd end up with bellies full of babies, slaving after their families, worrying about their mortgages. Andi wasn't going down that track. No way. Though she did like kids, especially the little ones. How could you not? But you could give other people's kids back again, which you couldn't with your own.

Anyway, she'd made some new friends lately, who were good fun to go out with, if a trifle expensive. And they'd introduced her to a club where the music was excellent and the drinks quite cheap, considering.

Maybe she'd go round to visit her mother tonight. It was only a few stops away on the Underground. She could usually count on bringing back a chunk of home-made cake these days, which would do for tomorrow's lunch. She didn't share her mum's cakes with her flatmates, they were too good to waste on others.

Thank goodness she could eat what she liked and didn't have a weight problem like her mum, who was fat by today's standards. It was no use Mum talking about that old film star Marilyn Monroe. People knew better these days than to let themselves put on any weight. Andi had suggested dieting, but her mum didn't care what size she was, didn't seem to care about anything except her stupid books.

On that thought Andi picked up her mobile and dialled. 'Hi, Mum. How's the writing going?' She listened to the news of her mother's latest book sales, studying her nail varnish as she did so, then when a suitable amount of chit-chat had been got through, asked, 'Can I come round to see you tonight?'

There was silence, then, 'I'm afraid not. I'm busy.'

'Doing what? Something interesting?'

'Just staying in with a friend — chilling out, don't you call it?'

'Oh.'

'Another time, Andi.'

She put down the phone, wondering who her mother's friend was. Probably another oldie. These middle-aged women certainly stuck together. Her mother had probably forgotten what it was like to go out with a guy but at least she hadn't remarried. Andi hoped she never would. It'd be — wrong. That was the one thing she agreed with her brother about. No one could live up to their dad and anyway, neither of them wanted a stepfather spending all Mum's money, which would be theirs one day.

What a boring life her mother was leading, though, staring at a computer day after day! What was the point of earning big time if you didn't go to glamorous parties, hobnob with celebrities or jet around the world? Actually, Andi didn't really enjoy the books her mother wrote. They weren't at all like real life. Ordinary people didn't meet their Prince Charming. The breed was extinct. Frogs had completely overrun the male world, frogs that pestered you for sex when you didn't want it.

Sighing, she finished cooking and called the others down to eat. Not even a bottle of wine to take the edge off the evening. Ross and Ginny only drank occasionally, so booze didn't come out of the housekeeping budget, and Andi couldn't afford to buy any this week.

Life sucked lately, absolutely sucked, had done ever since her father died.

* * *

28

When she was too tired to write any more, Sophie ate a simple meal and sat down to enjoy a book she'd been meaning to read for ages.

The phone rang and she checked the caller ID, relaxing when she saw it was William. Her son usually rang once or twice a week and popped across to see her sometimes at the weekend with Kerry and the children. He was so like his father physically it hurt sometimes to look at him, but he was more like Sophie's father than Bill, clever but tight with his money and watchful for the best advantage whatever the situation. She had no doubt he'd already calculated what she was worth, what he'd inherit one day.

As for her daughter-in-law, try as she might Sophie couldn't like her, or the way she was bringing up their children. The oldest girl was nearly three, a quiet little thing, too quiet if you asked Sophie. The new baby was only two months old, so the family visits hadn't been as frequent as usual lately. Which was a relief.

'Hi, William. How lovely to — '

'Are you all right, Mum?'

'Yes, of course. Why do you ask in that tone?'

'Did you know you were on the television news tonight?'

'Oh, no! They didn't!'

'Are you really having an affair with Jez Winter?'

'Of course not!'

'I didn't think you were, but that's what they implied. You're not his type, not glamorous enough, and anyway, you're a bit old for him.'

29

She stiffened. Why did both her children seem to think she was too decrepit and unattractive to get a sex life? 'Forty-nine isn't that old, actually, and Jez Winter is about the same age.'

'Oh.' Silence, then, 'So there is something in that news item?'

'I'm not having an affair with him, or with anyone else. Jez Winter took refuge here today when those horrible paparazzi were chasing him, that's all.'

'I didn't know he was an acquaintance of yours.'

'He isn't. He was looking round the house next door, which is for sale, and they cornered him. All I did was give him shelter.' It was amazing how disapproving silence could sound. 'William? I can hear your brain ticking. What are you thinking?'

'I'm just — surprised you'd get involved, that's all. I've told you to be careful who you invite into the house, but you don't seem to listen to me. And have you done anything about a security system yet? What you should really be doing is downsizing. That place of yours is far too big for one person. I never could understand why you bought it. A flat would have been much more sensible at your age.'

She wasn't going down that path again. She liked spacious houses and gardens and would hate to live in a flat. William was no doubt quoting his wife, who was jealous of the house and always made snide remarks when she came round. 'The police recommended me to get a security system, after they'd sent those horrible paparazzi away, so I suppose I'd better do something about it.'

'They were right. Do you want me to look into it for you?'

'No, thank you. I'm quite capable of doing that myself. Now, enough about me. How are Kerry and the children?'

'They're well. I'll email you the latest photo of the baby. She's gorgeous, just as pretty as her big sister.' A sharp voice sounded in the background and he said quickly, 'I won't keep you. I hadn't intended to ring tonight but when I saw you on the TV, I was worried.'

After she'd put the phone down, Sophie looked at her watch. The late-night news would be on in ten minutes. Surely she wasn't important enough to be on it again? Surely it had just been a passing shot of her earlier on and William had picked up on it because he knew her?

But to her dismay, she was *featured* on the news, looking scared stiff as she tried to close the door. Groaning, she watched it to the end then switched off.

The phone rang again. Andi. She picked it up reluctantly.

'Mum, you didn't say it was *Jez Winter* you were spending the evening with. He's really cool, for an oldie. How long have you known him? Will you introduce me?'

Sophie explained yet again what had happened, then cut Andi off. 'I was just going to bed. Got a lot to do tomorrow.'

'Can I come over tomorrow night and get the

31

hot goss on Jez Winter?'

'No. I've just started a new story and I don't want any interruptions.'

'I bet you'll be seeing *him* again.'

'I won't, actually. Bye.' She slammed the phone down and started getting ready for bed. It rang twice more, girlfriends she'd known since school, but she didn't feel like speaking to them or anyone else, so let the answering service take care of it.

She had trouble getting to sleep, kept wondering if she'd heard an intruder. She'd definitely have to get a security system installed now. It wasn't that she couldn't afford one, she just hadn't wanted the disruption to her daily life that installing it would bring.

Admitting that the encounter with the pushy journalists had spooked her, she got up and shoved a chair behind the door. Feeling safer, she fell asleep, but dreamed of Jez Winter, seeing again how sad he was. In the dreams she put her arms round him and gave him a good hug, as you would an unhappy child.

Honestly, how stupid could dreams get? As if he'd want her to hug him. As if she'd even see him or hear from him again.

★   ★   ★

Jez was in his new hotel suite when the TV news came on. He was about to switch it off but heard his own name and stared in horror at the screen. Sophie had opened the door again and been cornered by those sods. She looked terrified, poor thing. Why had she not checked who was outside?

He remembered her transparently honest face. She probably didn't understand how the gutter press could hound you. Oh, hell, this was all his fault! He should have followed his instincts and gone back to make sure she was all right. Those devils wouldn't stop bugging her for days now. What a sorry return she'd got for helping him.

Kevin, who was on duty tonight, came in from the other bedroom. 'Seen it?'

'Yes.' Jez waved one hand at the screen. 'We have to help her out, make sure it doesn't happen again.'

'She'll probably be glad of the publicity, sell a lot more books.'

'She's not like that.'

Kevin made a rude noise. 'Of course she is.'

'No, this one isn't. She's — otherworldly, naive even.'

Kevin screwed up his face in thought. 'She's certainly not with it as far as clothes are concerned and she needs to lose quite a bit of weight. You'd think her publicist would have told her that.'

Jez was surprised by this comment. 'I don't think she's overweight. She's just right. I'm tired of scrawny women who live on salads and bottled water. It's like cuddling a bag of bones, making love to them. And your wife isn't all that skinny, Kev.'

'My wife isn't a celebrity, thank goodness.' He studied Jez. 'Do you fancy this Carr woman?'

'We've only met once, for heaven's sake. I just

33

. . . like her . . . very much. And she was kind to me. So I owe her.'

Kevin shrugged. 'Not your concern now. She'll probably dine out for years on the story of how she gave you refuge.'

Jez seemed to hear Sophie's voice, saying, *If I can do a good deed — for anyone, anyone at all, rich as well as poor people — I do it willingly.* 'I think it *is* my business. She'd not be having this trouble if it weren't for me.'

'You can't go round there again. That'd make things worse.'

'No, but I'll send Donna to see her tomorrow.' His personal assistant was a capable young woman, loyal, intelligent and very with it. He paid her and his other staff well over the odds to keep their loyalty. 'She can help Sophie sort out what to do.'

'Good idea.'

'I'm going to bed now.'

'About time. The doctors said you should take things easy.'

'That's what I've been bloody well doing. I'm fed up of lying around. I need to get myself a proper home, and the sooner the better. We'll put Donna back on the job of finding me a house after she's seen Sophie.'

With that settled, Jez went to bed, sighing in relief as he lay down between the fine cotton sheets, his body aching more than he'd admitted to the doctor or Kevin. He wasn't sure he'd fooled either of them, though.

In the middle of the night he woke, as he often did, lying in the darkness with the day's events churning round in his mind. But most of all it was Sophie Carr who was occupying centre stage in his thoughts. He really hated to think of such a gentle person suffering because she'd helped him out.

He couldn't dismiss the incident, whatever Kevin said. He was responsible for her present troubles.

Who was responsible for his own troubles? Himself? Partly. He'd wondered so many times how he'd got to this point in life, alone in the world, no family or *significant other*, as they called it these days. And no idea of where he was going next. What were ageing pop stars supposed to do with themselves when they retired from public life? If they were wise enough to retire, that was.

But even if he stopped performing, he could never retire from the music that continually ran through his head. He didn't want to.

Actually, he did have a family, sort of — an illegitimate son, the fruit of a misspent youth. He'd not married the mother, though he'd offered, but she hadn't wanted to. She was from a very religious family and their brief affair hadn't changed her devotion to her church. She'd tried to get him involved, but he wasn't into religion.

He felt sad that he'd never known the boy, though, because it also meant he'd never met his two young grandchildren. He grinned, amused at how fans would react to the news that he was a grandfather twice over.

His main problem in life was that he was

lonely. He had more than enough money, but no one to enjoy it with. He wasn't getting married again, though. He might not be the world's worst husband, but he wasn't in the A league, that was sure.

He wondered what Sophie's husband had been like. Her expression had been so warm and tender when she spoke about him. It must be wonderful to love someone like that and be loved in return.

Oh, hell, he was becoming maudlin. He plumped up the pillow, trying to get more comfortable. He wasn't taking one of those sleeping tablets. They left you feeling lousy all morning.

As opposed to feeling lousy in the middle of a wakeful night.

★　★　★

The following morning just after ten o'clock, Donna Baxter turned into Sophie's drive and knocked on the door, looking forward with great interest to meeting the woman who'd made such a good impression on Jez.

She heard footsteps inside and a voice called out, 'Who are you? What do you want?'

'I'm Donna, Jez Winter's personal assistant.' She flashed a business card. 'He said I should mention how good your almond cake was if you were at all doubtful that I was genuine.'

A woman Donna recognized from the TV news as the one who'd helped Jez opened the door, looking in dismay towards the people hanging around near the gate.

'Come in quickly.' Sophie slammed the door shut and locked it. 'Did Jez want something?'

'He sent me to have a chat. If we can sit down somewhere, I'll explain.'

'I can't think why. But I was due for a break. Would you like a cup of coffee?'

'I'd kill for one.' Donna looked round with interest as she followed her hostess into the kitchen.

'Are you as fond of cake as your employer?'

'I didn't even know he was fond of cake, actually. He doesn't usually bother much about food.' She looked at the remains of the almond cake longingly, thought of how much she'd weighed that morning and sighed. 'I daren't accept a piece, thank you anyway. Got to watch my weight.' She had sturdy peasant genes and try as she would, couldn't achieve anything approaching a fashionable, sylph-like figure. 'And I take my coffee black, no sugar, please.'

Donna saw Sophie smile wryly, as if she'd expected this. She watched her hostess making the coffee. She'd studied the author photo inside the cover of one of the books she'd bought for Jez earlier this morning, but in the flesh Sophie Carr was much more attractive, ultra-feminine somehow, the sort of woman you could imagine wearing frilly, floaty clothes, whatever the fashion.

When they were seated Donna took a sip of coffee and sighed with pleasure. 'That's seriously good coffee, thank you. Now, if we could get straight to work?' She waited for a nod, then continued. 'Jez is very upset about the trouble he's caused you and sent me round to see how we can help.' She noted the surprise on the other woman's face.

'I don't need any help, thank you.'

'Are you used to dealing with the gutter press?'

'No. I've usually dealt with the more reputable newspapers and magazines. The journalists I'd met before yesterday were very kind, but these — well, they seem like a different breed.'

'They are. Um — you don't appear to have a security system here. Risky, that.'

'I'm going to do something about it just as soon as I get a minute to spare. Look, Miss Baxter — '

'Donna.'

'Donna, then. I'm grateful to your employer, but I'm really busy at the moment starting a new book and — '

'Let me arrange for the installation of a security system, then.' Donna could see refusal in Sophie's eyes and added quickly, 'It'll be easier in the long run for you to agree to that, because once Jez thinks he should do something, he doesn't stop until he succeeds. Stubborn plus, that's him. You have to be to succeed as a rock star.'

Sophie smiled. 'Same thing goes for novelists.'

'Well, you'll understand then. At the moment, he feels he owes you and I'm trying to find some way of satisfying him.'

'There really is no need.'

'I know. But would it hurt to let me do this?

I've done it before for Jez, so I know exactly what to arrange, security-wise. And if you don't mind my not getting several quotes, which would mean reps coming and tramping round your house, there's a company we've used before who do excellent work and they can monitor the system for you afterwards. Just one visit from their rep and then the installation.' She could see that she was winning ground and stopped talking, letting her arguments sink in.

'We-ell, as long as it's understood that I'm paying for this myself.'

That surprised Donna. Jez was rich beyond most people's dreams, even after the slice his ex-wife had taken from his finances, and he wouldn't even notice such a minor cost. Many other pop stars had been ripped off by their managers or agents, but Kevin had told her that Jez had grown up poor and had a shrewd northern streak to him, so had always kept a careful watch on his money — still did, as far as she could see. He might spend lavishly on occasion, but he lived well within his means and invested wisely. 'I'll make sure Jez understands that.' She waited again, watching Sophie.

'Well — all right. Thank you.'

Donna took out her PDA. 'Could you give me your private phone number? And when would be the best time for them to come and inspect the house? Tomorrow morning, perhaps?'

'Afternoon. Morning's my best writing time.'

'How about this afternoon, then?'

'Would they come so soon?'

For Jez Winter? The woman had to be kidding.

39

Donna studied her face. No, she wasn't. She clearly didn't understand how people *fawned* on Jez. 'If not, they can come another afternoon.'

'Very well.'

'There's one other thing. If you speak to any of the press about your meeting with Jez, would you let me know, please? Perhaps even let me tag along? I'm paid to protect his interests, you see, and I do understand how things work.'

'Why should I speak to anyone? I want nothing further to do with people like them.'

'They're still hanging around the house. As long as Talbin stays, so will the rest of them.' She saw that the name meant nothing to Sophie. 'He's a little weasel-faced man. He's not well thought of. I wouldn't trust him an inch.'

'I remember him. He was horrible.'

'Yes, but he's known to be tenacious when he thinks there's a story to be had, so if this goes on, it may be better for you to make a press statement to get rid of them.'

'As long as they stay on the street and away from my front door, they can hang around all they want. At this stage in a book, I don't even *want* to go out of the house.'

Donna stood up. She knew when to let something drop. She'd sown a few seeds — well, she hoped she had. 'Since you're busy I won't intrude any longer, but please don't hesitate to call me if there's anything, anything at all, that I can do for you. Jez's instructions.'

'He's doing more than enough already.'

Donna was thoughtful as she drove back. A nice woman, Sophie Carr, but too soft for her own good. She'd borrow one of the books from Jez, see if it gave any clues to the author's personality. He seemed very concerned about his rescuer, which had surprised those who knew him. *Otherworldly*, he'd called her, and his voice had been warm when he spoke about her.

Maybe he was right, and she was otherworldly, but there was a hidden strength in the woman too, if Donna was any judge — and she was well paid to be a judge of character. Sophie Carr wasn't whining and complaining about the annoyance the paparazzi were causing, she was quietly getting on with her life.

As she drove away, Donna reviewed the rest of her day's work. After she'd sorted out the security thing, she had to find Jez somewhere to live. She'd enjoy that. She loved looking round houses.

3

To Sophie's surprise, the security firm could come and do the preliminary planning on her house that very afternoon. Sighing, she agreed to let Donna bring them round at two o'clock, then went back to work again.

The afternoon post fell through the letterbox on to the tiled hall floor at one o'clock, bringing an envelope addressed to her by hand. She didn't recognize the sender's writing so opened that one first, smiling at herself. Curiosity was undoubtedly one of her besetting sins.

Dear Ms Carr

I hope you've recovered from your unpleasant experience of yesterday.

I just wanted to set the record straight, in case you think I was at your house yesterday to hound you — I wasn't, though it must have looked that way. I was there because I'm doing an article for 'In Depth' on the ways of the paparazzi.

I hope you'll keep this to yourself or I'll not be able to continue my observations.

Yours sincerely
Peter Shane

Sophie frowned at the letter. It seemed strange that he'd taken the trouble to write to her. She remembered clearly the man who'd helped her close her door, and she still had the business card he'd given her. Now she came to think of it, he had seemed different from the others, but she hadn't expected to have anything to do with him again.

Shrugging, she set the letter aside and checked the rest of her post. Bills, statements, catalogues. Nothing else of real interest. Most of her personal communications were by email now.

At five to two the doorbell rang and she let Donna in. Peter Shane's letter was still lying on the hall table and on impulse she picked it up and showed it to the younger woman.

Donna read it quickly, then read it again more slowly. 'What exactly did he do?'

Sophie explained. 'What I don't understand is why he even bothered to write to me.'

'Keeping sweet with you in case he needs to interview you one day.'

'Oh. Because of Jez?'

'And because of who you are. You're famous in your own right, remember. Shane's got a good reputation, so he could also be worried about damaging that.' Donna tapped the piece of paper. 'If Talbin continues to harass you, maybe we should offer Shane an exclusive on what really happened. He'd have a better insight because of being there.'

'I'd rather not. I don't want to speak about Jez's distress.'

Donna looked at her sharply. 'Jez was *distressed*?'

'They'd upset him, yes.'

'He's not fully recovered from the operation

yet. They've made a good job of his face, haven't they?'

'Yes. I could see he was exhausted, though. Strange to meet him that way. I've loved his music for years.'

The doorbell rang again and she forgot everything as she went round the house with the security planner, discussing what was needed.

When they'd finished, Donna said, 'I can take over from here, Sophie, if you like.'

'That'd be good. As long as it's understood that I'm paying for this myself.' She looked at both of them and didn't move until each had nodded.

★ ★ ★

Two mornings later Donna arrived again, ready to deal with the men fitting the security system. 'Can I just interrupt you for a minute, Sophie? After that, you can go back to work until they need to do this room.'

'Yes, of course. What is it?'

'This . . . and this. Sorry.'

Sophie grimaced at the headlines on the two newspaper articles Donna had laid in front of her.

WINTER'S PA VISITS NOVELIST

LOVERS USE GO-BETWEEN

Muttering under her breath, she screwed up the pieces of paper then realized they weren't hers to ruin and tried to smooth them out again. 'Sorry.'

'I don't want them back. I just thought you ought to know what's going on. I've discussed it with Jez and Kevin, and we think you should definitely give an exclusive to a reputable journalist, explaining what really happened. Would you mind if we offered it to Shane, since he was here and could see what was going on?'

'Do I have to do this?'

'Not if you're dead set against it. But we're trying to get them off your back, make sure you can go out and about without being pursued.'

Sophie sighed. 'I suppose I'd better do it, then. All right. Go ahead and arrange something, but not — '

'Not for a morning. I know. That's your best writing time.' Donna grinned. She didn't forget important facts.

★ ★ ★

Mary Prichard took one look at the headlines and shoved the newspaper away with an exclamation of loathing.

Her son, who'd brought the scandal rag he'd noticed at the newsagent's round to show her, picked it up off the floor and folded it carefully, avoiding her eyes as he spoke. 'I've been thinking of going to see him.'

She turned on him. '*What?* After all I've said to you.'

'Hell, Mum, Jez Winter's my father and I've never even met him. You won't tell me much

45

about him, so how else can I find out. You get tight-lipped if I so much as mention his name.'

'I brought you up decently and *normally* by keeping you away from him. Just be thankful for that.'

'I am. You've been a wonderful mother. And Brian's a great stepfather. But I want — *need* to know my real father as well.'

'You *don't* need him.'

'I do.' Tom looked at her earnestly. 'Believe me, I do, Mum.'

She sighed and her shoulders slumped. 'I wish you'd never found that birth certificate.'

'I don't. I'd always wondered who my real father was. And I'd have had to see it eventually, wouldn't I?' He hesitated, then asked the question that was burning inside him. 'What I need to know is, did you persuade Jez to stay away from me all these years or was that his own choice?' His voice broke on the words, he couldn't help it.

Her lips tightened into a thin, bloodless line.

'You're doing it again. You always get that expression on your face when I try to talk about him. That's when Brian usually steps in to prevent me continuing. Only I deliberately chose a time he wouldn't be here. Mum, if you won't tell me anything, do you have a contact address for Jez Winter? I really, really need to meet him. He's my father.'

'No, I don't.' She raised one hand to stop him speaking. 'I never wanted one. He and I agreed on a clean break and I kept to that promise.'

'Did he *never* show *any* interest in me?' Tom

turned his back to her, breathing deeply a couple of times, trying to control his emotions but quivering with the violence of them.

She laid her hand on Tom's shoulder from behind, saying nothing.

He raised his own hand to cover hers. 'Could you answer that question, please, Mum? It's important to me. Hasn't my real father shown *any* interest in me at all?' His voice cracked again on the last words.

The hand slipped off his shoulder and he turned to see her shaking her head blindly, tears in her eyes. But this time he didn't weaken and stop asking. This time he was determined to find out what had happened between his biological parents. It was doing his head in. He was twenty-six, dammit, a grown man, and should be over this. But he was a man with pain in his heart whenever he thought of his real father, the pain of rejection, and no amount of reasoning would take the sharp sting of that away. Only the truth would do it. He hoped. 'Well?'

She threw him a reproachful look.

'If you don't tell me, I'll definitely go and ask him myself, if I have to camp outside his hotel to do it.'

She let out a long, shuddering breath and sank down on the nearest chair. 'You promised me last time that you'd let the matter drop for good.'

'Brian said you had a heart problem and we mustn't upset you. He was lying, wasn't he?' Tom waited a moment, then repeated, 'Wasn't he? I watched you play with my children last Sunday. A woman with a heart problem couldn't have run around the garden like that. So it was a lie.'

She nodded, avoiding his eyes.

'Why? Why do you work so hard to keep me from meeting my father?'

'Because I want you to be happy. He . . . never was.'

'Well, I'm not happy. I need to know where I come from. And I need to know why he rejected me.'

'*I* can tell you that, you don't need to ask him.' She took a deep, sobbing breath and said rapidly, 'He didn't reject you. I had a lawyer's letter from him when you were five, asking for regular access.'

'*He wanted to see me?* Why didn't you let him?'

'I reminded him of the promise he'd made to me, to leave you to grow up *normally*. No one knew he was your father. Your grandparents were the only ones who knew who'd fathered my illegitimate child, apart from me and Brian. Now they're dead, there's only us and we're certainly not going to tell people.'

'Is it so shameful? He's not a bad guy, from all accounts.'

'He's into drugs and who knows what else. He's had two marriages fail. He doesn't seem like a good guy to me. We're just a normal, ordinary family and I want us to stay that way.'

Tom fought to control his temper. What was normal? He no longer knew. He'd been brought up in an unremittingly Christian household, one that was very different from most of his school friends' families. His mother had even tried to choose his friends and leisure activities for him, all based at her church. How normal was that?

Her loving supervision and careful indoctrination hadn't worked, though. From his friends and teachers at school he'd learned about the wider world, and he no longer believed in the sort of religion he'd been taught at her church, wasn't even sure he believed in a god at all. He'd not told his mother that, because he knew how much it'd hurt her.

He'd been brought up to believe that religion, marriage and family were the most important things in life, and that if you did the right thing, you'd be happy. His mother was indeed happy with Brian, who was a nice guy. Lucky her.

Tom no longer believed in happily ever after, or even in *for better for worse*, not after his years with Gail.

'So my father backed off, just because you asked him to?' he asked at last.

She hesitated visibly.

'This time I want the truth, Mum.'

'Not quite. He asked to be sent copies of all your childhood photos and I had to promise I'd keep him in touch with what you were doing, at school and — in general. I kept that promise by writing to his solicitor every quarter, but we didn't take any money from him. And I refused to open his letters.'

'He wrote?'

She nodded.

'To you or to me?'

She hesitated again.

49

Indignation made it hard for him to speak calmly. 'They were to me, weren't they? And you kept them from me, never said a word. Mum, how could you?'

'It'd only have caused trouble. He was godless, into drugs and whatever those people do. My parents warned me against going out with him, but I thought I could save him, help him. And . . . I loved him. They were right, though. He was beyond help. And my love wasn't enough. Before we split up, he tempted me into sin. I've never forgiven him for that.'

'Sin?'

She blushed. 'Fornication.' She seemed to forget Tom for a moment. 'Why should I have passed on his letters? They'd have upset you. Who knows what he'd have tempted *you* into if I'd let him near you? I had to keep you safe.'

How Tom kept his voice steady he didn't know, he felt so full of hot anger. 'You should have given me those letters because they were addressed to me, Mum. And because he's my father.' He asked another question that had been puzzling him. 'Did he refuse to marry you?'

Her blush deepened. 'I couldn't marry someone who didn't share my beliefs. I just — couldn't. He did offer, but I listened to my parents, thank goodness. What sort of life would I have led with a man like that, a man who refused to give up his music and settle down? It was a pity he insisted on being named as the father on the birth certificate, but he said he'd take me to court if I didn't do that, so I had no choice.'

Tom couldn't actually imagine his straight-laced mother making love, even when she was young. 'You still shouldn't have destroyed my letters.'

'As your mother, it was my duty to protect you, yours to obey and accept my guidance. *Honour thy father and thy mother.*'

She'd always quoted the Bible to him, always expected absolute obedience. She'd given her only child a lifetime of love, yes, but a lifetime of restrictions too. What she'd done made rage boil up inside him and overflow. 'I'll never, *ever* forgive you for that.'

He stepped back, as far away from her as he could. He could understand now why people lashed out at others in anger. His father had wanted to see him, he'd been desperate to meet his father, and *she* had kept them apart all these years.

'Son.' She reached out one hand towards him, her expression pleading, her lips trembling.

He had to leave before he said something that would damage their relationship irrevocably. She hadn't acted out of malice, he knew that, but it'd had the same effect. Ignoring her plea to stay, he brushed past her and left, slamming the door hard as he went.

But that small act of violence didn't relieve his feelings, nor did it stop the fury roiling in his stomach.

All those years! She'd kept his father from him for twenty-six years! He'd lain awake night after night as a teenager, wondering what was wrong with him, why his famous father not only didn't

51

want to see him, but never even mentioned to the world that he had a son.

What she'd done wasn't just from love. It was from a need to control him, to keep him tied to *her* world. She'd rejected his father when he wouldn't enter her world.

But she'd failed with Tom as well.

And he was definitely going to contact his father.

★　★　★

When he got home from work the next day, Tom found his wife drunk again and his children, two-year-old Ryan and four-year-old Hayley, still in their nightclothes, with dirty, tear-streaked faces.

He stood in the doorway for a moment, looking at Gail, hating her. His mother insisted marriage was for ever. Yeah! Like his marriage was going to last much longer. Like he even wanted it to.

Only, you needed money to separate and divorce, and he had none. Besides, he wasn't leaving the children with his wife, had to have somewhere decent to take them. But for that you needed money.

Since Ryan's birth Gail had drunk or frittered away all he earned, however hard he worked, pawning household stuff to get booze if he kept her short of money. She'd even pawned his Jez Winter albums one day. He'd lost it then and hit her, frightening her so much she'd never touched them again. He'd had to borrow money from his mother to get them back.

He'd frightened himself as well as her, didn't want to turn into the sort of man who beat his wife.

Why had he never told her that Jez was his father? He'd never told anyone, actually, perhaps because he was ashamed of being unwanted.

Well, Gail would be even shorter of money from now on because today he'd lost his job. Downsizing, they'd told him brightly, a sound economic measure. The company hated to let him go, his manager would give him a glowing reference, blah, blah, blah!

He didn't know what to do next. If he didn't find a job and tried to manage on social security, he'd not have the money to bring the kids up properly. And heaven alone knew what lengths Gail would go to in order to get hold of booze.

He'd hidden her drinking from people up to now. Gail's parents had moved to Spain and they didn't come back very often, so they weren't in the picture. Tom's mother expected you to go and visit her, not the other way around. The only one who knew was his neighbour Jane Burtill, who'd helped him out a few times, rescuing and feeding the children.

On that thought he went across to give them a cuddle. 'Are you hungry, my little hobbits?' They nodded and he wondered if they'd been fed at all today. He worried about that every day, so made sure they ate well in the mornings and evenings. He got out the biscuit tin, but it was empty. There were two pieces of stale bread left, so he put them on to toast then filled the kettle. He'd have to get some fish and chips.

He leaned over the sink, holding the edge of it, wishing he were a woman and could howl his eyes out. But men weren't supposed to cry. He had no one he could turn to. His mother wouldn't offer the sort of help he needed now, that was sure. She'd grown increasingly dogmatic over the years and now claimed she didn't believe in divorce for any reason.

Oh, hell, what was he to do? His children were dirty and ill-fed, poor loves. He was hungry too, and at the absolute end of his tether. He buttered the toast and found a scraping of jam to put on it, then wiped the children's hands and faces before sitting them down at the end of the table.

Gail raised her head and smiled owlishly at him, saying in a slurred voice, 'Is it teatime already?'

'Yes.' He'd have snatched the bottle of wine from her, but it was empty and she was cradling it out of habit.

'What time is it?' She pulled herself into a sitting position and squinted at the clock. 'You're home early.'

'I've lost my job, been made redundant.'

It took a minute or two for that to sink in, then she frowned. 'You'll get another one, though, won't you?'

'I can't even go looking while you're like this!' he yelled at her, snatching the bottle out of her hand and nearly, God help him, smashing it over her head. 'Go to bed. Just — go to bed and sleep it off.'

'Don't want to.'

He thrust his face near hers. 'If you don't go to bed, I'll carry you up there myself and lock you in. *Get — out of — my sight.*'

When she shrank away, he felt guilty, but when he looked at his children, also cowering from his loud voice, he grabbed Gail's arm, thrust her towards the stairs and repeated, at a slightly lower rate of decibels, 'Go and sleep it off, damn you!'

While the kids were eating their toast, he counted his money, made some plans, then rang his mother. Whatever their differences, she loved her grandchildren and would look after them for him if she thought he was off for a job interview and Gail was ill.

They said alcoholism was an illness. Well, if so, his wife was extremely ill and refusing treatment.

And he'd had enough of coping with it, more than enough. He wanted out — for himself and his children.

★   ★   ★

With a can of lemonade in his hand, ignoring the fancy crystal glasses in the hotel suite's bar, Jez sat watching TV. He flipped it off with the remote when Donna came in. 'How did it go?'

'It went well. The security system is fitted but she still insisted on paying for it.'

'You can usually persuade people.'

'She's not short of money, she wouldn't hear of you paying for it, so I didn't waste my time trying to persuade her.'

'How did she look?'

'Well. She fed everyone cake and coffee. She's a seriously good cook, even tempted me to a piece.'

He smiled reminiscently. 'Yeah. What sort of cake was it this time?'

'Coffee cake.' Donna waited a minute then changed the subject. 'About finding somewhere to live, I've seen three houses now plus the one next door to Sophie. That's undoubtedly the best, but we can't buy it.'

'Why can't we?'

'Because it'll start the gossip going again. You're trying to get Sophie *off* the hook, not impale her on it.'

'I suppose so. Tell me about the other places, then.'

She summarized what she'd seen.

'We'll drive past them tomorrow. If I like where they are, I'll go inside.'

But, he admitted to himself, the house next to Sophie's was a pretty house and Chestnut Lane was a lovely street. He'd really liked the look of it and had been very taken by the huge horse chestnut trees dotted here and there. He'd spotted one in his garden, another in Sophie's, their upper branches interwoven above the high wall that separated the properties.

It'd be nice to have a neighbour like her. He couldn't remember the last time he'd bothered to make friends with neighbours. He and Sophie might have a drink together occasionally, chat over the wall, use that old gate near the chestnut trees to visit one another.

She couldn't write all the time, surely?

But would she want to make friends with him? He wasn't at all sure of that, had never really made friends with a woman before, just seen them as wives and lovers.

★　★　★

The following day was the monthly lunch with her girl friends. Sophie got ready, humming to herself, the first chapter of the book now sorted out. She loved these lunches, which made her feel young and carefree for an hour or two.

Her heart sank as she was followed to the café by two cars. She asked for a table out of sight of the street. The waiter looked at her and at the men standing on the pavement.

'Aren't you — ?'

'I'm just a customer meeting friends. If you can't accommodate me in privacy, I'll go elsewhere.'

'OK, OK. Come through to the back room.'

He brought her friends to join her a few minutes later.

Soon after that a waitress showed the men who'd followed Sophie to a table nearby.

She stopped speaking in mid-sentence. Lisa and Ashley followed her gaze.

One of the men was Talbin. He made a flourishing gesture of greeting with one hand.

She didn't respond in any way. 'It's the paparazzi,' she said. 'They're probably recording every word we say. Come back to my place. We'll get some takeaways instead.'

She got the waitress to parcel up some food, paid for the bottled water they'd drunk and ran to her car.

As she got into it, she saw her friends being pestered but couldn't think how to help them, and at least there were two of them. Switching on her engine, she drove quickly off into the traffic, heading for home.

She was furious about this. Had those idiots nothing better to do than hound her?

When her friends joined her at her house, they thought it was a bit of a laugh.

She didn't.

Lisa and Ashley pestered her for information about Jez, but she didn't give them anything that wasn't already known, nothing personal. It'd have felt like a betrayal.

She hoped this stupid fuss would soon die down. How did the poor man stand it, year after year? No wonder he looked sad.

But his music wasn't sad — well, most of it wasn't. His music ranged over every human emotion she could think of and touched all of hers. She smiled wryly — hers and those of thousands of other women of all ages. As did his looks, that wonderful hawk-like face and those deep-set dark eyes that seemed to brood and smoulder.

★   ★   ★

Before Jez could leave the next afternoon to look at some houses, the room phone rang. Since Donna was on her mobile, gesticulating and talking earnestly, Jez picked up the call himself. No danger in speaking to hotel staff, just the irritation of their always being so damned obsequious.

'Reception here, Mr Winter. I'm so sorry to disturb you, but we have a young man down here who says he's your son.'

The room spun round him and Jez had to clutch the table to steady himself. 'What — ' He had to swallow hard before he could finish the sentence. 'What's his name?'

There was a mutter of voices, then, 'Tom Prichard.'

He still felt dizzy with shock, but he forced words out. 'Get someone to bring him up and please, not a word about who he says he is to anyone.'

'Of course not, Mr Winter. You can rely on our discretion absolutely.'

Jez put the phone down and closed his eyes for a moment, then realized he was wasting time. He went across to Donna, who had her back to him, and tapped her shoulder.

'Just a minute,' she said into the phone and looked at him enquiringly.

'My son's turned up at the hotel. I've never met him before, and I'd like this meeting to be private. Could you and Craig go somewhere else for a while? And obviously, I shan't be going out now.'

She stared at him wide-eyed, mouthing the word son in shock. Then she nodded and said curtly into the phone, 'Something's just come up. I'll ring you back in five.' She looked at Jez sympathetically. 'I didn't know you had a son.'

'No. His mother kept him well away from me.'

'That's sad. Will you be all right?'

Even in the midst of his turmoil, he could tell that she really cared about how he felt, and was touched by that. She'd only been with them for five months, on a year's contract, but she'd been brilliant as a PA, the best he'd ever had. 'I don't know. But this is something for me to do alone.' He couldn't imagine what had suddenly brought Tom to London to see him, but it could only be trouble.

Soon after she'd left, there was a knock on the door. He wanted to rush across the room and down the suite's short corridor to fling open the door, but hung back, trying to get his emotions under control. He wasn't sure how to face this.

The person knocked again and he went to answer it, his stomach lurching.

The young man standing there was so like himself at that age, he knew at once this was no impostor. 'Come in.' He smiled at the concierge. 'Thank you.'

Tom followed him into the living area of the big suite without a word. He hardly glanced at the luxurious room but kept staring at Jez as if he'd devour him.

'It's wonderful to meet you at last, Tom.'

'Don't you want to see some ID?'

'Your face is enough ID for me. I used to see a face like that every day in the mirror when I was your age. Haven't people commented on the likeness?'

'Sometimes. I just make a joke of it.'

'Come and sit down.'

They took two big, comfortable armchairs stationed at right angles, the smooth cream leather and braided satin cushions contrasting with Jez's dark clothes and Tom's scruffy jeans and worn leather jacket. For a moment neither of them spoke, then Tom cleared his throat and said with a marked northern accent, 'I didn't know.'

'What?'

'That you'd wanted to see me when I was a kid, that you'd sent me letters. Mum never told me. She did it out of the best intentions but — '

The bitter words escaped before Jez could stop himself. 'Mary always does things out of the best intentions. That's what makes her so hard to deal with.'

Tom scowled at him. 'I love her very much.'

'I did too, once. It wasn't enough, though. Even when she was pregnant, she wouldn't marry me unless I went to her church and gave up my music — as if I could. Sorry. That's ancient history now. Tell me why you came.'

Tom took a deep breath. 'I've been wanting to meet you for years. It's important to know your father, don't you think? But also, at the moment I need your help — desperately. I know that sounds grasping and I'll pay you back every penny, I swear, but I didn't know where to turn and when I found out you'd *wanted* to see me, I — just came.'

Jez tried to sift the sense from this jumble of words. 'You're in financial trouble?'

Tom shrugged. 'Going to be soon. But I'd

have wanted to see you anyway. I *needed* to.' His voice choked to a halt and he swallowed hard, staring down at his legs.

'I've needed to meet you for a long time, too, Tom.'

'You have?'

'Yes.' Jez couldn't stop looking at him, wanted to see and know everything about his son, didn't know where to start. 'Let's — um, make ourselves comfortable. Are you hungry, thirsty? I don't drink alcohol, but there's coffee, tea, soft drinks of all kinds.'

'She said you were a drunkard *and* took drugs.'

'I was. I did. When I was your age. I grew out of it, thank goodness, before I killed myself.'

There was silence, but each man was studying the other. Then Tom's stomach rumbled.

'If I could have a sandwich and a cup of tea, that'd be great? I'm a bit hungry. I only had enough money for a single train fare, you see, and we didn't have much food in the house.'

'Of course you can have something to eat. Excuse me a minute.' Jez picked up the phone and ordered lunch to be brought up to the suite, then went back to join Tom, who was sitting on the edge of the chair, legs apart, staring down at his clasped hands. Jez hesitated, then patted his son's shoulder, the first time he'd ever touched him since he was a baby. He'd only been allowed one visit to see his new-born son, then Mary had vanished and her parents wouldn't say where she was. She'd gone back to live with them once Jez had left the area, though. She'd been a pretty girl. He wondered what she looked like now. The baby had turned into this sturdy young man with Jez's face.

Tom looked up at him, tears spilling from his eyes and running down his cheeks. 'I didn't mean to come and ask you for money straight off. It must sound awful.'

Jez could bear it no longer, but pulled his son to his feet and hugged him. 'Whatever the problem is, we'll sort it. I promise we'll sort it. But don't apologize for coming to see me. I've longed for this day.'

For a moment the younger man stood rigidly in his father's embrace, then he burst into strangled sobs and leaned against him. 'I don't know — what to do.'

'Neither do I.' Jez hugged his son even harder, bitterly conscious of all the years of hugs he'd missed out on, not sure if he'd ever be allowed to do this again.

After a few moments, Tom pulled away, wiping the tears with the sleeve of his sweater and muttering, 'Haven't even got a tissue.'

'Here.' Jez pulled a fistful out of the box that sat at one end of the bar, thrust them into his son's hand then grabbed more for himself.

There was a knock on the door and he cursed under his breath. He went to answer it and found two waiters with a trolley. 'Set up lunch as quickly as you can in the dining area, please. We'll serve ourselves.'

He paced up and down impatiently while they fussed about getting things just right. For some reason he couldn't fathom, he kept remembering the simple meal Sophie had provided and how good that had tasted. Would this fancy one taste any better? He doubted it.

Shutting the door behind the waiters, he turned to Tom, who had kept his back to the room, as if staring out at the view of the Thames. 'You all right?'

His son — *his son!* — turned and gave a faint smile. 'I didn't expect that to happen. I'm not usually — so out of control.'

'If we can't be moved about meeting one another at last, I don't know what we can weep about. I'm sorry I've not been there for you over the years, but your mother — well, she was sure it was the best thing to do.'

'She didn't even tell me who my real father was until I was fifteen and needed my birth certificate to get a passport for a school trip. When she wouldn't give me it, said she'd changed her mind about the trip, I went hunting through the cupboards and discovered my birth certificate. And I only found out you'd wanted access two days ago. She destroyed all the letters you sent as I grew older, *all of them*. I never saw a single one.'

It was hard not to say what he thought of that gratuitous cruelty, but Jez managed to keep his comment mild. 'That was . . . unfair.'

'Yes.' Tom frowned at his father. 'You look pale, but the scars aren't as bad as I expected. Shouldn't you sit down now? I don't want you fainting on me.'

Jez nodded. 'I'd better. I still tire easily.' He touched his face. 'This won't show much at all when the scars fade, they tell me.'

'How about your hand? It said in one article that it was damaged. Can you still play all right?'

'You've been following what happened to me?'

'For years.'

'Then why the hell didn't you contact me sooner?'

'Mum. And then I got married. Setting up a home and having kids can be pretty time-consuming.'

'I've seen photos of Ryan and Hayley. I'd love to meet them.'

'You know their names?'

Jez fumbled for his wallet and pulled out the photos.

Tom's eyes filled with tears again and he touched the photos with one fingertip, very gently, his love for his children showing clearly. 'It's because of them I've come to you. My wife's — she's turned into an alcoholic. I want to leave her, take the kids away from her, keep them *safe*. She doesn't even feed them properly, and she pawns our stuff. Only I've just lost my job. I feel so *helpless*.'

'We could get her into rehab. They can work wonders.'

Tom fiddled with a thread hanging from his sweater sleeve. 'That'd be good. For her, I mean. If we can persuade her.'

'She has to want it or it won't work.'

'Even if she does, I still don't want to stay with her. It was a big mistake, marrying her — lust, not love. She's pretty, but stupid. And sneaky. Like with the second baby. I thought she was on

65

the pill. I was thinking of leaving her. She guessed and got pregnant on purpose to keep me with her. She doesn't really like looking after kids but for some reason she won't let go of me.'

'Sounds a bit of a mess.'

Tom sighed. 'Tell me about it.'

'Let's have something to eat now, then we'll talk some more.' Jez put his arm round his son's shoulders as they walked across to the dining area, wanting desperately to do this right, be a good father, make up for lost time. *If you ever could.*

And Tom didn't flinch or move away from his grasp.

Please let this work out! Jez prayed. *Please. Please.*

4

Andi turned up that evening without warning. Sophie checked who it was and sighed before opening the door.

'Hi, Mum. Surprise!'

Was it her imagination or was Andi just a little unsteady on her feet? 'I thought I'd asked you not to come without checking with me first.'

For a moment a scowl darkened Andi's face. 'Other mothers are *glad* to see their daughters any time.'

'Other mothers don't have books to write and deadlines to meet.' And other daughters came visiting regularly, even when they didn't need something. But Sophie didn't say that aloud, just wondered what Andi wanted this time.

'Shall I go away again?'

'No, of course not. Come in.' She didn't try to hug Andi, who had made it very clear a few years ago that she wasn't into that touchy-feely stuff, though she'd always hugged her father. Since Bill's death, Sophie felt that she and her daughter had grown further apart, which upset her. She'd even stopped trying to get closer to Andi lately, she realized suddenly with a jolt of shame. Though you could only beat your head against a brick wall so many times before the pain stopped you trying again. 'Want a piece of my coffee cake?'

'How come you've time to cook and not to see me?'

'I've told you before: baking is what I do when I'm trying to think things out in my plot. Any mindless activity would do really, just to keep my hands occupied. I thought of a really good twist while I was beating the eggs for this cake.' She didn't pursue the point. Her daughter's eyes always glazed over when she talked about her writing and Andi had only read Sophie's first two novels, then said when offered others that sentimental stuff wasn't her thing.

In the kitchen, Andi took her usual place at the breakfast bar and waited to be served. She might have got out the mugs to help, Sophie thought as she put the kettle on and cut her daughter a slice of cake.

'Aren't you having some?'

'I've just eaten.'

'No visitors tonight?'

From the avid look on Andi's face, this was part of the purpose of the visit, at least, to find out more about Jez. 'No.'

'What's he like?'

Sophie didn't intend to make it easy for her. 'Who?'

'You know. Jez Winter.'

'Nice. Look, he's not a friend or anything, and I'm not seeing him again. I just gave him shelter that one time.'

'How long did he stay?'

'A few hours. He was avoiding the paparazzi. He had a piece of my almond cake.'

'And . . . ?'

'And nothing. His minder came and picked him up once it was safe. End of story.'

'I don't believe you.'

Sophie frowned at her daughter, seeing the enlarged pupils, the slightly glassy expression. 'Have you been drinking?'

'Just a couple. It's been a long, hard week. I'm going clubbing later, only . . . Look, I had a few expenses this week. Could you lend me a bit, Mum?'

'How much?'

'A couple of hundred? I'll pay you back.'

'You never have before.'

'You're so *mean*. You've got all that money and you grudge me a tiny bit.'

'I work for the money, so it's mine to do what I please with, and it doesn't please me to spend it on getting you drunk.'

Andi laughed openly and squealed in a high voice, 'Oooh. Drunk. How about joining the twenty-first century? Bladdered, trolleyed, slaughtered. A writer should be in touch with the words people really use, shouldn't she?'

'Being rude to me won't get you anywhere. Besides, you should be working for your own money at your age, not trying to cadge mine.'

Andi's face turned red and her voice grew shrill. 'I'll never get anywhere in that dead-end job, or earn enough to live even half comfortably. Dad wouldn't have wanted me to spend my life slaving for idiots. *He* really cared about me. *He* didn't nag me. And anyway — they sacked me today. So I can't earn my own money at the moment.'

'*What?*'

She shrugged. 'They gave me the push, the

69

heave-ho, say byesy-bye, don't call us we'll call you.'

'Do you have another job in mind?'

'Of course I don't. I didn't know they were going to sack me, did I?'

At times like this Sophie felt lost. She didn't know how to deal with her truculent daughter, but didn't dare let her go homeless — and Andi knew that, had traded on it before. 'I'll pay your rent for a few weeks, but I'm not paying for you to waste money on booze and clubbing. You'll have to register for social security for your living expenses and — '

Andi jumped to her feet, shoving the empty plate away so hard it slid off the surface and smashed to the ground. 'Put that on my bill!'

'Sit down and — '

'And what. Let you lecture me again? I've had enough of your bloody lectures. That's all you do when I come round, criticize me. I'm going off to see my friends. They want me to be happy and have fun.'

She rushed out towards the front door.

Sophie followed and found her fumbling with the new deadlocks, kicking the door in her frustration. 'Come and sit down again, Andi. We need to talk about this.'

The face her daughter turned on her was twisted with anger and . . . surely that wasn't hatred? What had she ever done to deserve that?

'Let me out of here, you stupid bitch!'

'Calm down.' Sophie reached out to touch her daughter but Andi slapped her hand away, then kicked out at her.

'Selfish — fat — bitch! Why are you still alive

and Dad dead? It's not *fair*.' She suddenly started belabouring her mother and kicking her.

Sophie was so taken aback it was a minute or two before she responded, then she fought back, shoving Andi away so hard she bounced against the wall. After she'd opened the door, she had to wrestle her daughter outside, then slammed the door on her and locked it.

Panting, rubbing her calf, which felt bruised, she watched over the security system as Andi stood there, yelling and cursing for a few moments, then stamped off down the drive.

If anyone was still out there watching, they'd have enjoyed that.

Oh, hell, were they there? Had anyone taken photos? Would they stop Andi and get her side of the story?

But no one stepped out of the shadows near the gate as Andi stopped to make a rude sign at the house. No engine revved up in the street as she started walking down it into the evening shadows.

As Sophie went back into the kitchen, reaction set in and she began to tremble. She stumbled across to the nearest chair and collapsed into it, weeping. Her daughter had been like a madwoman tonight. She'd suspected before that Andi was taking drugs, now she was certain of it. Her daughter had always had a sunny, optimistic nature but that had been changing for a while now. Tonight she'd been virulent, her eyes staring, her skin blotchy.

Like a stranger. A violent stranger. A stranger who hated her.

When she'd finished weeping, Sophie made herself a cup of drinking chocolate, trying to think what to do as she waited for the kettle to boil. But what could you do when someone was legally an adult and had the right to go to hell in her own fashion?

Should she give her daughter the money she clearly craved? No way. Everything in Sophie revolted at the thought of pouring down a bottomless drain the money she'd worked so hard for. She'd been brought up with the so-called Protestant work ethic, but she'd clearly failed to pass that on to Andi. The poor girl had never come to terms with the loss of her father. Well, Sophie missed him too. But life was like that. It kept chucking things at you. She knew that better than anyone.

She wished she could think how to put things right, how to help her daughter. She couldn't, hadn't the faintest idea what to do, where to start. That made her feel so sad.

Picking up the mug, she went to sit in her living room and put on a CD. She didn't look as she switched on the player, which was already loaded with a few favourites. Of course the first track was 'Tears May Fall'. She sat with her eyes closed, letting the music carry her away, thinking of Jez now and how much she'd liked him.

It helped banish the ugly memories of tonight. Well, it helped a bit.

Strange how Jez Winter had stayed in her mind ever since his visit, just as his music had threaded through her life for years.

'Oh, come on!' she said aloud. She was too old

to fantasize about pop stars, for heaven's sake.

Reaching out, she switched off the CD player and in the silence walked slowly along to her meditation room.

She sat down on the quilted rug, switched on the outside light to shine through the stained-glass window, then ran her forefinger round her favourite pattern on the rug as she let her body slowly calm down.

An hour later she went to watch a favourite TV programme, then got ready for bed, feeling she'd exorcized her demons — as much as you ever could with a problem child.

But that night she dreamed of Jez. How pitiful could you get?

She'd been without a man for too long, and her body had been letting her know that for a while. That must be the reason. She wished she had someone to love, everyone did, but pop stars didn't fall in love with middle-aged women. They married a series of beautiful young women.

Sophie felt very alone, in spite of her friends. Her son was firmly under his wife's thumb; her daughter seemed to hate her.

Was this what things would be like for the rest of her life? She hoped not. Sophie heard no more from her daughter and when she rang her at home the next day, the guy who shared the house with her said Andi was out. He sounded calm, as if nothing was wrong.

Out where? Sophie wanted to ask, and she also wanted to know where Andi was going to find the money to live comfortably?

But she didn't ask him that. Instead she rang

up the letting agent and agreed to pay Andi's rent until further notice, giving them her credit-card details.

It was all she could think of to do.

*   *   *

Two days later, Sophie tried to go grocery shopping and was followed the minute she drove out on to the street. They didn't even try to hide what they were doing.

When she stopped in the car park of the local supermarket, three other cars did too, one right next to her. The guy with the vicious expression jumped out of it, what was his name? Talbin, that was it. His camera flashed before she could cover her face.

'Where's lover boy? Not with you today?' he jeered.

Cringing at the mere thought of going round with her trolley while they embarrassed her publicly with their horrible questions, Sophie started up the car and drove home again. There she got online and arranged for food to be delivered.

After thinking about it, she rang Donna and told her what had happened. 'If you think it may help, I'll do an exclusive interview with someone like Peter Shane. This is starting to seriously disrupt my life. I can't go out for lunch with friends. I can't even go shopping.'

'It may help. Nothing's guaranteed, I'm afraid. I'll check whether Shane's interested and get back to you. Jez told me to say hi, by the way.'

'Oh. Well, tell him hi from me, too.'

'He'd have been in touch personally but he's had a family crisis — something good's happened, but it needs his attention.'

'I've had a crisis too, but not a good one.'

'Anything I can help with?'

'Thanks but no. It's a mother-daughter thing.'

After she put the phone down, Sophie turned to the computer and tried to start work. But she couldn't settle.

When the phone rang again, she snatched it up and agreed with Donna to do an exclusive interview the following afternoon with Peter Shane.

More interruptions, she thought wearily. But somehow she had to get the paparazzi off her back.

She didn't get as much work done as usual because she kept wondering what her daughter was doing, whether she was looking for another job, how she was managing for money. But you couldn't watch over them every minute of the day, not once they'd left home.

Her daughter was twenty-two and loudly proclaimed that she was an adult, not a dependent child. Then next minute she'd be asking for money and acting exactly like a spoiled, immature brat. She'd always been difficult, going her own sweet way once she got an idea fixed in her mind. She'd changed her name at the age of twelve and refused point-blank to answer to Andrea any longer, either at home or at school. Sophie had never liked the shortened form, Andi, but Bill had just accepted it.

If only he were here to help. He'd always been able to manage their daughter better than Sophie had. Only he wasn't here, never would be again. She still missed him dreadfully, his calmness in the face of crises, his support, his wry sense of humour, someone to touch you and cuddle you. And, of course, making love. She was a normal, healthy woman and missed that, too.

Should she ring William and tell him about his sister, ask him to keep his eyes and ears open? No, waste of time. The two of them weren't the best of friends these days and rarely saw one another. And to say her daughter didn't get on with Kerry was an understatement. They were like two cats when they were together, claws unsheathed, ready to strike.

She abandoned the writing and began to play solitaire on the computer, a sure sign that she was upset. She never normally played during the daytime, only when she'd finished writing for the day.

★   ★   ★

The following morning it took Tom a minute or two to work out where he was when he woke up. The children! Oh yes, they were with his mother. They'd be well looked after.

His head felt heavy and his eyes were a bit sore. He suddenly remembered what had happened the night before and sat bolt upright in bed. He was in his father's hotel suite, in a very elegant bedroom with his own bathroom.

When he got up, he put on the towelling gown

76

hanging on the door, for lack of anything else. He'd been too distraught even to think of packing a change of clothing, had half expected a rejection and having to hitchhike back.

When he peeped into the main area, he saw Jez — his *father* — sitting there with a cup of coffee, which smelled wonderful. 'Is there any more of that?'

'Of course. Over there. Help yourself.'

As Tom went back to the sitting area with a mug of hot coffee, Jez waved one hand towards a pile of clothes. 'I wondered if you'd like to borrow something to wear, since you didn't bring anything. I'd guess we're about the same size. If you don't like these, we can send out for something else.'

Tom stared at him, then shook his head slightly. This still felt unreal. *Send out* for clothes, for heaven's sake, not nip out and buy something. 'I don't mind borrowing something of yours, if that's all right with you.'

'Of course it is. I've arranged for my lawyer to come here at ten but I think we ought to phone your mother before then. She won't be happy about us meeting but unless she's changed greatly, she'll prefer to know what's going on.'

'She's not changed.' Tom sipped the coffee and eyed a big platter of pastries and fruit, set out like a work of art, with just a couple of gaps in the pattern.

'Help yourself to food. I've had my breakfast and anything left over will only be thrown away.'

Tom ate heartily then picked up the pile of clothes and took it into his bedroom. They fitted him well. Classy, they were, and obviously expensive. He stroked the beautiful material of the trousers and fingered the soft wool of the sweater, smiling at himself in the mirror. He felt a bit more confident dressed like this. People were wrong when they said clothes didn't matter. You had to feel right for the company you were keeping and his scruffy jeans were completely wrong for this posh hotel.

After that, they rang his mother, something that set his stomach churning. She was definitely unhappy about what he'd done, but he managed to calm her down and explain why he'd lied about going for a job interview, also why he'd not dared leave the children with Gail.

There was silence then, 'I knew something was wrong with her, but I didn't realize what it was. Why didn't you tell us sooner, Tom?'

'It's not the sort of thing you broadcast and she kept promising to give up the booze. Only she didn't, well, not for more than a week, anyway. She had a psychotic incident when she tried smoking pot, which frightened her and kept her off it from then on. That was when she went into hospital for a few days when Hayley was two, remember?' He heard her sigh.

'Yes. I do remember. We wondered why you didn't want us visiting her. We thought she must have had some kind of surgery, something embarrassing.'

He still shuddered to think of that time. He'd had a scary week or two until Gail came out of it, and didn't know what he'd have done without his neighbour Jane to look after Hayley. He didn't want to go into any more details about Gail with his mother, so he changed the subject. 'How are the kids?'

Her voice grew softer. 'Beautiful as ever. They had a good breakfast, then a bath and now they're playing with the toy box.'

'I knew you'd look after them well. Can I speak to them?'

After he'd finished chatting to Hayley and Ryan, and got his mother back on the phone, Jez signalled to him. 'Jez wants a word with you.' Tom handed over the phone.

'I'll look after him, Mary.'

Angry, staccato sounds at the other end.

'I don't drink or do drugs these days, haven't for years. I saw too many people dragged down by them, one way or another. And they got in the way of my music. Look, I'll help Tom in whatever way he wants and we'll be in touch with you after we've seen a lawyer.'

'It's a doctor Gail needs, not a lawyer.'

'The lawyer is to protect Tom and make sure he gets custody of the children while she's — er, incapacitated. For their safety.'

'And no doubt you'll be telling him to divorce such an unsuitable wife!'

'Is she unsuitable?'

Silence, then a sigh. 'Yes. I never liked her. But Tom swore in church to take her *for better for worse*.'

Jez wasn't getting into that sort of argument. 'We'll ring you again after we've spoken to the lawyer, Mary.'

He put down the phone and looked at his son.

'Do you want to phone your wife now?'

'No.'

'Might be wiser.'

'Even if I wanted to, she'd still be sleeping it off. She doesn't rise early these days. Some days she doesn't rise at all.'

Tom's sense of unreality continued until the lawyer arrived, asking questions that struck straight at the quivering mass of pain inside him. He had a hard time keeping it together as he talked. He'd been hiding his problems for a long time and it was even harder than he'd expected to reveal all the sordid details.

After a while, the lawyer turned from him to Jez. 'Shall I send someone up north to sort it?'

'Have you got someone suitable?'

He smiled and said in his plummy voice, 'Oh, yes. One of our junior partners, Stephen Perriman, is very sound and specializes in divorce.'

'Then get him on to it. The sooner the better.'

'Mr Prichard will need to be there too.'

Jez turned to his son. 'I can send you back in a car as soon as you're ready.'

Tom knew then that the bubble was about to burst, so he nodded, trying to look as if he wanted to go back and leave his father, with so much yet to say. He didn't want to go. No way.

After the lawyer had gone, Jez sat looking thoughtful and Tom didn't dare interrupt him, so fiddled around with another cup of coffee.

'There's a lot to decide,' Jez said at last. He wasn't looking at Tom as he added, 'I hope I can keep on seeing you — and the children?'

Tom lost it again, nodded, could only make a gruff sound. He was near to howling like a baby from sheer relief that his father did want to keep seeing him. He found Jez sitting next to him again patting his shoulder. Blinking furiously, he sniffed and hunted for a tissue. One was pressed into his hand.

'It must have been bad.'

'Yeah. Worst of all, I've been worried she'd hurt the kids. Though she never has, I'll give her that. But she's neglected them badly, and when she's drunk she doesn't know what she's doing. They've learned to hide when she's like that. Hayley's very ingenious about finding places to hide and looking after her little brother.'

'I'm dying to meet them.'

'You'll love them. You know . . . I was worried about meeting you.'

Jez smiled. 'I know. I was terrified. But that's all right now, isn't it?'

Tom turned and glanced at him, only able to nod. He hadn't expected meeting his father to affect him so strongly. More silence, then Jez asked, 'What we need to decide is where you want to live after you separate from your wife. She'll be entitled to half your present house, I should think, but I can buy you another wherever you like — if that's all right with you. Up north or down here.'

'Buy me a house?' Tom gaped at him.

'Or you could come and live with me. I hate hotels, and I'm negotiating to buy a big house, one with room for a small recording studio in it. This place I've seen has some self-contained flats for live-in staff. You and the kids could have one — if you like. And my housekeeper could provide meals for all of us. We'd get you a nanny . . . but that's only if you want. I'm not trying to take over your life.'

Tom swallowed hard, trying to take all this in. Finally he managed, 'Yeah. That'd be great. Really . . . great.'

'You wouldn't prefer to stay near your mother?'

He didn't hesitate. 'Definitely not. I want to — get to know you. Let the kids get to know you. If that's all right?'

'That's great — just great.' It was Jez's turn to struggle for self-control, Tom's turn to pat his father and allow him time to pull himself together.

Sometimes, Tom thought as he watched Jez, there simply weren't any words that fitted. He'd never spent two such emotional days, wouldn't have missed them for the world, but he felt gutted now, absolutely exhausted by it.

It suddenly occurred to him that it might look as if he was after the money and he added hastily, 'I'll need to find a job as soon as possible, mind. I don't want to sponge off you.'

'We can find you something in one of my companies.'

The words escaped before Tom could hold them back. 'Just like that. Job from Daddy?'

Jez's voice suddenly became harsh. 'No, not *just like that*. They'd give you aptitude tests, make sure you had any training you needed, and I'd expect you to work hard. I don't run the companies myself, but I trust the people who do. And anyone who works for me earns their pay or we say goodbye.'

'Sorry. I didn't mean to sound ungrateful. That'd be wonderful. I did get a degree. Business Studies. Oh, you know that, don't you? But I didn't do very well. I got a bit drunk on the freedom of university, you see.'

'Freedom from your mother?'

'From her church, more than anything. They interfere too much, narrow your horizons, try to keep you *safe* from the real world. As if you can cut yourself off from reality!'

They looked at one another, then looked away. Tom was damned if he knew what to say or do next. But he felt a warmth within him about his father's instant, unquestioning support. He'd prove himself worthy of it, he vowed, whatever it took.

And he'd make sure Hayley and Ryan were loved and looked after properly from now on. Gail didn't deserve kids as nice as them.

5

When Jez had seen Tom leave for the north with the young divorce lawyer, he went to find Donna.

She smiled at him. 'Everything all right now?'

'I think it's going to be.'

'I like the looks of your son. He's very like you. Is he musical too?'

Jez looked at her in surprise. 'I don't know. It didn't even occur to me to ask. We've barely touched the surface of getting to know one another.' But it was rather a nice idea, a father and son making music together. He realized she was waiting for him to speak. 'Now, I want to go and look at that big house in Hampstead again.'

'The one in Chestnut Lane?'

'Yes. It's the only one that suits my needs now.'

'It'll start the gossip up again if you go and live next door to Sophie.'

He spread his hands helplessly. 'What choice do I have? I don't want to live out in the depths of the country, but I do need a big place, which you don't get many of in town. My son needs a home, I've two grandchildren I want to get to know — and dammit, I need a home, too. Besides, I always did like that house best.'

'Well, then, we'd better go and look it over carefully. And I'd better warn Sophie.'

'Perhaps we could pop in to see her afterwards?'

Donna rolled her eyes at him.

'Not a good idea?'

'No way, José. Not if you want to protect her reputation.'

Pity, Jez thought. But if they lived next door to one another, he'd definitely see her again. If she wasn't angry with him for drawing attention back to her, that was. Surely she'd understand about Tom?

Jez was surprised how much he wanted to see Sophie, how often he thought about her. All this after one meeting. He hoped he wasn't going to make a fool of himself again, then smiled. Been there, done that. Could survive it again, if he had to. But perhaps . . . He didn't let himself finish that thought. Not yet.

★　★　★

When Tom arrived back in the north with Stephen Perriman, he and the divorce lawyer went to his house first to see Gail and formally tell her he was instituting divorce proceedings. He couldn't bear to do anything in an underhand way.

He led the way inside and found to his embarrassment that his wife was lying in the front room. She'd obviously passed out and it wasn't yet teatime. There were two bottles lying nearby, one empty, the other almost empty, with a damp patch next to it on the carpet where it had fallen over.

The lawyer studied her, then turned to Tom. 'If you can bear it, we could do with another witness to this.'

He looked down at his wife. Her hair was lank,

her clothing dishevelled and dirty, her mouth open as she snored slightly. He hated to bring in a witness, but the thought of the kids made him agree. 'Jane Burtill next door has seen it all before, and she's helped out with the kids quite a lot. She's like an extra grandmother, really. She's a widow and never had children of her own so she says she enjoys it. I've — um, relied on her quite a bit in the past few months. I don't know what I'd have done without her.'

He fetched Jane, who nodded as the lawyer explained the situation.

When Perriman had finished, she said quietly, 'Well, I'll testify to what I've seen, of course I will, though I hope it won't be necessary. It's not good to have children in a tug of war.'

'I'm grateful.'

She looked at the still figure on the floor. 'Can we get Gail to bed now, Tom? Whatever she's done, she needs looking after.'

'She'll be offered rehabilitation as part of the settlement, all expenses paid,' the lawyer said quietly.

'She won't accept it. She'll either continue downhill till she's shocked into stopping or she'll drown in the booze.' Jane looked from one man to the other. 'I've some experience with this. My husband was a drunkard and it killed him.'

'My client wants to help his wife if he can,' the lawyer said smoothly.

'He's a good lad, Tom is, but he has to think of his children now.'

Tom and the lawyer carried Gail up to bed, then Jane shooed them out. 'I'll clean her up.

She's wet herself and needs changing.'

Tom avoided the lawyer's eyes. It had happened before.

After that they left her to sleep it off.

'I'm going to miss those kids of yours,' Jane said as she went towards the front door.

An idea struck Tom suddenly. 'You don't want a job as nanny, do you? Only, we have to hire someone and I'm sure Hayley and Ryan would be happier with you. It'd mean you moving to London, but my father said he'd provide accommodation.'

She gaped at him for a few seconds then a smile crept slowly over her face. 'I'd not mind a bit of a change. Life can get very quiet for an older widow without children or grandchildren, and my place is only rented. Look, you know my phone number. If you're still willing when you've thought about this, and if your father agrees, let me know when you want me and I'll be there. I'd better leave you to it, now.'

'Mrs Burtill seems a sound woman,' the lawyer said. 'Very useful her seeing what your wife was like today. She'll make a good witness.'

Tom wished there need be no witnesses, no court proceedings, for his children's sake. But he knew Gail would make a fuss about the divorce, because she had nothing else in her life except him and the alcohol.

★　★　★

The chauffeur dropped Tom at his mother's and took the lawyer to a hotel for the night, promising to bring him back the following morning.

He gave Tom his mobile number. 'I'll find somewhere to stay in town. Mr Winter says I'm at your service for as long as you need me.'

'Thanks.' Tom took a deep breath and knocked on the front door, then went inside, calling, 'It's only me.'

'So you're back,' his mother said sharply. 'I saw the fancy car. Are you sure you can be bothered with us ordinary folk now?'

'Don't be daft, Mum.' He hugged her then the kids, delighted to see them looking rosy and well looked after, for once. They were just going to bed, so he went up with them, kissing them goodnight and listening to them repeat their prayers after his mother. He remembered doing the same thing, but the words had been completely meaningless to him, just a ritual to please his mother.

As he followed her downstairs again, he could feel the butterflies in his stomach. It was one thing to talk of going against her wishes and making a new life for himself, another thing entirely to do it, mainly because he didn't want to hurt her. 'Where's Brian?'

'Thursday night. Church elders' meeting.'

'Oh, yeah. I'd forgotten what day it was.'

'Are you hungry?'

'Not really. We — um, need to talk.'

She led the way into the sitting room, instead of using the small sunroom off the kitchen, so he knew she regarded this as a very serious occasion.

'Tell me,' she said once they were seated.

He explained more fully what had been happening lately, not glossing over Gail's drunkenness this time, telling her how worried he had been about the kids and how despairing about his own future.

'You took her for better for worse.'

'And it's been getting worse, not just for me. It's actually quite dangerous for the kids to be left with her, because she ignores them.' He took a deep breath and said it as plainly as he could, 'Whatever happens, I'm not staying with Gail, Mum. Nothing will change my mind about that.' He saw her open her mouth and repeated quietly but firmly, 'Nothing. Only I didn't know how to manage it and then when I lost my job . . . '

After he'd finished explaining about Jez's offer, she bowed her head and he waited, knowing from past experience that she was praying for guidance and would do nothing until she'd finished.

It was a few minutes before she raised her head. 'Didn't you think to come to us for help?'

'Yes. But I'm too old to live here again, besides which I've changed, don't want the same things in life as you do.'

'You've been skipping church for a while now. Don't think I haven't noticed. Brian said to leave you be.'

'Yes. Well, your church doesn't feel right for me any longer.'

'Would you — talk to the pastor about that? Please?'

'No, definitely not.'

89

There was the sound of the front door opening and Brian came in, so everything had to be explained all over again. He listened with his usual quiet attention, then turned from the man he considered his son to his wife.

'Mary, the boy needs to know his biological father. We've disagreed about that for a while now.'

Tom looked at them in surprise. He hadn't had the faintest suspicion of this.

'We have to trust that we've brought him up to be a decent human being,' Brian said, 'and wish him well.'

She cried then, something Tom had rarely seen before. He felt racked with guilt, nearly said he'd stay, but bit his tongue. If he said it now, he'd only have to unsay it tomorrow. And would.

He slept better that night on their sofa than he had for a long time in his comfortable bed next to Gail.

In the morning, he lay wondering what his wife was doing. Had she woken up and gone out for more booze, then drunk herself senseless again — or simply stayed in bed? There seemed no pattern in her behaviour from one day to the next.

He didn't want harm to come to her, but if he never saw her again it'd not upset him. And that was sad, given the high hopes with which they'd married. Was everyone the same at the beginning? Why did some marriages fail so quickly? It had taken only a few months of living with Gail to disillusion him, but by that time she'd been pregnant, and the love he'd felt for her had gradually transferred to Hayley. And then Ryan had come along and he'd loved his little son on sight. How could you not?

He wondered how Jez would get on with such little children. Would he enjoy being a grandfather? He carried their photos in his wallet, Tom's too, so maybe he'd like having a family.

So many things to wonder about, so many things in a state of change.

For the first time in ages, though, Tom felt hopeful about the future.

★ ★ ★

The following afternoon Sophie got ready for her interview with Peter Shane, trying on three outfits and not feeling right about any of them, wishing she'd had her hair trimmed, wishing she had the sort of hair you could do fashionable things with, instead of hair so thick and heavy she could only find a good hairdresser to cut it just so, then let it hang loose. Well, at least it wasn't very grey yet, which was something to be thankful for at her age. Most of her girl friends dyed their hair now. She wasn't sure she could be bothered to do that.

When the doorbell rang half an hour before the interview, she was still in her casual clothes, still dithering. She let Donna in with relief.

'Just thought we could discuss what to say or not say, if you don't mind. And what to wear. He'll be taking the photo himself. He's quite a good photographer, actually.'

'I don't mind at all going over it with you. You

know far more about this sort of thing than I do.' Sophie hesitated, then asked, 'How's Jez? I hope he sorted out his crisis. I was worried about him the other day, he seemed so tired and sad.'

'He's still tired, but not as sad. Sends his best wishes every time he knows I'm coming to see you and talks about your cake. You certainly made a good impression on him.'

Sophie could feel herself blushing and saw Donna's amusement at that. 'That's nice. I'll give you a chunk of my latest cake to take back for him.' She couldn't hold back a sigh. 'I can certainly sympathize about family problems. You don't want to hear about that, though.'

'Do you still have a problem? I'm a good listener.'

Sophie explained about Andi. 'I don't know what to do.'

'There's not much you can do except be there if she needs you.' Donna gave Sophie a wry smile. 'Oh, and you can worry. Mothers do a lot of that.'

'You're not a — '

'No, I'm not a mother, but my sister's a single parent and she's having a lot of trouble with her son. He's only eight, so she's still got some control over him, but he's a cheeky little devil, always into fights, in trouble at school. He needs a father, really.'

'Your sister has all my sympathy. Now, could you please help me decide what to wear? Come and see what I've got.'

They chose a simple outfit, black skirt and top, and a patchwork jacket in velvet, with flowers in jewel colours on the patterned pieces, but still mainly black. Sophie had once bought it at a colourful market stall and never found the right occasion to wear it. But Donna loved it and somehow it looked right today.

The doorbell rang. She took a deep breath and went to answer it.

Peter looked smarter than last time, a well-dressed urbane man, tall, with prematurely silver hair.

'Please come in.'

The interview was easier than she'd expected. He didn't ask any leading or awkward questions and Donna, sitting watchfully to one side, didn't have to step in.

When Donna's mobile rang, she excused herself and went to answer it in the kitchen. Her 'Oh, damn!' rang down the corridor loud and clear.

She came hurrying back. 'I have to go.' She looked fiercely at Peter. 'Can I trust you not to lead her astray?'

'I promise.' He smiled as her expression remained stony. 'I mean it. It'd not suit my purpose at all to get on the bad side of the Jez Winter machine, now would it? I'd really like to do an in-depth interview with him one day.'

Donna relaxed. 'All right. I'll trust you. We'll see about the interview when he's more settled. I'm making no promises, though. And make sure it's a flattering photo today.'

'Easy to do with that face and hair.'

When Sophie escorted her guest to the door, not forgetting to pack a chunk of cake for Jez,

93

Donna whispered, 'Remember, there's no such thing as off the record. Don't say anything you don't want publishing, whether he's put away his recording gadget or not.'

Sophie felt vulnerable and apprehensive as she walked back to the sitting room.

Peter looked up and chuckled. 'I'm not an ogre and I promise not to try to trick you.' He sketched a cross over his chest. 'Shall we do the photo next?'

It took very little time and he showed her his shots on the digital camera.

'You're good. I should have something more like this on my book covers. I don't really like the one they're using. It looks like a wax model of me, with no life to it.'

'I could sell you one of these, if you like. I never mind making extra money.'

So they chose one photo for the article and another for her next book cover, agreeing a price which was half that of the studio portrait she'd disliked. By the time she sat back, she felt much more relaxed with him. 'Would you like a drink? A glass of wine, maybe?'

'That'd be nice. I don't mind what sort it is. I like both white and red, and I'm not a wine snob.'

'That's a good thing, because I'm not either. I just buy quaffing wine, not vintage stuff. I don't drink very often, but the occasional glass is nice. Why don't you come through into the kitchen? If you've finished, that is.'

'I just need the information about your novels that you promised me. I'm sorry I've not read any of them, but I will have before I finish writing this article.'

'I don't expect everyone to have read my books. I'll get you a press handout from my office and a copy of my latest book.' When she led the way into the kitchen to get the wine, she saw him look at the tray she'd set out. 'I'm into making cakes. I was going to offer you both refreshments after the interview, though I don't think Donna lets herself eat cake very often.'

'I'd love a piece. I didn't get much lunch.'

She found she was enjoying herself. He was good company and talked about all sorts of things, not asking any more questions about Jez Winter.

'Would you like to go out for a meal one night?' he asked suddenly. 'Strictly social.'

She stared at him in surprise, not knowing what to say. Then Andi's scorn about her being too old to enjoy life made her say, 'That'd be nice. If we can avoid the watchers, that is.'

'I think the article on you will set their nasty little suspicions to rest.'

'Are you really writing an article about them?'

He grinned. 'I am. Bit of role reversal, don't you think? The biter bit. Especially Talbin, who's a very strange man. I can't quite figure him out. Anyway, who cares about him? How about going out with me next week? That'll give this fuss a few more days to die down.' He drained his glass. 'I'd better leave you in peace now, and anyway I've got to visit my mother in hospital. She's a fearsome old bat, but I'm rather fond of her.'

When she was alone, Sophie changed out of her interview clothes into something old and extremely comfortable. She looked in the mirror and grimaced. She looked positively scruffy now. Then she forgot about her appearance as she started writing again.

This time she managed to work steadily. Things were going to get back to normal soon and the paparazzi would stop chasing her, she was sure.

As for the problem with Andi, things would settle down, of course they would. They always had before.

That was what happened when you lived alone. You got things out of proportion.

★   ★   ★

Jez went to see the house again and it was, as he'd remembered, very suitable for his present needs, far better than any of the others. He had quite a retinue now, something which both amused and irritated him. Due to that damned intruder, Kevin and Craig took it in turns to stay the night, with a third man filling in as necessary to give them a break.

The house really appealed to him, and though it was shabby and in need of modernization, the rooms were big, the ceilings high, and quite simply it felt right.

'Buy it,' he told Donna, strolling over to a window to look wistfully towards the house next door. That one was much smaller, but still bigger than average. The estate agent had told Donna that another of these huge old houses had been demolished there and the land split into four building plots with a new 'executive residence' on each. Strange that Jez had never noticed the other three houses before, but he could see them all clearly from the upstairs window. He could see the old gate too, which had led him to Sophie.

He leaned forward a little, smiling as he saw her come out into her garden, hair gleaming like molten honey in the sunlight. She tipped something from a packet into a bird feeder, nipping off a couple of dead flowers as she moved away. On the lawn she stood still and lifted her face to the sun, a gesture of such natural pleasure that he ached to join her and do the same.

'Don't even think about it,' Donna said from behind him.

He spun round. 'Is it so obvious?'

'That you fancy her? Yeah.' She hesitated, then added, 'Stop me if I'm out of order, Jez, but I've never seen you so taken with a woman, not since I joined the team, anyway. She's not your usual sort of female, either.'

No, she wasn't. His eyes were drawn to Sophie again as he tried to understand his feelings. Was this just a casual physical attraction, easily satisfied by a few nights together? He'd not bothered about women much lately, not for lack of offers, but for lack of interest. Why did it feel different with Sophie? He didn't know, only that he wanted to spend time with her and find out what there was between them.

He didn't want to do anything that might hurt Sophie, though. He hadn't made women happy in the past, why should it be any different in the future?

Donna nudged him to get his attention. 'You still with me, Jez?'

He forced himself to turn away from the window. 'Yes, sorry. Go on. About the house . . . '

'You'll let me do the bargaining, won't you? We can get it for much less than they're asking, because it's such a monstrosity. Most people would only buy it to knock it down, only it's been listed so they'd have trouble doing that.'

He waved one hand. 'Whatever. Just buy it for me quickly.'

'Right. Let's get you back to the hotel, then I'll make a start.'

He took one last glance at the garden next door, not wanting to leave. But Sophie had gone inside again. Oh, hell, he was being stupid today, absolutely stupid.

Donna gave him one of her serene professional smiles as they got into the limo. 'Peter Shane wants to do an in-depth interview on you. I said maybe.'

'I don't need any publicity.'

'But it might help with this Sophie thing if you explained what you were doing at her house that day.'

He sighed. 'Slave-driver. I'll think about it. I'm promising nothing, though.'

The hotel felt stuffy. He was bored, wanted to make loud music, send it shivering along his veins and filling his head with sound. But he didn't have his electric guitars here, just a couple of acoustics.

He stood by the window looking at a magnificent panorama of the Thames. He'd rather see Sophie among her flowers, go out and draw her into his arms and . . .

Stop it! he told himself. But the image wouldn't go away.

In the end he toyed with some food then went to bed for a nap, waking heavy-eyed and unrefreshed.

* * *

The hotel phone rang early that evening. Stephen Perriman, Tom's divorce lawyer, was reporting in from Lancashire.

'Did you fix it?' Jez asked.

'I can, but she wants money. I think her cousin's been putting inflated ideas into her head.' He summarized the legal ins and outs.

'Just get on with it. Pay whatever it costs to set Tom free — and to get him custody of the children.'

'Nothing is ever guaranteed, Mr Winter. Mrs Prichard could sober up and weep all over a sympathetic judge, who might then give her another chance with the children. But we did get the neighbour in to witness the state the wife was in, which may help. It won't hurt if you have a home ready for them.'

Which meant pushing this house purchase through as quickly as possible. He'd impress that on Donna first thing tomorrow.

Jez fell asleep that night to dream of his grandchildren. How would it feel to play with them? Would they want to be with him? Hell, what did he know about little children anyway, except for what he'd seen on the TV or in movies?

But it was good to know your blood was being carried on down the generations. It surprised him how satisfying that felt. And he now had photos of them and Tom openly displayed in his suite. That felt good, too.

★ ★ ★

Tom rang his father the next morning, hesitant to talk about money, though clearly it was going to be the key to freeing him.

'The money's not important to me,' Jez said impatiently. Tom's voice grew harder. Jez could imagine that at that moment his son would have a look like his mother.

'Well, it is to me. Whatever you spend, I'll pay back as soon as I can.'

'Why? Don't you think I'm glad to help?'

'I suppose so. And I'm grateful. Very. But I'm *not* a scrounger. I prefer to stand on my own feet.'

'Right. Sorry. I didn't mean to imply that you were — you know — only contacting me for the money.'

'As long as that's clear.'

Jez was touched by this. His son was the second person he'd met lately who didn't care about money. It was strange — hard to believe.

100

'Can you and the children stay with your mother till I get into this house I'm buying?'

'Yes. And I may have found a nanny for the kids. It's our neighbour. She's looked after them from time to time and she's like a second grandmother to them. Would there be room for her as well in this new place?'

'Of course.' And if there wasn't, Jez would make room. 'If you change your mind, you can bring them down and stay at the hotel with me. The nanny too.'

'There are things to do at my own house, stuff to sort out and pack, so I need to stay up here for a few days, I think. And small kids don't go well with posh hotels.'

Jez smiled. 'In this hotel, given the price I'm paying for my suite, they'll accommodate children or anything including a pet elephant, believe me.'

Tom chuckled. 'Well, actually, I'd love a pet elephant.'

★　★　★

Tom went round to his house to get some clean clothes the next day, waving a greeting to Jane as he walked up the path. When he got inside, he stopped for a minute, feeling uncomfortable, like a visitor.

He found Gail yawning over a cup of coffee, looking as if she'd just got up, though it was ten o'clock in the morning. 'I need to get some of my clothes.' He thought it better not to mention the kids' things.

She scowled at him. 'My cousin came round last night. She's been divorced twice now and she gave me some very good advice. I'm not doing anything or agreeing to anything till I find myself a lawyer. So don't think you can cheat me out of my rights.'

'Cheat you? How am I doing that?'

'I don't know. But your *daddy* can afford fancy lawyers and everyone knows rich people get away with murder. I might want to clean up my act a bit and look after the kids myself. I'm the one who had them, after all, and you'll be out at work, because I'm sure *Daddy* will find you a job.'

He didn't believe her about cleaning up her act. She'd promised that too many times already, and anyway, she'd never been a good mother. But she could be a nasty bitch when she felt herself the injured party, so he didn't argue, just went up to their bedroom.

To his annoyance, she followed him up. He turned to look at her and something in the way she was standing worried him. Suddenly it didn't seem such a good idea to come here on his own with her. 'I'll — um, I left something in the car.'

He had to push past her and for a moment they were pressed closely together in the doorway. She raised one hand to touch his cheek and wriggled her hips against him. He realized with disgust that she was trying to tempt him sexually, which was her answer to everything. But she hadn't attracted him in that way for a while now and he drew back from her unwashed body. He couldn't even bear to touch her.

His revulsion must have shown in his face, because her expression turned ugly. 'Too good for me now, are you? Throwing me away now you've got a rich father to look after you?'

He ran down the stairs, with her words stabbing the air behind him.

'I'll make you sorry for dumping me, Tom Prichard. See if I don't.'

He stood by the front door wondering what to do, then saw that Jane was still in her garden so hurried across. She'd been there when he arrived. 'Did you see me going into the house a minute or two ago?'

She nodded.

'And coming out again?'

Another nod. 'And I can see Gail watching us from the bedroom window at the moment. Have you two quarrelled?'

'Permanently.' He twisted round to look up at his wife, but she must have ducked back again. 'I think I was foolish to come back on my own.'

Jane looked at him in surprise then shook her head sadly. 'I don't like to see couples breaking up with such acrimony, but you've had a lot to bear. Do you want me to come inside with you?'

'I think it'd be better still to have a lawyer or a police officer there.'

'My nephew Dean is a policeman and he lives nearby. Shall I give him a call? If he's off duty, he'll come into the house with us as a favour to me, I'm sure. You couldn't get a more credible witness than a policeman.'

To Tom's relief, her nephew was free and came round at once.

When the three of them went into the house, they heard hysterical weeping from upstairs. Tom led the way up and found Gail lying on the bed, her face bruised and scratched.

'Don't let him hit me again!' she yelled as Tom stood gaping in the doorway. She put up one arm as if to protect her face.

He couldn't move, so shocked was he by this accusation.

Jane moved forward. 'What happened? I saw you standing at the window *after* Tom left. You weren't hurt or upset then.'

'You couldn't have seen me. He hit me and left me lying on the bed.'

The nephew cleared his throat to get their attention. 'I think I should call someone in, if she's alleging assault. Perhaps you'd come downstairs with me, Mr Prichard? And if you could stay with Mrs Prichard, Auntie Jane?'

Tom sat numbly on the couch, listening to the nephew report the alleged assault to his sergeant. Gail had promised to make him sorry and was doing it already. But surely she couldn't make this accusation stick? He hadn't touched her.

He waited in silence for the police to arrive, then answered their questions with the simple truth. The woman officer looked down and he saw she was studying his hands.

'You haven't washed your hands recently?'

He looked at her in puzzlement. 'No.'

'Don't wash them.'

Tom could only stare after her in puzzlement as she took Dean aside and spoke earnestly to him in a low voice.

When she came back, she asked, 'Is there anyone you want to ring?'

His mind refused to function for a minute or two then he nodded. 'My father. Um — my biological father, that is. He's in London. Is that all right?'

'Go ahead, Mr Prichard.'

He took out the card with Jez's number on it and prayed that his father would answer. But it was Donna. She took the details and advised him to say nothing further to the police. She'd get a lawyer on the case straight away to represent him.

Tom sat in numb dread, unable to think clearly, while people came and went, going up and down the stairs, tending Gail. Time seemed to pass very slowly.

He couldn't believe this was happening.

What if his damned wife got the children and had him prosecuted? How could he protect them then? And what would his father think?

★   ★   ★

Donna phoned Jez's lawyers straight away and they promised to find a colleague in the north who could step in. Only then did she go and wake Jez, who was having another of his naps.

'I'm sorry. It's bad news.' She explained what had happened to Tom.

'He didn't do it.'

'You can't be sure of that.'

Jez looked at her. 'You've met him. Does he look like a wife-beater?'

105

'What do they look like? If you ask me, appearances are nothing to go by.'

'Well, I can't and won't believe Tom did it. Has anyone rung his mother?'

'I don't know.'

'I'll do that now.'

Mary didn't answer the phone till the sixth ring. 'It's Jez.'

'What do *you* want?'

'To let you know what's happened to Tom.'

Her tone changed instantly. 'What do you mean? Is he all right?'

'His wife has accused him of beating her up. The police are at his house, questioning him.'

'He'd never do that, not my Tom.'

'I don't believe he would, either. I've arranged for a lawyer to go and help him. I just thought you'd better know.'

There was silence, then a grudging, 'Thank you. I'll call Brian at work, get him to go round to be with Tom.'

'Good idea.'

As he put the phone down, Jez cursed the fact that he was too far away to help. Still, Tom had turned to him. That was a good sign — wasn't it? It must be.

And whatever Donna said, whatever *anyone* said, he was absolutely certain Tom was innocent.

★ ★ ★

Tom looked up as someone knocked on the door. More police? Were they coming to take him

106

to the station and lock him away? He hadn't a clue what the procedure was in this situation.

A man was shown into the room. He looked tired, his clothes were rumpled and he seemed to know the female police officer.

'Has Mr Prichard been charged with anything, Liz?'

She shook her head. 'We're still investigating the complaint, Morrie.'

'Can I speak to my client alone, please?'

She nodded and left them in the small sitting room.

'I'm Maurice Yetherby. Jez Winter has hired me to look after your interests.'

'I didn't do it,' Tom said at once.

'Tell me every single detail.'

When he'd finished, Yetherby also studied his client's hands. 'You've no signs of bruises or grazing.'

'Because I didn't hit her! I didn't touch her in any way, though *she* rubbed herself against me. Gail's a good liar and she'll do anything to get her own way, even hurt herself.'

There was a knock on the door and the policewoman came in again. 'The doctor's here to examine your wife and he'd like to see you too afterwards, Mr Prichard.'

'Do we need a doctor of our own?' the lawyer asked in a low voice.

She hesitated, looking over her shoulder, then shook her head quickly, even as she said, 'I can't discuss the case at this stage, you know that, Morrie.'

Tom looked from one to the other, bewildered

107

at the subtext in this conversation.

There was another knock on the front door and they showed his stepfather in.

'Did you ring Winter?' Brian asked Tom.

'Yes.'

'Why didn't you ring me?'

'I don't know. But he sent someone to help me.' He introduced the lawyer.

Brian scowled at Yetherby. 'Is it all right if I stay?'

'Yes, of course.'

A few minutes later the doctor was shown in, examined Tom's hands with a magnifying glass, then turned to the police officer. 'Couldn't have attacked her like that without doing some damage to himself. There's no sign of it whatsoever.'

'I think we'd be wise to make sure of the evidence,' she said.

'OK.' He took swabs from under Tom's nails and photographed his hands. 'I won't get these analysed unless we need to.'

At Yetherby's prompting he took extra swabs and sealed them in an envelope, handing them over to the lawyer.

Tom couldn't seem to think straight, was still shocked to the core by what had happened, so just did as they asked.

They heard footsteps going upstairs and voices in the front bedroom. All at once, there was a scream of fury, then Gail began crying loudly.

Tom jerked to his feet. 'What are they doing to her?'

The lawyer smiled. 'Probably telling her not to

waste police time.' He patted Tom's shoulder. 'It was plain you didn't hit her, but it had to be proved. They'll probably thank you for your help and release you shortly. If I were you, I'd make sure I was never alone with her again.'

'I need to get some clothes. And the children's things. And knowing Gail, I'd better get as much as I can. She's liable to take her anger out on my things. She's chopped up my shirts before.' Worst of all, she'd smashed his guitar a few weeks ago, knowing how much that would hurt him. He'd had it since he was fifteen, missed it.

The lawyer looked at his watch. 'I'll wait a little longer. As soon as they release you formally, pack as much as you can and we'll take it away with us now. Then stay right away from her.'

When the police came back to confirm that Tom had been cleared of suspicion and no charges would be brought, he felt numb more than anything else. He seemed to have been on an emotional rollercoaster lately — and it was all too much.

His mother would be furious with him for going to Jez for help. And he'd need to live with her until he could join his father in London. That wouldn't be easy. Her silences could be as disapproving as other people's words.

6

By the time Donna left the hotel, it was getting dark. Jez fiddled around with his guitar, striking chords, playing snatches of melody, but couldn't settle to playing anything even half decent. He put it down and switched on the television, but there was nothing worth watching.

At last, giving in to temptation, he phoned Sophie, his heart beating faster as he waited for her to respond. 'It's Jez.'

'Oh. I didn't expect . . . How are you?'

'Upset. I wonder — could I come round for an hour? We'll do it discreetly. I'll go next door and come through the gate. I just — I'd like to talk to you again. Am I asking too much?'

He waited a long time for her answer.

'I'd like that.'

Relief sang through him. 'I'll be about half an hour.'

He went to find Craig, who was on duty tonight, and of course his minder protested about the outing, but Jez didn't care.

Hidden in the back of Craig's small car, he left the hotel. He knew it was foolish to get mixed up with Sophie Carr again, but he didn't care. He wanted to make sure . . . to find out . . . he didn't know what he wanted, except simply to be with her.

He smiled. And maybe to enjoy another piece of her wonderful home-made cake.

After parking on Chestnut Lane, Craig studied the other vehicles, then switched off the engine. 'I'll just scout round. Keep the car doors locked.'

Reluctantly Jez did as he was told. The memory of the intruder with the knife slashing his face was still horribly vivid and ensured that he took care.

Craig returned and slid into the car. 'I don't think there are any watchers tonight but we'd better not approach her house openly. Come on. We'll go through the gardens of your new place.'

'You don't need to come with me. I know my way.'

'You know better than that, Jez. Don't worry. I'll stay outside in the garden.'

'Good thing it's a fine evening.'

Craig didn't bother to reply. He didn't joke about his job.

Creeping through the darkness and trying not to make any noise felt ridiculously theatrical, cops and robbers stuff. The gate creaked a little and Craig muttered under his breath.

When they approached the side door of Sophie's house, Jez expected a security light to come on, but it didn't. He knocked and waited, keeping his eyes open to what was happening around him, even though Craig was watching his back.

The moonlight was bright enough to show the curtain moving slightly at a nearby window then dropping into place again. Wise of her, Jez thought, but felt sad that she'd had to learn this lesson the hard way. When she opened the door, he slipped inside without a word.

Once the door was closed she switched on the light and they stood staring at one another.

'You look even more tired and stressed than last time,' she said at last.

'Been an eventful few days.'

'Come and tell me about it.'

The urge to gather her in his arms was very strong, but he resisted it. He had no right and anyway was unsure how she'd react, though he was certain she was attracted to him. You couldn't miss that flare of energy. 'I shouldn't be here, really, only — well, I enjoy talking to you.' He saw her tense expression soften into a smile.

'I like talking to you too, Jez.'

Amazed at her lack of pretence, he followed her into the kitchen, which again smelled of something delicious.

'Shall we start with a piece of cake and a glass of wine, maybe?'

'The cake would be wonderful, but I don't drink. I'm an alcoholic, recovered I hope. I don't touch a drop these days.'

'It must have taken a big effort to get off the booze.'

'Yeah. And the drugs.' Perversely, he didn't want her to have any illusions about him.

She studied him gravely. 'How long have you been clean?'

'Twelve years.'

'That's wonderful. A huge achievement.'

He could feel himself relaxing. 'You're doing

the same as last time, making me feel better about myself.'

'Good. That's what friends are for.'

'Are we friends?'

Again the air shivered around them. He definitely wasn't imagining it. There was this current of attraction flowing between them.

'I hope we're friends.' She handed him a plate with a large piece of chocolate cake on it. 'You shouldn't be so hard on yourself. It's counter-productive, produces negative energy.'

He smiled at her earnest expression, winning an answering smile from her, then he looked down at the plate and his mouth watered. 'How do you make cakes without wheat flour?'

'That's the challenge. Rice and potato flour mainly. There are ways. I may write a cookery book on cooking for people with cereal intolerances one day.' She took a jug out of the fridge and poured them both a glass of what looked like fresh lemon juice, then led the way into the living room.

He stopped in the doorway to stare round. 'I kept thinking about this place, but it's even nicer than I'd remembered.'

'I can't imagine why you think that. You must have lived in some magnificent places.'

'They were houses, not homes. Yours is most definitely a home. You've got such a peaceful atmosphere and the colours are pretty. Pretty isn't the *in thing* these days, I know, but I like it. With your permission, I'll send my interior designer across to look at this house before she starts on mine.'

113

'Why don't you plan your own colour schemes?'

'I don't know enough about it.'

She chuckled.

He was entranced by the rich sound, the way her eyes danced with amusement. 'Why are you laughing?'

'You of all people can afford to make a few mistakes and correct them, Jez. Unless you're too busy, of course.'

'No, I'm not busy. I'm bored out of my tiny, actually. Why didn't I think of doing that myself?'

'Probably because you're not fully recovered yet. Eat your cake then I can start on mine.'

He took a mouthful and closed his eyes in bliss as he chewed it slowly. 'Even nicer than the almond one.'

Only when they'd finished eating did he tell her about his son and the assault charges his wife had tried to lay against Tom.

'You must be worried about him and his children.'

'I am. But I didn't need the police to tell me he didn't do it. He has one of those sane, wholesome expressions, just as you do.' To his delight she blushed. He was entranced, couldn't remember the last time a woman had blushed at a compliment from him.

'Oh. Well, thanks for that.'

They continued eating in silence but when she wasn't talking her face settled into slightly sad lines. He waited till he'd finished. 'That was wonderful. Thank you, Sophie. Now, turn and turn about. Tell me what's putting the sadness behind *your* smile tonight.'

This abrupt switch surprised Sophie and she couldn't think how to respond, then decided on the truth. 'My daughter.' By the time she'd finished telling the tale, she was in tears. She didn't notice him move to sit beside her but suddenly his arms were round her and she melted against him in a way she hadn't done with anyone except Bill.

And when Jez kissed her — so gently, so delicately — she didn't pull away because she wanted him to. It felt right, wonderfully right.

It was he who drew back. 'Do you mind?'

'No. Should I?'

'I don't know. I've wanted to kiss you since we first met. Your skin is so soft, and you're not wearing make-up, which makes it a pleasure to touch.'

His next kiss was much more passionate, but he was still holding back and she was glad, because the warmth and urgency of her own response had surprised her and this was one area where she had little experience. She'd met Bill at eighteen, had only had a couple of boyfriends before him, and she'd been with him till he died. They'd been comfortable and happy together, but her life with Bill was the sum total of her sexual experience with men.

She didn't object, though, when Jez shifted to sit more comfortably. She nestled against his side with his arm round her. Sitting like this was another thing that felt *right*. Which shocked her rigid. 'I — um, don't know what to say.'

'Do we have to say anything?' He looped a

lock of her hair round his finger, studying it. 'I love your hair.'

Even that slight touch made her senses swirl. 'If people are attracted, they usually talk, get to know one another.'

His smile was a caress in itself. 'Let's talk about ourselves, then. How did you come to be a novelist? And your family. I already know about your problems with your daughter. But you have a son as well, don't you?'

'Yes. He was very disapproving about my helping you.'

'And he'd disapprove of us too, I suppose.'

It was out before she could stop herself. 'Is there an us?'

'I hope so. Who can tell at this stage? I warn you, I'm not a good risk. I don't seem to be able to sustain relationships. My marriages were both disastrous, that's the only word for them.'

'Why?'

'The first time it was drugs, on both sides. I was unheeding of anything else except gratifying my senses. The second time, well, the papers called her a gold-digger and they were right. She'd have stayed married, though, if I'd let her, because she loved the celebrity life. Only she slept around and that upset *me*. Whatever rumour says, I don't sleep around when I'm with someone. It's one of my few good points as a lover.'

His laugh was so bitter, she asked lightly, 'Should I run for my life?'

'Probably.'

She cuddled against him. 'Sadly, I have this

116

dreadful curiosity. It used to get me into trouble as a child, and although I control it better now, it's still there.'

'What are you curious about?'

'Anything and everything. At the moment, you. I've loved your music for years. But what's behind the music? Why am I attracted to Jez Winter, the man? What's he really like?'

'He's a selfish person, jaded, tired, not sure where he's going in life.'

'You're very hard on yourself.'

'I'm trying to be honest with you, Sophie. I don't want to hurt you.'

'I appreciate that. But life hurts all of us from time to time. No one can prevent that.'

'How did you become so wise?'

'I'm not wise. I'm as foolish as the next person.' Particularly foolish tonight. What was she doing with a man like him? However, since she intended to carry on being foolish for as long as this lasted, she reached out to take hold of his hand and watched as his long elegant fingers twined with hers.

They sat without speaking for a few more moments, then, as a clock chimed the hour somewhere in the house, he groaned and pulled away. 'I promised Craig I'd not be more than an hour. That damned clock of yours moves too quickly.'

'You can't have been here that long already!'

'I have. Sophie . . . can I see you again? Can we continue getting to know one another? Can we find out if this is going anywhere?'

She didn't let herself say yes, but she wanted

to, wanted it so much. 'I don't know. Maybe we should be careful, think about it for a while.'

'I'm not feeling at all careful where you're concerned.' He pulled her to him and kissed her again, then brushed her cheek with his curled fingers and stood up. 'I'll ring you. My movements are a bit uncertain till we get into the house next door and sort something out for my son.'

'All right.'

She walked with him to the back door, letting him kiss her again before she opened it.

As he went outside, a shadow moved and a man appeared from underneath the chestnut tree.

'My minder,' Jez whispered and gave her hand a final squeeze before letting go of it.

Only after the two of them had disappeared through the gate did she remember her coming date with Peter Shane. She wished she'd told Jez about it. She didn't want him to think she was seeing someone behind his back.

No, why should she tell him? It was none of his business. They didn't even have another meeting planned. He didn't own her.

But he was attracted to her. And she to him. And he'd made a big point about being faithful.

She went to stare at herself in the mirror, turning from side to side. She wasn't slender, didn't dress fashionably, but still he fancied her! How wonderful was that? And she fancied him, too. Not with a fan's adoration, but as a woman reacting to a very attractive man.

Then her smile faded and she looked at herself

again, one hand brushing briefly against her right breast.

This thing with Jez probably wasn't going anywhere, but if it did, it wasn't going to be easy. They both had secrets.

She would keep her date with Peter because she needed to see how she felt with another attractive man.

She was terrified of making a public fool of herself. She was a very private person these days, lived a quiet, peaceful life. And Jez Winter seemed to live his life in a bright public spotlight.

Only — she was also terrified of doing what her children clearly expected of her, stopping being a woman, stopping having adventures, sitting quietly at home writing, and visiting the grandchildren from time to time, when allowed.

She was too young, too filled with life to settle for that. And if she continued to live so quietly, her writing would suffer and that would upset her too. Her writing had pulled her through bereavement and illness. Without it she wouldn't be here.

If she started going out with Jez Winter, there would be problems, she had no doubts about that. The paparazzi would come back and pester her. Or he'd leave her high and dry. No, surely not? She wouldn't be attracted to someone so shallow. But he wouldn't be an easy person to live with, she guessed.

Well, she wasn't easy to live with, either. When she lost herself in her writing, the rest of the world blurred and she didn't notice things she should. Andi had often pointed that out, complained of her lack of attention. Bill had understood, though. Dear Bill. What would he think of Jez?

She took a moment to consider that and decided he'd probably like Jez.

Going back into the kitchen, she poured herself a glass of wine and took it into the living room. She sipped it slowly, trying to relax.

She couldn't think of anything but Jez tonight. He was . . . she smiled into the wine . . . very attractive. Like a good wine, he'd aged well.

She dreamed of him, of course, dreamed of his kisses, his quiet voice, his sad eyes.

Had he dreamed of her? She hoped so.

★　★　★

The next day when the phone rang, Sophie checked the caller ID, mildly surprised when she saw it was Donna. She'd thought all business between them was completed. Perhaps it was a message from Jez. Only if it was, surely he'd have phoned her himself?

Donna's voice was crisp. 'Something's cropped up, and I know morning's your best writing time, but can I come round? I'll try not to disturb you for long.'

'Yes, of course.'

This urgency worried Sophie. What had happened when Jez got back last night? Was he sending his PA to tell her he never wanted to see her again? It surprised her how much she didn't want that.

She wandered round the house, unable to

settle, relieved when someone buzzed at the new automatic gate. She pressed the button to open it, a car came up the drive and Donna got out.

Suddenly desperate to know if Jez had changed his mind, Sophie flung open the front door. 'What's wrong?'

'Do you want me to tell you on the doorstep or can I come in?'

'Sorry.' She led the way inside, gestured to a chair and waited expectantly.

'Jez has bought the house next door and the media have found out. I thought you should know. It's bound to stir up trouble again, I'm afraid.'

'Oh.' Sophie frowned at the younger woman, wondering if she knew about last night's visit. It didn't sound as if she did. 'It's a pretty house. I've always liked it. I've been expecting somebody to buy it and knock it down, but it's listed and anyway it's hard to get planning permission to build flats in this district. Too many influential people live here.'

'Is that why you moved here?'

'No. I bought this house because it suited my needs. I love having plenty of space. My family thinks it's ridiculously large for one person, though.'

'It has a lovely atmosphere. Very peaceful. Jez has been raving about it.'

'Oh. Well, that's nice. Can I offer you a coffee?'

'No, thanks. I'm going next door now to do some careful planning. Jez needs to move in as quickly as he can because of his son.'

Her visit left Sophie with a lot to think about.

What would the paparazzi say about Jez's move? Would they start following her again? Could she face living in a spotlight?

As if she hadn't enough on her mind already with Andi!

* * *

When the phone rang later that day, it was Andi. Sophie sighed. She didn't need any more hassles, had a book to write. But she picked it up anyway.

'Mum?'

'Yes.'

'I'm sorry about the other day.'

'Are you?'

Silence, then, 'Yes. Can I come round to see you?'

'Come round for tea at about six. I've got a chapter to finish first.'

'All right. And Mum — thanks for paying my rent.'

Sophie forgot her troubles and immersed herself in her work. She was surprised when the buzzer rang to find it was six o'clock already. Damn! She hadn't done anything about tea. Well, she'd send out for takeaway or pull something out of the freezer.

She went to let Andi in.

They stared at one another in the hall, each very stiff, then Andi swallowed hard. 'I really am sorry.'

'Yes. So you said.' Sophie waited till they were in the kitchen to ask, 'You'd been taking something, hadn't you?'

122

Andi looked at her warily.

'I know you had. I could see it in your eyes and your speech was slurred. It's no use denying it.'

'It was only something to brighten me up a bit when I went clubbing. Everyone's into recreational drugs these days, Mum.'

'No one I know is.'

'I'm not talking about oldies. Anyway, your friend Jez Winter was into drugs big time, probably still is.'

'He isn't. He doesn't even drink alcohol these days.' Sophie realized what a giveaway that was, and was furious at herself for saying it.

Andi looked at her, eyes narrowed. 'You've seen him again, haven't you?'

'Just a brief meeting.'

'I'm surprised he'd bother with someone your age. No offence, Mum, but you're not exactly this year's model and you don't even try to lose weight or keep up with fashion.'

'I don't feel I need to lose weight. I like the size I am.'

Andi shrugged. 'Whatever. Anyway, good luck with him. It'd be quite a feather in your cap to have an affair with him.'

'I don't regard Jez Winter as a feather in my cap. I try to get on with all my neighbours and — ' She broke off, aghast that she'd done it again.

'Neighbours? He's not coming to live next door, is he?'

'Yes. But I don't think it's public news yet, so keep it to yourself.'

'Yeah, yeah. Wow, imagine living next door to *him*.'

Sophie sought for some way to lead her daughter's thoughts in another direction. 'Actually, I've got a date next week with another guy, someone I met recently.'

Andi looked at her in puzzlement, as if unable to believe her own ears.

'This one's a journalist and he's rather dishy.' Might as well lay it on thick.

'So you're not *dating* Jez Winter?'

'I keep telling you: he's going to be a neighbour and, I hope, a friend.'

'Oh. Right. Makes more sense. Good luck with this journo guy, then.' She looked round, sniffing. 'What's for tea? I can usually smell something delish when I come in but there don't seem to be any smells wafting from the kitchen.'

'I forgot the time.'

Andi brightened. 'Can we go out, then?'

'I would normally, but wherever I go at the moment, those stupid paparazzi follow me. It's embarrassing.'

'There wasn't anyone there when I drove here.'

'They seem to appear miraculously the minute I set foot outside.' She went to look in the freezer, but her stocks were low and she didn't feel in the least like cooking. 'We'll have to go out.'

'Fine by me. I could murder a curry.'

'So could I. Oh, let's do it. If they follow us, they'll see only a mother and daughter out for a meal.'

Sophie and her daughter were halfway through

their meal when the restaurant door opened and Talbin came in. She groaned. Did that man never go off duty?

Andi followed her gaze. 'They really are following you! How cool! Don't you ever — you know — talk to them? You'd get your photo in the papers and they'd pay you a fortune for the hot goss on Jez Winter.'

'I wouldn't dream of gossiping about him and I don't want my photo in the papers, thank you very much. Just ignore them.' But her pleasure in the meal was destroyed and she was glad when Andi declared herself 'stuffed' and they could leave.

'Who's the friend?' one of them called as they walked outside. 'I hadn't figured you as being into women.'

'I'm her daughter, silly.' Andi posed obligingly for the camera.

Sophie grabbed her arm and yanked her towards the car. 'Do not encourage them!'

'It doesn't hurt to set the record straight.'

'It upsets me even to talk to that man. He's the worst of them all.'

When they got back, Andi fidgeted about then got to the point and asked her mother to keep on paying her rent until she found a new job.

Sophie agreed, of course. What else could she do? But she refused to pay Andi an allowance as well as the rent. 'You need to get on social security, and let them help you find a job.'

'They don't give you enough to live on.'

'You'll have to economize, then. Other people manage.'

'I don't want to take another dead-end job.'

'You do what you have to in order to earn a living. If you'd finished your degree, you'd have had more choice, made more money.'

Andi opened her mouth to argue, then snapped it shut again and contented herself with a dirty look. 'I'd better go.'

She'd come mainly for the money, Sophie admitted to herself as she closed the door. Again. And the evening hadn't really brought them any closer.

She felt lonely, the silence seeming to echo around her. She hadn't thought about that till she spent time with Jez.

But it was because of him that she'd been followed tonight and if she continued to see him, this would go on. She didn't think she could live like this. She'd be better stopping things now, before they went too far.

★ ★ ★

Jez tried ringing Sophie, but got only her answering machine and she didn't call back.

He tried the following day, with the same result and wondered if she'd been having second thoughts about seeing him. The thought of that upset him more than he'd expected.

If she didn't return his calls by the end of the week, he'd go round to see her again. He wasn't going to let what was between them die still-born. Meeting her had given him more hope for the future than anything else had for a long time.

It surprised him how much he wanted to see her again, how often he thought about her. He didn't usually feel so — overwhelmed by the need to see a woman.

A woman! She wasn't 'a woman', she was Sophie, a very special person.

⋆　⋆　⋆

As Sophie got ready to go out with Peter, she felt absurdly nervous. The days had flown by while she was working, but the evenings had seemed — empty. She'd decided not to answer the phone at all, merely checking her message bank — feeling guiltier each day as she heard Jez's voice asking her to return his call.

He'd rung her every single day!

When Sophie opened the door to Peter, after letting him bring his car into her drive, she felt tongue-tied and was glad he wanted to leave at once.

'I've parked my car round the back. Maybe you should leave by the back door?'

She nodded and he left by the front door, while she crept out of her house like a criminal. His comfortable car smelled of leather and peppermints.

'Um . . . ' He hesitated. 'You might want to slide down as we drive out and put my coat over yourself. They won't have seen you get into the car, but they could still be watching carefully who goes out.'

'OK.' She felt ridiculous as she crouched on the floor with his jacket over her head and pressed the gadget that opened the gate. There were no flashing cameras this time, at least.

'You can sit up now. No one seems to be following us.'

She wriggled back into place, fastening the seat belt and trying to tidy her hair. So much for making it look smoothly stylish. It'd be all over the place now.

He shot a smiling glance sideways. 'I like your hair with the mussed look. It suits you.'

'Oh.' She didn't know what to say and was relieved when he made easy small talk about a film that had just been released.

With Jez she'd had no difficulty talking. *Stop thinking about him!* she ordered herself. *You're with Peter tonight.*

He drove round to the rear of the restaurant and moved a cone blocking a marked parking bay before occupying it. As he helped her out, he said, 'A friend owns this place and I asked him to save me a place out of sight of the road.'

'Good.'

'We'll go in the back way, if you don't mind.'

'I'd prefer it. I've not even been able to go shopping without them hassling me lately.'

'Must be frustrating. I wonder why Talbin has his teeth into you?'

'I don't know. He's a real pain.' He was another reason not to continue this thing with Jez. There she went again, thinking about him. She was a fool, an absolute fool!

The meal was excellent and Peter's friend coped happily with the changes to dishes on the menu necessary to handle her cereal intolerance, always the sign of a good restaurant. The conversation was interesting — but the spark simply wasn't there between her and Peter, which taught her what she'd needed to know.

After they'd finished the luscious desserts, he leaned back and said with a smile, 'He's a lucky man, whoever he is.'

She could feel her face growing hot. 'I don't . . . how did you *know*?'

'I'm not conceited but I do usually manage to elicit some response from a woman I fancy. And keep her attention during a meal.'

She looked down at the tablecloth for a moment or two, then told herself she was being cowardly again and raised her eyes. 'I'm sorry.'

'Do I know him?'

'I'm not even sure *I* know him.'

'It's Jez Winter, isn't it? Talbin's sure there's something between the two of you. He's right, isn't he?'

She stared at him, panicking. 'You won't say anything. It isn't — we haven't . . . '

'I understand. It's early days. And I'm not like Talbin.' He reached out to lay his hand on hers. 'Be careful, though. Winter doesn't have a very good reputation with women.'

'I know. He warned me of that himself. I'm so sorry, Peter. I wish it were you instead. It'd be much easier.'

'I do too, but perhaps we can still be friends? A person can never have too many real friends. And if I can ever help you in any way, don't hesitate to ask.'

'Why are you being so kind to me?'

'Because I not only find you attractive, I like you.'

Which made her feel worse than ever.

Only as they turned into her drive did she realize she'd forgotten to slide down again, and by that time the cameras were flashing.

'Damn!' he said. 'Sorry. I should have remembered.'

'It doesn't matter. It's not a crime to go out with someone.'

'No. But they'll twist it round, see if they don't.'

7

The next morning she heard the buzzer and muttered in annoyance as she finished typing her sentence. When she heard Donna's voice on the intercom, she pressed the gate button and went to open the door.

Her visitor was grim-faced.

'Is something wrong?'

'May I come in?'

From Donna's expression, Sophie knew something was definitely wrong so didn't bother offering refreshments.

'Have you seen the newspapers today?'

She shook her head. 'I've been avoiding them this week.'

'Better look at the front page of this one, then.'

She took the newspaper and stared at the photo of the house next door in horror.

WINTER BUYS LOVE NEST NEXT TO NOVELIST

Heading a side column on the same page was:

TROUBLE ALREADY IN PARADISE?

There was a photo of herself coming back in Peter's car and the article speculated about her being unfaithful to Jez, comparing her to his ex.

That article had the name Gene Talbin at the bottom.

'I can't believe this!' she gasped.

'Neither can we.' Donna's face was still grim. 'How did they find out that Jez is buying the house next door? We certainly haven't told anyone and the estate agent swears blind that no one at their end has said a word to the press. They're a reputable firm, so how could anyone have found out?'

'Just a minute. Let me see what they say.' Sophie skimmed through the two articles, feeling soiled before she'd finished the first paragraph, but persevering to the end. Who else had known about him buying the house? She hadn't said a word. Then she suddenly guessed who it must be.

'Oh, no! It's my fault, I think.'

'*You* told them?'

'No. I let the information slip when I was talking to my daughter. But I asked her not to say anything . . . '

'Could you ring her and find out if it's her? The thing is, if there's some other leak, we need to plug it.'

Sophie dialled her daughter's number and waited. Just as she'd decided that Andi wasn't there, someone picked up the phone and a sleepy voice mumbled something.

'Andi? Is that you?'

'What? Oh, Mum. I was asleep. What's wrong? You never ring in the mornings.'

It was no use asking on the phone, she had to see Andi's face to know whether her daughter was lying or not. 'Could you come round straight away, please? Something's cropped up. Take a taxi. I'll pay for it. You can have breakfast here.'

'I'm not even up yet.'

'Please hurry. I desperately need to talk to you.' She set the phone back in its cradle and turned to Donna, explaining why she'd asked Andi to come round.

'You think it's her? Why would she do that if you asked her not to?'

'She's just lost her job and if that horrible man offered her money — well, she'd probably have taken it. She and I don't — um, get on all that well.'

'What about the other thing in the article?'

'What other thing?'

'This fellow you're dating. Peter Shane. I thought — and Jez thought — that you were interested in him, that you weren't the sort to string two men along at once.'

Scorn rang in her voice and that made Sophie cringe. 'That's between me and Jez. All I'll say is that it was one date, which had been arranged for a while, and there is nothing between me and Peter Shane.'

'You didn't return Jez's calls.'

'Do you always help him with his relationships?'

Donna flushed and looked embarrassed. 'No. And he doesn't know I'm asking about this. It's just that I care about him. He's been through a lot lately. We thought he was getting better and now today he's depressed again.'

Sophie calmed down. 'It's good that his employees are so loyal. Look, I'm still trying to

133

sort out how I feel about him.' She hesitated, than added, 'As a woman, surely you understand that I don't want to set myself up to be hurt. So as I had a date already with Peter, I went on it. I wanted to see how it was with another attractive man and . . . ' She sighed.

'And how was it?'

'Not the same. I like Peter and I think we'll become friends, but you know how it is sometimes: a man can seem everything you need, but the magic just isn't there.'

Donna's expression softened just a little. 'Yes, I know.'

'That's all I'm going to say about me and Jez. Now, you might as well have a coffee while we wait for Andi.'

★　★　★

Half an hour later the buzzer rang and Sophie let her daughter in. Andi looked half-asleep still — or could it be the residue of something she'd been taking?

'Is that coffee I smell, Mum?'

'I'll get you some.' She led the way into the kitchen. Donna was no longer there, nor was her mug, so Sophie didn't say anything about her other visitor.

Andi took a big gulp, sighing in pleasure. 'You make the *best* coffee.' She slid on to a bar stool. 'So — what's wrong?'

'Did you tell the press about Jez Winter buying the house next door?' Sophie watched her daughter's mouth fall open, then saw the soft lips clamp together hard and those baby-blue eyes shutter over in a way that was all too familiar from the rebellious teenage years. 'You did, didn't you?'

Andi shrugged. 'Why not? They paid me really well for the information, and it'd have come out one way or another, so why shouldn't I be the one to benefit?'

'I asked you to keep quiet about it.'

Another shrug.

'How *could you* betray a confidence?'

'If you will keep me short of money, I have to find other ways to get some, and I do *not* fancy going on social security, thank you very much, and being forced to go for interviews for jobs I don't want. I shouldn't have to, either, with a rich mother.'

'What makes you think you have a right to my money?'

'The years you vanished into your office, typing away. The years Dad and I hardly saw you at weekends.'

Sophie opened her mouth to protest then closed it again. She hadn't realized Andi had resented it so much. 'Bill understood my need to write.'

'He might have understood but he still missed you. And mothers are supposed to be there for their children. You weren't.'

'I was most of the time. Do you mean I should have given up my life to support yours?'

'Other mothers do.'

'Your father still kept his job. Should he have given it up?'

'It's different for men.'

'You have a very old-fashioned attitude to life. And I deeply resent your selfishness.'

Andi drained her mug, thumped it down and held out one hand. 'You owe me twenty quid for the taxi. And another twenty to get back. I've got things to do.'

Sophie didn't try to continue the discussion. She got her purse, taking forty pounds out and thrusting the money into the outstretched hand of this hard-eyed alien who had taken the place of her daughter.

Andi left without a word of farewell, didn't even turn round as she strode down the drive. She was dialling a number on her mobile phone as she walked.

After Sophie closed the front door, Donna came out of hiding and returned to the kitchen. 'Sorry. I thought it might be better if you faced her on your own.'

'Yes. And you got the information you wanted. I apologize for what my daughter did, and for my own carelessness in letting her know about Jez.' Sophie blinked her eyes, but the tears wouldn't be held back for much longer. 'I'd like to be alone now, if you don't mind.'

'I'm sorry about this. I'll — um, tell Jez what happened.'

'Do what you want.' She escorted Donna to the door then walked back, tears running down her cheeks, wondering where she'd gone wrong with her children. Blindly she walked into the meditation room, her refuge in times of trouble. Once she would have walked into Bill's arms.

Wished she still could.

But even her beautiful room failed her today and in the end she lay on the rug and howled her eyes out.

It hurt to be so at odds with her daughter. And to know that she'd made things more difficult for Jez. It hurt that they were printing this rubbish about her in the sleazier newspapers.

Everything seemed to hurt today.

On that thought she got up, went to wash her face and came back to meditate. She of all people should know better than to give in when the going got tough.

★   ★   ★

The next morning Sophie couldn't settle to work. Her conscience was bothering her and she had to do something before she could get on with her life. She picked up the phone and dialled the number Jez had given her.

To her surprise, he answered in person.

'Jez? It's me, Sophie. Please don't hang up until I've apologized.'

His voice was curt. 'There's no need. *You* didn't contact the press.'

'But I let my daughter know you were buying the house next door.'

'Just a minute.'

He must have covered up the phone because there were only faint sounds. She waited.

He came on again. 'Sorry. I've got an urgent call. Can I ring you back later?'

'There's no need. I just wanted to say I was

sorry.' She ended the call and went back to her work. But she felt sad that things had ended like this, that she'd let him down.

She was quite sure now that she'd wanted to go on seeing him.

★   ★   ★

Tom stared at his mother in horror. 'Say that again!'

'Gail came to see me this morning at church. She remembered it was my day to attend Ladies' Bible Class. She wanted to talk about your marriage. She's ashamed of what she's done, is seeking your forgiveness and promises to mend her ways.'

'You didn't believe her, did you?'

'I'm willing to give her a chance. I asked her to speak to our pastor, and he told me afterwards that she'd listened with great attention. She's agreed to go back and speak to him again. She desperately wants to save your marriage, which is more than you do.'

Tom groaned. 'She's just trying it on, using you, pretending to repent.'

'If she is, then there is surely a chance that true repentance will follow. It won't hurt you to give her a chance, will it? After all, you are still married to her.'

He knew better than to argue when she got that evangelical tone. It would hurt her, and anyway it would be a waste of time. A woman so honest and naive would never understand someone as devious as Gail.

He waited until his mother had gone shopping, settled the children down to play and rang his father. It was Donna who answered.

'I need to speak to Jez.'

'He can't be disturbed, but perhaps I can help?'

'Look, if he's there, I'd really appreciate you asking him to speak to me. It's very urgent.'

'Worth interrupting an important phone call for?'

'Hell, yes.'

'Hold on.' She went into the living area and signalled to Jez, who covered up the phone and listened to her quick explanation.

'I'd better speak to him. Ask him to hold on and give me a few seconds to finish this call.'

When Jez ended his call to Sophie, Donna put his son on the line.

★   ★   ★

Tom sagged against the wall in relief when he heard his father's voice.

'What's wrong?'

He explained what had happened. 'You offered to put me and the children up at your hotel. I think we need to get away from here as soon as possible. Gail's a good actress and my mother doesn't realize how tricky my dear wife is. Well, *I* didn't until after we were married.'

'I can arrange for accommodation easily enough and send a car to pick you up. When?'

Tom thought rapidly. 'Tomorrow afternoon. Mum goes out to choir practice at her church at two o'clock.'

'Is it really necessary for you to sneak away?'

'It's better than having a confrontation with either my wife or my mother, believe me. I don't want to upset the children. I'm not giving Gail the chance to pull any more tricks to keep me here. I will have to contact Jane, though, to make sure she can come too. Only — she lives next door to Gail so I don't want to pick her up.'

Jez's voice was amused. 'It's like playing cops and robbers, isn't it? We can send a taxi for Jane once you've left safely and you can meet her somewhere.'

Tom heard his voice wobble as he said, 'Thanks.' He couldn't help feeling shaky. This was the worst thing that had ever happened to him. You didn't walk out on a marriage, a house you'd been renovating bit by bit, and a mother who loved you — not without some qualms, not without a lot of pain.

'Tom? Are you still there?'

'Yes. Sorry, Jez. I'll be ready by just after two. Um — I'll only have bin liners to pack our stuff in. It'll look a mess.'

'I don't mind if you come with only the clothes you stand up in.'

'Thanks. I'm grateful.'

As soon as he'd switched off his phone, Tom began making plans in his head, working out what he'd take.

★ ★ ★

The phone rang an hour later and Sophie hesitated, then went to see who it was. Jez. She'd

140

not answer it. Then she changed her mind and snatched it up at the last minute before the answering service took over.

'Sorry about ending our call, Sophie. Tom needed my help urgently.'

'That's all right. We'd just about finished anyway. I'd only wanted to apologize to you.'

'Well, *I* hadn't finished speaking. Look, we can't talk properly on the phone. How about doing lunch?'

'Pardon?'

'Come and have lunch with me here. Unless you've got something going with this Shane fellow?'

'I haven't got anything going with him.' She wasn't sure she had anything going with Jez, either. But she couldn't resist the chance to see him again. 'OK.'

'Good. We can talk properly over lunch. Since there's no hiding anything from the press, don't try to drive yourself. I'll send a car for you. Twelve o'clock suit?'

'Yes.' She stared at the buzzing phone then set it down carefully. She shouldn't be doing this. Every time she went near Jez Winter something awful happened to her. Only . . . she'd been the one to mess things up by not telling him about Peter . . . and Jez was probably lonely . . . and it wouldn't hurt to take a couple of hours off, because she wasn't doing very well with her writing today, simply couldn't settle into it.

He hadn't sounded angry.

Oh, heavens, what was she going to wear? She rushed up to her bedroom and started pulling clothes out of the wardrobe.

The car Jez sent was a limo. Of course. It took her to an elegant London hotel. There was no sign of Jez, but the driver of the limo said quietly, 'If you'll go inside, madam, someone will be waiting for you.'

The foyer was small but beautifully appointed, with a mammoth flower arrangement just inside the door. A man smiled at her from behind the reception desk and beckoned to a young woman in black, who came towards her.

'Ms Carr? If you'd follow me, please.'

They went up in a lift that gave almost no sign of movement, stopping on the top floor.

'This way, ma'am.'

Sophie walked along a carpet so thick and soft it muffled all sound and made everything seem unreal. Her guide knocked on a door at the end of the corridor and it was opened by a man who looked vaguely familiar.

'Welcome, Ms Carr. You may remember me: Kevin, head of Jez's security?'

'Yes, I do. Nice to meet you again.'

'Won't you come in?'

He ushered her along a short internal corridor and opened another door, not entering with her but closing it behind her. She took a hesitant step forward, staring round a huge sitting room with a panoramic view of the Thames.

Jez was standing by the window and held out one hand to her. 'Come and look at the view. It's costing me an arm and a leg, so we may as well enjoy it.'

She walked slowly across another thick carpet, feeling a little shaky, unsure of what he wanted from her today.

He smiled as he took her hand. 'Don't look at me as if I'm going to eat you.'

'I'd deserve it. I feel so guilty about what my daughter did.'

He put a fingertip on her lips. 'Don't. My purchase of the house would have come out sooner or later. As long as we know *we* don't have a security leak, that's what matters most.' He studied her face. 'I'm sorry your daughter treated you like that, though. She's hurt you, hasn't she?'

'Yes. And she wasn't at all repentant. I don't know where we went wrong with her.'

'Sometimes children have to make their own mistakes. I was a rebel myself and I reckon I made more stuff-ups than most, probably put my parents through hell. I was able to make it up to them before they died, thank goodness.'

'You're very understanding,' she said.

'I'm more bothered about this Shane fellow. Donna says he's not really in the picture. Is that right?'

'No, he's not in the picture. He'd asked me out a few days before your second visit. I should have told you, though. But Jez, I *needed* to go out with him, to see if . . . ' Her voice faltered, because it was hard to explain. 'I'd not been out with anyone for a while. I needed to see if that was why I reacted to you.'

'And was it?'

She could only shake her head.

'So you'll not be seeing Shane again?'

'Only as a friend. I really like him but there's no spark — not on my side at least.'

Jez let out his breath in a sudden whoosh. He must have been nervous too. That was so amazing she stared at him in wonderment.

'There is definitely a spark between you and me.' He reached up to caress her cheek briefly.

His touch made her struggle for breath and all she could do was nod.

'But we'll let the spark burn up slowly, if that'll make you feel better.'

'It will. I thought . . . Well, that Andi's action might have destroyed our friendship.'

'No, it hasn't. We are still friends, aren't we?'

'I hope so.'

He gave a wry smile. 'I've never started a love affair with a friendship before. I'm not sure I know the rules.'

'Any rules I ever knew would be well out of date.' She took a step away from him because being so close seemed to stop her breathing properly.

'Are you hungry?'

She considered this, then smiled. 'Yes. I was too nervous to eat a proper breakfast.'

'I'll ring for the food to be sent up. Can I offer you a drink in the meantime? A glass of wine, perhaps?'

She shook her head. 'I don't drink at lunchtime. And anyway, wouldn't that be difficult for you?'

'No. If it upset me to watch others drink, I'd have sunk back into alcoholism long ago.'

They ate a wonderful meal. He'd remembered her food problems and ordered accordingly. There was a gateau afterwards, which the waiter assured her contained only potato and tapioca flours.

After the staff had cleared away the meal, they chatted lazily, talking of anything and everything.

She was shocked when a little gold clock chimed again and she saw it was nearly five o'clock. 'Where has the afternoon gone?'

'Do you have to leave?'

'I'm afraid so. I'm hoping to write another thousand words or so before the end of the day. I try to write every single day so that I can stay inside the story. I couldn't settle down to it this morning. And anyway, you're looking tired.'

'Happily tired, for once. Can I see you again?'

She couldn't lie to him. 'I hope so.'

'Would you like to see over my new house?'

'I'd love to.'

'Donna says afternoons are best for you, because you like to work in the mornings. I've got something on tomorrow, so how about the day after? Three o'clock suit you?'

'Yes.' You'd think someone who earned her living with words could manage more than monosyllables!

'I'll get Kevin to meet you at the side gate. We've got the perimeter secured now.'

'Like Fort Knox!'

His expression was bitter. 'More like Alcatraz. It sometimes feels like being in prison.'

'I'm beginning to understand that.'

'I'm sorry getting to know me has done this to

145

you.' He rang a bell. 'Someone will have to show you out again. This is a very secure hotel.' At the door, he put his arms round her. 'Am I allowed to kiss you goodbye?'

He didn't wait for permission but drew her towards him and kissed her until her knees grew weak. He smiled as he drew back a little, continuing to hold her. 'I think the spark is glowing quite brightly, don't you?'

She had trouble speaking coherently. 'Yes. It's surprised me.'

'Me, too.'

The same woman was outside the suite ready to show her down to the limousine, which was waiting at a side entrance this time.

There had been no sign of the paparazzi on the drive back but a car was parked outside her house when she got home, which made her stomach lurch in apprehension.

Inside the house the phone light was blinking and when she listened to the message from her son asking her to call him, she thought he sounded angry, so she didn't do it. William always expected her to drop everything when he wanted to see her, usually to give her a lecture about something.

She went up to change into comfortable working clothes, feeling all at sea again. When she was alone with Jez everything felt so simple and right, and she wanted to see him again — and again.

But once the world intruded, their relationship seemed so full of complications it was difficult to believe in a happy outcome.

* * *

As soon as Sophie had left, Jez asked Donna to pull out all the stops to get his new house ready for occupation.

'That sort of thing takes time.'

'Doesn't sound as if we've got a lot of time with Tom and the children coming to London in a few days, so if throwing money at it will help us move in quickly, do it. We don't need everything to be perfect, just to have basic furniture and make sure all the bathrooms work.'

'And to hire domestic staff, who'll need vetting, not to mention finishing setting up the internal security. Jez, it's a huge house and there are all sorts of details to sort out.'

'Hire yourself an assistant if necessary. I mean it, Donna. Oh, and I'm showing Sophie over the place the day after tomorrow in the afternoon.' He flushed slightly under her amused gaze.

'You've forgiven her for letting the information out?'

'It was her daughter.' He frowned. 'Maybe we should look into that young woman's background.'

'Kevin's already on to that, just in case she's still intending to feed information to Talbin.'

Donna left Jez to rest. Sophie's visit must have gone well today from the way he kept smiling. She hoped that would continue. She really liked her employer, but had found out that Jez didn't let people get close to him easily, not even the staff he worked with every day, like her and Craig. Kevin was a bit different because they'd known one another from way back.

It was easy to get fond of Jez, because he was kind and thoughtful — and sometimes even shy.

And because he was always faintly sad. Money and fame hadn't made him happy. What would? She wondered. It'd take a very special woman to deal with a man like him and the life he led. She wouldn't like to marry someone famous.

8

Jez listened to Donna's summary of the arrangements she'd made for his son at the hotel, leaning his head back to consider them when she'd finished.

'Why are you smiling?' she asked.

'I'm thinking of the reaction of the staff here to two small children.'

She smiled reluctantly. 'And I know who'll have to smooth things out.'

'Will you mind?'

'No. I'm paid to solve problems.'

He looked at her, his brow wrinkling. 'But do you *enjoy* working for me?'

She nodded. 'Very much.'

'Why? It's been nothing but mayhem since you joined us, what with the intruder then the accident.'

'And I've not been bored once.' She shrugged. 'I hate being bored.'

'You've done well. Kevin and I were wondering if you'd like to join the permanent staff? I know we said a year's trial, but we really like having you on the team.'

She didn't hesitate. 'That'd be great.'

★ ★ ★

William rang up from his place of work as Sophie was waiting for Kevin to arrive to take her to see the house next door — he often rang from work, presumably so that his wife wouldn't know how often he called.

'Mum? How are you?'

'I'm well. Look, I'm expecting someone. We can talk till he arrives, but I may have to end the conversation abruptly.'

His voice suddenly grew sharper. 'Oh? Who is it? Not that pop-star fellow, surely? Andi says you're *seeing* him.'

'Don't talk to me about your sister!'

'What's she done now?'

'I can't tell you. It's confidential, someone else involved. But she let me down, broke a promise and we've quarrelled — rather badly. If you can keep an eye on her, though, and let me know if she needs anything, I'd be grateful?'

'We don't see much of one another either. She's so rude to Kerry. Dad would be horrified at how she behaves.' A pause, then, 'And why should Andi *need* anything?'

'She lost her job and . . . oh, William, I think she's on drugs. She says they're just recreational, that she only takes them now and then, but even that sounds bad to me.'

'Oh, no! I thought she'd given them up.'

'You knew?'

'Yeah. It's why we were on particularly bad terms last year. I met her one evening at a café and, well, it was obvious she was spaced out. I was so worried about her so I took her straight home and gave her hell about it. And she let me drag her home, which shows how bad a state she was in. It's dangerous to be so out of control.

She said it was a new sort of tablet she'd taken and she hadn't realized how it'd affect her, and she promised me faithfully that she'd stop.'

'Oh, dear. I don't know how to help her, but if money is what's needed — '

'Money can't do anything without her changing her attitude. But I will go and see her, since you're worried, though I doubt it'll do much good. I'm more worried about *you* at the moment. That's why I rang. Mum, you're crazy if you get mixed up with Jez Winter. He has a dreadful reputation. He's into drugs in a big way, the hard stuff. Don't you ever read the papers?'

'Not that sort of paper. And actually, he's been clean for years.'

'So Kerry was right. That's why he's buying the house next door, so he can be near you.'

Thank you, Kerry! Sophie thought, but as she opened her mouth to explain, someone knocked on the back door. 'Sorry, William. My visitor's just arrived. Have to go.'

She put the phone down, cutting off his protest, and went to answer the door.

Kevin stood there, smiling. 'Are you ready?'

'Yes. I'll just get my handbag and keys to lock up.'

As they went through the gate, he asked, 'Would you mind if we put in a special security system on this gate? A numberpad lock, I think.'

'Is that really necessary? I mean, the gate's not in a public area. Jez must be spending a fortune on this house.'

He smiled. 'I think he can afford it. And yes, it is necessary, at least until we catch the lunatic

151

who threatened his life. I take such threats very seriously, believe me.'

She stopped moving to stare at him in dismay. 'Surely it was a one-off incident?'

'We don't know. So I'm continuing to take precautions. In the meantime, if you don't mind my saying so, Sophie, you're good for Jez. We're all pleased for him. He's been a lot brighter since he met you.'

'You're the second member of his staff to show concern about him.'

'He's a great guy.' He started walking again. 'And the gate?'

'Oh. Well. All right, then.' She followed Kevin through the neglected gardens, thinking how much she'd like to take them in hand. She stopped for a moment as they got to the lawn, staring across at the house. 'It's a beautiful old place, even the rear elevation. The builder worked hard to make it attractive, didn't he? Look at those fancy roof-capping tiles, with the little gargoyles at each end. And I love the double row of gables.'

But Kevin was frowning at it. 'Everything's very shabby inside. It'll need a lot of work.'

'Shabby can be cured. And Jez needs something to occupy himself with, as well as his music, don't you think? Besides, if the inside is half as attractive as the outside, it'll make a lovely home. I bet it's got moulded plasterwork ceilings and covings.'

'It has. You're obviously an enthusiast.'

'I don't like most modern buildings. So many of them look like piles of boxes dumped together

152

by very young children. Architecture from the second half of the twentieth century is *not* something to be proud of.' The back door opened before they got there and Jez appeared, beaming and nodding dismissal to Kevin before offering Sophie his arm.

'I was worried you'd change your mind.' He bent to kiss her cheek.

'I'd have told you if I had. Actually, I'm dying to look round. I've never been inside.'

He set off, walking with his usual long-legged stride, and she tugged his arm to slow him down. 'Don't rush. Let's take our time.'

They walked round the main reception rooms, discussing them animatedly, then along to a wing containing a former library. It was now a sad skeleton with bare shelves and a musty smell.

'Such a pity,' she murmured. 'I wonder what happened to all the books. And there would have been a sliding ladder attached to that rail to get to the upper shelves. Why would anyone take that away? You must try to get a period piece to replace it.'

'Yes, ma'am.' He gave her a mock salute and a grin that made him look years younger. 'And I think I should ask you to fill the shelves for me. I noticed you had rather a lot of books in your house.'

She pulled a face. 'Too many. I'm always running out of space for them and having to buy another bookcase. But you should fill your shelves with things *you* like reading, Jez, not buy them by the yard or ask someone else to do it. It doesn't matter what they look like, it's what's inside a book that counts.'

'I'll bear that in mind. The first one to be shelved can be your latest book.'

'You're reading my book?'

'I've read it. And enjoyed it. As you said, it had a happy ending and left me feeling good. I wish life was like that. I've started on another one now.'

'I feel flattered.'

'You'll have to sign them for me, just as I sign CD sleeves. Now, come and see the other wing. I'm going to make it my music suite.'

They spent longer in that area as he explained exactly how he was going to set it up. Half of what he said was meaningless to her, but she nodded and encouraged him to continue because it kept that happy light in his eyes.

'When do you move in?' she asked once he slowed down.

'As soon as the internal security system is running properly and we've got some furniture and domestic staff. We've got nightwatchmen on duty at the moment. It'll be ready enough in a few days, I hope.'

She didn't say it, but she thought how sad it was that he had to protect his privacy so carefully. Then it occurred to her that she did too now.

'Let's sit down a minute. I want to tell you what's been happening to my son.' He explained Tom's dilemma.

'It'll be nice for you to have family with you.'

'I hope it will. I don't know much about young children . . . or about Tom, either. Though I like what I've seen of him so far.' He glanced at his watch. 'Have you time to look at the staff cottages and flats? I thought one of those would suit him and the children. They'll want their own space — and I will, too.'

'Of course I've got time.' Fancy having several cottages and flats for staff! When she and Bill had got married, they'd lived in a one-room flat for the first year — and been happy there, too.

Neither cottage was large enough to give the nanny her own sitting room, but Sophie suggested knocking a door through from the upper flat next to it.

'You're good at that sort of thing,' he said as they walked back to the big house.

'I like making houses into homes. My internal courtyard was my own idea. I had it added on and it works well, don't you think?'

'It's lovely. I'm thinking of having a private garden made outside my studio. Will you help me design that?'

'If you wish.'

He smiled. 'What you mean is, if we're still together.'

She stopped dead. 'Isn't it rushing things to say we're together?'

'No. We're together already. Have been almost from the first.'

She stared into his eyes and saw nothing but warmth there. 'You're right. I can't understand how it's happened so quickly, but it has.'

'Hoy!'

They swung round.

Kevin was standing at the door of the big

house, grinning at them. 'If you lovebirds can tear yourselves apart, Jez has a physio appointment.'

Jez looked at his watch. 'Damn. I can't believe time's gone so quickly. I hate to say goodbye.' He pulled Sophie into his arms and simply held her close, heedless of whether Kevin was still watching. She went willingly. She'd missed touching and being touched, had read about 'skin hunger' in people living on their own.

'I love holding you,' Jez murmured into her hair.

She tightened her arms round him and took another risk. 'Would you like to come for dinner at my place tomorrow night?'

'I'd love to. What time?'

'Six. We can chat over drinks before we eat — and I do know how to make interesting non-alcoholic ones.'

'You don't have to limit your drinking for me. Truly.'

'I enjoy good company more than alcohol.'

'*Jez!*'

He pulled away. 'Sorry. Got to go.'

But he refused to leave till he'd seen her safely home.

It took her a while to settle down to her writing again. There were no phone calls for the rest of the day, and time itself seemed suspended, as if she were encased in a bubble, living in a world apart. It took her a while to work out that was because she was happy.

★ ★ ★

When they got back to the hotel after the physio appointment, Jez said, 'I'm going to have dinner with Sophie tomorrow evening. At her house.'

Kevin frowned. 'Is that wise?'

'I don't know. But it's what I want and it'll help keep me sane.' He looked round with distaste. 'I'm going stir-crazy here. I want to start my life moving again.'

'Be careful what you wish for.'

★ ★ ★

The following evening Jez went to his own house and walked across the gardens with Kevin to visit Sophie.

'Is this necessary? I should be able to walk through my own gardens without an escort.'

'There are a couple of security glitches to sort out first. And Talbin's still hovering.'

Jez sighed. 'What does that sod want?'

'Stories that bring him money. It seems to be his modus operandi to drum up a hue and cry by obnoxious behaviour then make mega-bucks by selling exclusive stories about the person in question.'

'Maybe I should just behave in a more open manner?'

'You'll still need protection until they catch the fellow who attacked you.'

Jez shuddered at the memory of those few minutes when he'd been at the mercy of a lunatic holding a knife to his throat, when he'd been sure he was going to die as the knife sliced into him. 'I'm trying to forget about that incident.'

157

'Don't. You need to remember it and stay vigilant.'

'OK, OK. You've made your point. I do still need protection. But once he's caught, I intend to live more openly.' He caught sight of a pitying look on Kevin's face. He hated having people feel sorry for him.

To his surprise, there was now a brand-new wooden gate in the shade of his chestnut tree, with a touch-pad lock embedded in the stone wall. He looked at Kevin. 'Your doing?'

'Yes. Watch carefully. This is the number.' He keyed it in and turned the handle.

The gate opened noiselessly. Jez preferred the creaky old one.

'I'll take you to the door. Ring me when you want picking up. Remember to tell Sophie what the security number is. They only just finished installing it this afternoon, so I've not had time to tell her.'

They arrived at the back door and Jez smiled as Sophie opened it, standing framed in a halo of light, her hair gleaming darkly golden, her dress made of a floaty material in shades of blue with a frill round the hem. His heart began to beat faster as he stepped over the threshold.

How had he ever thought those scrawny young women were attractive?

★ ★ ★

Sophie nodded a greeting to Kevin then closed the door and turned to Jez. Before she could move he pulled her into his arms and kissed her.

158

She hadn't known how sexy a slow, soft kiss could be. When he drew away she heard herself giving a low moan of protest as she looked up into his eyes.

'I've been waiting to do that all day.'

His voice was husky and yet he looked as shaken as she felt. 'Did the earth just move?' she asked.

'Definitely.'

'It's like a fire catching hold and consuming everything in its path,' she said. 'But I don't want it to get out of control.' She gathered her courage together, because she'd promised herself to ask this tonight, though she'd not expected to do it so early in the evening. 'What do you want from me, Jez?'

He stilled. 'Isn't that obvious? You. Me. Together.'

'For how long? A short affair? A long one?'

'I don't know. How can we tell?'

'I know the sort of person I am. I don't walk lightly into a relationship — or out of it, either. So if this is just a pleasant way to pass the time for you, well, better that you find someone else to play sex games with.' She could see the astonishment on his face, but she had decided earlier, as she got ready, that she had to be up front with him. If the idea of staying together long-term was going to put him off, better that it happened now, before she'd gone in too deeply.

Who was she kidding? She'd be devastated if he walked away. She'd been mooning around like a love-sick girl today, counting the hours till he arrived, preparing the best meal she could, changing her mind three times about what to wear, longing to be with him.

He took hold of both her hands but didn't pull her towards him. 'I'm not playing with you, Sophie. I'm not walking lightly into this relationship, believe me. But I'm — not confident about anything.'

'Why not?'

'Because I don't have much to offer you, not in the long-term way you want.'

'I don't understand what you mean by that.'

He let go of one of her hands to wave his scornfully. 'I can offer you money, more money than any sane person needs. That's not what worries me. I just — I feel to be emotionally crippled, Sophie, when it comes to long-term anything. The serious relationship with Tom's mother never got as far as marriage. I've had two wives since and each marriage failed quickly. If I ask you to marry me now, people will call you Number Three Wife and take bets on how long it's going to last, not to mention wondering who's going to be Number Four if I so much as glance at another woman. The press will be hurtful and the one thing I'm sure of is that I don't want to hurt you like that.'

'So are you saying you can't do relationships that last?'

'I don't know. No, wait. I'm trying to be honest here. It's *me* that's the problem, not you. I've failed three times. I know my own faults and I can't see anyone caring enough for me, warts and all, to stay for the long haul.'

'Couldn't we at least start out by *hoping* for

something permanent?' She stretched out her free hand to caress his face. 'That's what I'm doing.'

'Are you?'

'Yes, I am, Jez.'

The sadness was back in his eyes as he took hold of her hand again. 'Then let's hope and pray for that. If anyone can teach me how to love someone properly, it's you.'

They stood quietly for a few moments then she broke the silence. 'All right, we know where we stand and where we want to stand. Let's forget the heavy stuff now and enjoy our evening. Come and chat to me while I finish getting the meal ready. I've made some non-alcoholic cocktails. I found the recipe on the Internet. They're really nice, too.' She put ice in a tall glass and poured some mango-coloured liquid into it, then laced the top with red syrup and a pair of maraschino cherries.

He sat at the counter, sipping — it was delicious — and watching her assemble their starters. Was it possible to find someone who really did think long-term, who could be faithful and honest . . . who could love him more than his money? A month ago he'd have laughed scornfully at the mere idea. Now . . . well, a man could hope, couldn't he? Even without her prompting, he'd have been hoping.

'It's a very simple meal,' she said. 'I'm in the thick of writing so I didn't have time to do anything elaborate. This is rice bread, oven-crisped with cheese on top, and my version of French onion soup.'

His mouth was watering already. 'I remember how much I enjoyed your last simple meal, the risotto and cake. It tasted much better than the hotel chef's offerings.'

'You've a jaded palate, my lad.'

'It comes with the territory, I think.'

'And you're intense, broody. Somehow I hadn't expected that. It's fascinating to peer behind the scenes and meet the real Jez Winter, compare him to the media image — and to his music — learn his secrets.'

'What about the real Sophie Carr? Have you got secrets too?'

'Yes, of course. There are things I need to tell you about myself. But not tonight. Let's just enjoy ourselves now. Do you like to listen to music while you eat?'

'I always enjoy music.'

'Then go and find something to play while I ladle out the soup. My collection of CDs is in the living room.'

He chose Sting and she smiled to hear 'Fields of Gold', which was one of her own favourite tracks.

He ate every mouthful of the soup, to her delight.

The main course was casseroled steak, with vegetables and sweet potatoes. He ate two helpings, which filled her with even more satisfaction.

Just as she was about to serve dessert, the buzzer sounded from the front gate. She looked at the speaker in shock. Who could be visiting her at this hour of the night?

'Are you expecting someone?'

'No. I rarely do anything in the evenings.' She went to press the speaker button. 'Yes?'

'Mum? Since when have you had these fortifications built?'

'Oh. William.' She mouthed, 'My son,' to Jez then pressed the button. She couldn't very well turn her son away. 'Come in. The gates will close automatically behind you.'

She turned to Jez. 'I'd have preferred to wait to introduce you to my family, but it seems fate has taken a hand.'

'I can leave if you want.'

'I don't want. I don't like sneaking around and I *don't* turn my guests out.' But she was more worried than she'd admit about William's reaction to finding her sharing an intimate dinner with a notorious celebrity.

'He won't approve of me, and I can't blame him.' Jez's expression had changed again, become more guarded. 'Why are you always so down on yourself, Jez? It's not up to William to approve or disapprove of you, though I warn you he's a bit stuffy. It's up to *me* to approve of you.' She smiled and pressed a quick kiss on his cheek. 'And I do.'

'Very well. I'll stay.' But he still looked nervous.

'I'll go and open the front door.'

William was on his own and had his I'm-going-to-lecture-you look.

He kissed the air above her cheek. 'Just thought I'd pop in to see you, Mum.'

'Well, you might look happier about it. And

163

it'd have been better to ring and see if I was busy or not. I've got a guest tonight. Come and meet him.'

'Who is it?'

'Jez Winter.'

'So Andi was right!'

She swung round. 'About what?'

William glanced along the corridor and said in a lower voice, 'That fellow *is* taking advantage of you.'

'You must have a very low opinion of me if you think I'm such an easy mark.'

'Perhaps I'd better come back another time.'

'And perhaps you'd better come and be introduced properly. And mind what you say. I brought you up with some manners, I hope.' She led the way into the dining room. 'Jez, this is my son, William.'

The two men shook hands and William positively bristled, looking like a dog defending a bone as he said stiltedly, 'I'm — er, pleased to meet you.'

'And I'm delighted to meet Sophie's son.'

'Are you? I pop round quite often, so we'll no doubt meet again. I like to keep an eye on my mum. Don't want anyone upsetting her.' He moved closer to his mother, as if on guard.

In spite of the tension, Jez's lips twitched and his eyes began to dance.

Sophie had trouble holding back an answering smile. Her son was like a bulldog at times. 'I was just about to serve dessert. Come and join us, William. I'll bring you a plate and cup.'

He opened his mouth to refuse, caught her eye

and snapped it shut again, taking a chair and sitting in silence.

'I don't bite, you know,' Jez said quietly as she left the room.

William breathed deeply. 'But you have a bad reputation and I'm concerned for my mother.'

'So would I be in your place.'

'*What?*'

'I'm well aware of my reputation, but most of that's in the past. Just to set your mind at ease a little, I don't drink or do drugs, and haven't for many years.'

'But you do still play the field. Look at all those photos of you with slinky young models.'

Sophie came in on the tail end of this. 'You shouldn't believe all you read in the gutter press, William.' She set a piece of gateau on it in front of him, then moved on to set one in front of Jez. A quick trip to the kitchen brought her own plate and a jug of cream. 'Serve yourselves.'

Jez passed it to her. 'After you.'

She smiled wryly at him. 'I have problems with milk and cream as well as cereals.'

'It must make life difficult.'

'There are worse problems.' She shrugged and took a forkful of gateau.

William followed suit and closed his eyes in bliss. 'This is *wonderful*, Mum. It's a new recipe, isn't it?'

'Yes. I'll give you some to take home for the children, if you like.'

He hesitated. 'Kerry doesn't like them eating sugary things.'

'For yourself, then.' She saw his hesitant

165

expression. 'She doesn't let you have them, either, does she?'

'She's watching her weight. It isn't fair to eat such things in front of her.'

Sophie put a forkful of gateau in her mouth before what she thought about her daughter-in-law popped out.

'You can give *me* some to take home,' Jez said. 'You make brilliant cakes.'

'It's a personal challenge, to find ways of cooking delicious food with my limitations. I'm taking careful notes for that cookery book. It'd be fun to write it.'

'Strange idea of fun, writing a different sort of book. A real busman's holiday.' Jez's smile was so warm it made something inside her melt. She heard William mutter and forced herself to turn towards him. 'Was there a special reason for you coming here tonight?'

'We can discuss that another time.'

'No, we'll discuss it now, openly. You said Andi was right when you saw Jez here, so I'd guess you've come to warn me about the big, bad wolf.'

Jez let out a choke of laughter and tried unsuccessfully to turn it into a cough.

William looked from one to the other and Sophie was reminded of when he'd been a schoolboy trying to pluck up his courage to argue with her.

'Give me a ring, then, and we can arrange another time, but if it's to warn me about Jez, you're too late. We're seeing one another.'

He choked and she handed him a glass.

'I can't drink, I'm driving.'

'It's not alcoholic. Jez doesn't indulge. I think I'm going to have to investigate making non-intoxicating drinks that are interesting.'

'Mum.'

His voice was pleading. She laid one hand on his arm. 'William, I'm a grown up. I'm allowed to have a love life.'

Jez looked at her in surprise then gave her a smile so warm it curled her toes.

William finished his dessert and stood up. 'I'll come and see you another time, Mum.'

'If you must. And William — don't believe everything Andi tells you. She seems to have lost touch with reality lately.'

'She really has upset you, hasn't she?'

'I didn't give you the details when you phoned, but it was she who told the press about me and Jez, and was well paid for it.'

He stopped moving, shock making his mouth fall open. 'She didn't!'

'Have I ever lied to you?'

'No. I just . . . She didn't tell me that.'

'She wouldn't.'

At the door William whispered, 'Be careful. I don't want you to get hurt, Mum.'

'Few relationships are without thorns. Yours included.'

He reared back. 'Kerry is a *wonderful* wife.'

'Kerry is a miserable control-freak.'

'I shall forget you said that.'

She shouldn't have criticized his wife, she knew, but she was fed up of her daughter-in-law sniping at her and sending William round to lecture her.

When she sat down at the table again, Jez said mildly, 'I can see that you're a formidable woman when crossed.'

She smiled. 'I hope so. Be warned.' She raised her glass in a silent toast. 'Here's to rebelling against one's children!'

The rest of the evening passed quietly and happily. They listened to music. She found she fitted nicely against him when they cuddled up together on the sofa, and that their musical tastes fitted nicely too.

When it got to ten o'clock, she moved away. 'I'm going to send you home now. You're starting to look tired and it's my bedtime. I'm an early riser.'

His eyes gleamed and the breath caught in her throat for a moment. When they stood up he pulled her to him, but when she held back, he didn't try to stop her.

'I'm not falling into bed with you, Jez, even if I do fancy you. I've only ever slept with one man in my life and if that's old-fashioned, too bad.'

He was staring at her in shock. 'You've only ever slept with your husband?'

'Yes.'

'That's amazing. I've had a much more varied sex life, but not nearly as varied as the press would have you believe. I suppose I'd better tell you that I was tested for STDs last year and as I've not indulged since, I can be considered safe.'

'I've never even considered being tested.'

'I doubt you'd need it.'

'I agree. Bill was the faithful sort. I am too.'

'I'm beginning to understand that. What I

can't understand is why you say you have secrets. You life seems remarkably open.'

'I'll tell you when the time is ripe.'

He took out his mobile. 'Got to call Kevin. Makes me feel like a child to be escorted everywhere.' When he'd finished the call, he said, 'I hope you'll be extra-careful from now on.'

'I will.'

He smiled down at her. 'My son and grandchildren are arriving tomorrow, so I'll call you but I won't be able to see you. Is it all right if I call you every day?'

'More than all right. Evenings are best.'

She was very thoughtful as she finished clearing up. She'd enjoyed Jez's company more than she'd expected to. It wasn't just the physical attraction, either. He was interested in so many things. And it was a bonus that he had a sense of humour.

But she was annoyed with William. What made him think he had the right to tell her what to do, who to make friends with? She'd phone him at work tomorrow and make it very plain that she didn't welcome such interference.

9

On the Friday afternoon Tom waited on tenterhooks for his mother to go out. She noticed, of course.

'What's the matter with you today? There's something wrong, I know it.'

He shrugged and sought desperately for a reason to distract her. 'I'm looking forward to spending some time on my own, if you must know. I've been with people every minute of the last week or so. I'm used to quiet hours with a computer during the day, and I need my peace. The kids are having a nap, so I'll just sit and relax.'

She looked at him, shaking her head, and he didn't know whether she believed him or not. But at least she left.

He started to pack. Most of his own possessions were still in the bin bags he'd brought from his old house. He'd already put his laptop in its case. Now he had to go into the children's room to pack their things, which woke them, so he gave them a snack and a drink, before continuing to pile their toys and clothing into bags.

As he shoved Hayley's comfort blanket into the top of one bag, he heard a car draw up outside the house. He went to the window and breathed a sigh of relief as he saw a limousine waiting there and a uniformed chauffeur coming down the garden path towards the house.

He grabbed the bag he'd just filled and rushed downstairs, throwing the door open.

'Mr Prichard?'

'Yes.' He gestured to the line of bulging plastic bags along the hall. 'Can you start putting these into the car, please, while I pack the last few things?'

'Certainly, sir.'

The man's expression remained wooden, but his distaste for this job was obvious.

At the last minute, Hayley insisted she wanted another wee-wee and Ryan, who seemed terrified of the chauffeur, clung to Tom's leg as he took her upstairs again, making it even more difficult to act quickly.

Just as they were coming downstairs again, the front door opened and his mother walked in. Tom froze, feeling his face growing warm.

Her eyes seemed to miss nothing and the look she gave him was one of disappointment as well as annoyance. 'My neighbour rang me at church to ask if I knew a limousine was at our door and a man was carrying things out of the house. Can you imagine how I felt? Why couldn't you tell me to my face that you were leaving, Tom? Am I such a bad mother?'

Hayley began to cry and both children were now clinging to Tom's legs.

'I didn't want to upset the children,' he said, but even in his own ears, it sounded a lame excuse.

'Instead you've upset me.' She picked up the phone. 'We're doing this properly. I'm going to ring Gail and ask her to come round. You're not leaving until you've spoken to her and got her permission to take the children away from here.'

* * *

Jez fidgeted round the hotel suite, played his guitar but couldn't produce anything worth listening to.

Donna was out at the house, so was Kevin.

Craig was on minder duty today and was not noted for his chatty manner.

In the end Jez picked up the second of Sophie's books. He hadn't read many novels in his life, though he'd been forced to read a few at school. Those had always been miserable tales that depressed him. He'd not understood Shakespeare, whom he'd also studied in secondary school at the rate of one play a year. The only thing he'd enjoyed had been poetry, still did. He wrote his own lyrics and though he'd not class them in the same league as serious poetry, there were a few he was rather proud of.

It had surprised him how much he'd enjoyed the first of Sophie's books, and this one hooked him into the story just as quickly. He found himself caring about the characters, intrigued by their dilemma, keen to find out how they solved it. And as she had promised him there was always a happy ending, he even managed to enjoy the characters' tribulations en route.

He was so immersed in the tale he was surprised when Craig reminded him that it was lunchtime.

After lunch he gave in to the temptation to ring Sophie, even though she'd said evenings would be best. 'Been writing this morning?'

She chuckled. 'Yes. I was absolutely lost to the world. There were two phone messages left for me and I didn't even hear it ring.'

'Who were they from?'

'I haven't checked them yet. But I was just getting my lunch and when I saw it was you, I picked up the phone.'

He felt absurdly pleased about that. 'I'm sorry I can't see you tonight.'

'I hope it goes well with your son. The children will be very tired when they arrive. Don't be surprised if they're whiny and cling to their father.'

Jez glanced at his watch. 'They should be well on their way by now.'

They chatted for a while and he was still smiling as he put the phone down.

★   ★   ★

Donna left the new house with a list of essential furniture to buy. They'd retrieved the things from Jez's old flat, but they weren't nearly enough for this big place. And she had the staff cottage to furnish for Tom and his family, as well.

She went to a large department store, where she'd already made an appointment with a personal shopper. The man was probably getting a very hefty commission for his services but he certainly knew his way around the store. She was armed with the words 'pretty' and 'soft colours', which were Jez's only specifications. Both the shopper and the furniture department head pulled faces at this and tried to persuade her to buy something more 'in tune with the times'.

However, they stopped protesting when she offered to do her shopping elsewhere if they had nothing to suit. 'It's an Edwardian house and my employer has had enough of stark modern styles, which wouldn't suit it anyway.'

'Perhaps we should go and visit it, if we're to do it justice?' the department head suggested, his eyes lighting up.

'No. Just find me some furniture to start us off and get it there tonight.'

'*Tonight!*' they yelped in unison.

'Yes. It's a condition of sale. I presume your delivery team won't mind earning double money? We certainly won't mind paying it.'

She was exhausted by the time she got back to the hotel, but felt she'd done a good job.

Jez was looking twitchy, but she didn't comment on that as she brought him up to date on what she'd purchased today.

'I wonder where Tom is now?' he murmured afterwards, picking up his book again. 'I'd expected him to phone me.'

★ ★ ★

Mary gave Tom another of her stern looks. Other mothers yelled and grew angry, but his radiated disappointment and pain when she considered he'd let her down. That was somehow more daunting than anger would have been.

'I'm not giving Gail the chance to stop us going, Mum, or to upset the kids. I need to get away and start my new life and the children need stability. This decision has nothing to do with Gail.'

'They're her children too.'

'She's not a fit mother, which is why I've got temporary custody.'

'Don't argue with me. Fit or not, she's their mother and your wife and you're *not* abandoning her, you're doing this properly. If you won't phone her, I will.'

Almost he buckled down, the habit of years keeping him quiet, then he remembered how his wife had neglected Hayley and Ryan, and that gave him the courage to defy his mother. 'You can ring her if you want, Mum, but we're leaving now.'

He picked up Ryan and told Hayley to follow him out to the car.

His mother snatched Hayley's hand and dragged her back. 'I can't let you do this, son. It's wrong.'

He thrust Ryan into the chauffeur's arms. 'Strap him into the car seat.' Then he removed Hayley's hand from his mother's as gently as he could. 'I'm not letting her hurt them again.'

'She doesn't hurt them.'

'They go all day hungry and unwashed. Ryan has had a sore backside several times from wetting himself. Is that good care?'

'I'll help her more. I'll get the other women from the church to help, too. We'll set up a roster.'

'No, Mum. It's over between me and Gail and nothing you do will change that.'

She wept then, clinging to him and pleading with the Lord to make him see sense and keep him away from sinners. And it was so rare for her to weep like this, he hesitated once more.

It was Hayley bursting into tears that brought him to his senses. He picked up his daughter. 'It's all right, darling. Grandma's just sad to be saying goodbye to us. We're going for a ride in the car now.' Then he walked out, ignoring his mother's sobs and calls to come back.

He felt riven with guilt as he checked that Ryan was all right, strapped Hayley in and told the chauffeur to drive off. The man was po-faced and the rigidity of his spine spoke volumes.

As agreed, they met another limousine at the first service station on the motorway and Jane Burtill got out of it, beaming at them.

Once she and her luggage had been transferred, she took the children to the toilet. After that, they both settled down and were soon asleep.

'You're wonderful with them,' Tom said.

'They're lovely kids. You look upset, love. What happened?'

He explained. 'When I refused, Mum cried. That always upsets me.'

'Tears can be as much of a weapon as knives and guns.'

'She never sobs like that normally, though. I've really upset her.'

'You're the father and you have to do the best for your children. They *must* come first. I've seen

176

how Gail neglects them and I think you're doing the right thing. Eh, look at Ryan. He's a lovely little lad, isn't he?'

They both stared down at the child, whose thumb was in his mouth and who only looked this angelic when he was asleep. Tom found himself smiling involuntarily.

After a few moments, Jane said thoughtfully, 'We'd better tell that lawyer of your father's what happened, though. We don't want these two used as the rope in a tug-of-war.'

Tom took hold of her hand with its work-reddened fingers, the knuckles lumpy with arthritis. But somehow this wear and tear was admirable because he knew how hard a worker she was. He clasped her hand for a minute then patted it. 'Thank you, Jane.'

'What for?'

'Your simple common sense. Your lack of hysteria.' He let go of her.

'Common sense isn't found as often as people make out. But I do try not to get into a fuss. It doesn't solve any problems.'

'I shall try to follow your example from now on.'

'And in the meantime, let's enjoy our ride. I've never been in a limo before. Isn't it comfortable?'

All he could enjoy was the relief of having escaped from his mother, but he didn't want to spoil Jane's pleasure by saying that. He had, he realized with a feeling of shame, rarely defied his mother, even after he'd grown up, except about trying to contact his father and about marrying Gail. How pitiful was that for a twenty-six-year-old man?

He felt as if he'd grown ten years older in the past month. Once they were settled in London, he'd find a job so that he didn't have to live on his father's charity and . . .

★ ★ ★

Tom had forgotten how luxurious the hotel was. He felt as if he and the children were in the wrong place, even though the staff were clearly expecting him and fussed over him from the minute he walked through the door. But the concierge hadn't been quick enough to hide his amazement and scorn at the pile of plastic bags that were carried in, and Ryan had started crying the minute they entered the foyer, so that another guest turned his head to look at them with a pained expression.

Jane bent over to comfort the little boy while Tom kept hold of Hayley's hand. By some miracle, Ryan stopped howling and let his face be wiped clean of snot and tears.

The woman on reception gave Tom a professional smile. 'We've been expecting you, sir. I'll just get someone to show you up to your father's suite.'

Tom was terrified about what two small children would do to the beautiful rooms of the suite. Then his father came hurrying across the day area, beaming, arms outstretched to give him a cracking big hug. Suddenly things didn't seem as fraught.

'This is Jane, Mrs Burtill, who's going to look after the children.'

Jane shook his hand. 'Nice to meet you, Mr Winter. I need to get these two to the toilet straight away, if you don't mind.'

He showed them the two adjoining bedrooms she and the children would use, with their own en-suite bathroom. 'I'm afraid you'll have to sleep on the next floor down, Tom. Is that all right?'

'Fine.' He looked round. 'I'd forgotten how beautiful it is here. You could fit my mother's whole house into this sitting room.'

Jez shrugged. 'I've grown used to it now, but I grew up in a small house, too. What I'm looking forward to is moving into my new home. We can go and look at it tomorrow, if you like. There's a cottage for you and the children, and a flat next to it for Jane. They're sending some furniture round tonight. Donna — my PA — wondered exactly what the children would need, apart from beds.'

'So do I,' Tom said ruefully. 'We'll ask Jane. She's a very capable woman.'

'Good. And what about a meal? I know it's late for such small children, but surely they need to eat before they go to bed?'

Jane came back just then, leading Ryan by the hand, while Hayley flew ahead of them to clutch her father's hand and stare solemnly up at Jez.

Tom realized he hadn't prepared her for this meeting. 'Can we all sit down? I need to tell them who you are. I should have done it before, I know, but they slept most of the way down and I didn't dare say anything to them till after we'd left.'

Jane quickly pulled off the children's shoes

179

before they clambered on to the big white sofa. 'Perhaps we should order the food for them first, Tom?'

Jez picked up the phone, dialled a number and spoke to someone, then handed it to her. 'Order what you like.'

She blinked in surprise, then ordered so modestly he took the phone from her hands and said, 'And anything else you think might suit two small children, please. And we need it quickly.'

While they were waiting for the meal to arrive, Tom said, 'Hayley, love, I didn't tell you before, but this is your other granddad.'

She looked at Jez. 'He doesn't look like a granddad. He's not got a bald head.'

Jez couldn't hold back a snort of laughter.

'And where's the other grandma?'

'There isn't one,' Jez said. 'Just me.'

She frowned and eyed him again. 'Have you fallen over and hurt your face?'

'I was in a car crash and banged my face.'

She crawled along the sofa to the edge nearest to him to look more carefully, touching his face very gently. 'Did they sew you together again like Grandma sewed my teddy?'

'Yes.'

'Did it hurt?'

'A bit.'

She continued to study him with that unnerving gaze young children have, then crawled back to lie against her father with a tired sigh.

'Don't go to sleep, Hayley,' Tom told her. 'You need to eat some supper first.'

The food arrived shortly afterwards, wheeled

180

in on a trolley and set up under Jane's supervision on the table. Fruit in the shape of a face tempted Hayley, but Ryan wanted only toast and jam.

'They didn't make much impression on that lot,' Jez commented.

'It'll do fine for my supper after I've put them to bed,' Jane said.

Tom wandered over and began picking at the lavish display of food. 'It'll do for mine, too.'

Jez joined him, worried about his son's careworn expression, ate a piece of apple, then was tempted to another.

Jane came bustling in. 'You both need to say goodnight to them.'

Jez hesitated. 'What do I do?'

She smiled at him, such a motherly smile that his breath caught in his throat. 'Just watch what Tom does. It's mainly kiss them on the cheek and tell them to sleep well. Then you'd better come back here for a meal. You look to me as if you need feeding up.'

He found himself obeying her, marvelling at how soft a child's cheek was and feeling pleased that Hayley accepted his kiss with a murmured, 'Night, G'anddad.' Ryan had fallen asleep while being carried to bed.

Back in the living area, the two men wandered over to the table, leaving Jane to her final ministrations in the bedroom.

'You look unhappy. Was it bad getting away?' Jez asked quietly.

'Yeah. I usually do as Mum says and it was really hard to go against her. I think we'd better

181

talk to a lawyer in the morning because she seems to be on Gail's side.' Tom began to fiddle with his glass of orange juice. 'And after we've settled in, can we see about finding a job for me?'

'Of course. I've spoken to someone already. They can start the tests as soon as you're ready.'

'Tests?'

'Aptitude tests. We don't want to try to fit a square peg into a round hole, do we? But they were pleased to hear you'd done a business degree.'

'They were?'

Jez could see some of the worry shift from his son's face. 'You're pretty employable, you know. At least, they seemed to think so. But I think we should get the children well and truly settled in before you start work. That's the most important thing.'

As Tom hesitated, he added gently, 'Are you all right for spending money?' He saw his son's flush of embarrassment and added, 'I can lend you some to tide you over.'

'I'll need to pay Gail maintenance as well. I don't know how much I'll be earning, but it won't leave much to pay you back with, not at first.'

The money meant nothing to Jez but he didn't say so. Tom was clearly touchy about it. Instead he said, 'I'm sure you'll pay me back when you can. In the meantime, I'm delighted you're here. I've been rather lonely lately.'

It was the right thing to say, because Tom's expression brightened.

'I'd better tell you, though. I'm seeing someone. She's really nice. I'm sure you'll like her.'

'It's whether you like her that matters, isn't it?'

'Partly. But your opinion is important too.'

'What's she called?'

'Sophie Carr. She's a — '

'Novelist. My wife reads her books, or she used to before she started drinking so heavily.'

'It seems as if everyone knows about her. I've just read my first one and am into my second. I'm really enjoying them.'

'Is she pretty?'

For answer, Jez went to pick up the book and show Tom the cover photo.

'She's your age!'

'You sound surprised.'

Tom wriggled uncomfortably. 'I thought you only went out with beautiful young models.'

'I used to. But I never stayed with them for long.'

Tom studied his face. 'Is this one serious?'

'I hope so. I'm a bad risk and I've told her she should run away, but I'm rather hoping she won't.'

He was hoping a lot of things. His life seemed to be changing daily, and for the better. In fact, he felt happier than he had for a long time.

* * *

Jane joined them, smiling in that comfortable way she had.

'You must be hungry,' Jez said, standing up to

help her to a chair. 'Are you sure you don't want me to send out for something fresh?'

'I am hungry.' She looked at the table. 'No use wasting good food, however rich you are, Mr Winter. And this looks delicious to me.'

'Yes, ma'am.'

They sat round the table, eating the simple food prepared to tempt a child's appetite.

'I enjoyed it,' Jez said afterwards.

Jane smiled at him. 'Good. Now, I can see how tired you are, and it's been an eventful day for me and Tom, so we should all go to bed.'

Jez gave his slightly crooked smile. 'You sound like you're mothering us, too.'

She looked from one to the other and reached out to pat each man's arm in turn. 'You seem to need it — both of you. I've never had children of my own, but I wanted them very badly. And since my husband died, I've mothered quite a few lost souls. But you've only to tell me if I step out of line. I've not been a nanny before, not had anything to do with famous folk, either, so I don't know exactly what I'm supposed to do.'

Jez picked up her hand and raised it to his lips. 'Do what seems right to you, Jane. There are no rules and I don't need anyone to curtsey to me. I've really enjoyed your company tonight. But you're right: I am exhausted. So I'll leave you now.' Yawning, he wandered off to his bedroom.

Tom looked at Jane. 'He's kind, isn't he?'

'Very. But he's lonely. It's a good thing you got in touch with him. He'll help you to spread your wings and you'll give him family to love. Swanning around with young women who don't wear enough clothes and staying up late like he's been doing isn't good for anyone. Now, I'd better go and unpack.'

Tom let Craig escort him down to his own room on the floor below. When he was alone, he looked round and sighed. It felt empty and unwelcoming. Comfortable as the bed was, it took him a long time to get to sleep, because his head was spinning with the day's events.

But he was on the right track now, he was sure of it, and wouldn't waste this opportunity to make a new life for himself and his children.

His main worry was Gail. She was like a loose cannon. You never knew what she'd do next.

It'd be best if she accepted Jez's offer to go into detox.

No. He couldn't see her agreeing to that. But he desperately didn't want to drag his kids through the courts — and he didn't know what he'd do if he lost custody of them to her.

10

Andi didn't get up till eleven o'clock. She felt awful, her head thumping, her brain shrouded in a cloud of fog. Her friend Mandy had given her a happy pill yesterday, and she'd felt great at the time, but now felt worse than ever, really down.

She got herself a cup of strong coffee and sat sipping it. To her surprise Ross came downstairs on the same mission.

'Not at work?' she asked, not really caring, but feeling a need to fill the silence.

'I put in long hours last week, so I've got a day off in lieu. I'm working on something of my own.' He hesitated, then sat down with his cup of coffee. 'You look awful. Aren't you feeling well?'

She shook her head then wished she hadn't. 'Ouch. No. I — um — overindulged last night.'

'You're not into those fancy cocktails again?'

'What concern is it of yours? And no, it wasn't cocktails.'

'If it's drugs you're getting into, I'm outta here. I don't want to get mixed up with that.'

'It's me who's taking them, not you. You're not affected.'

'It's a downhill track. Once you get really hooked, you start stealing or whoring to support your habit. I've seen it before with my cousin. She died of an overdose. Twenty, she was.'

Andi scowled at him. She didn't like to hear stories like that. 'I'd not let it go that far. I'm only into occasional recreational use.'

'That's how they all start, what they all say. And you've lost your job. How are you going to manage? How did you pay for last night's pleasures? It's definitely my concern whether you can pay your rent and your share of the groceries.'

'I came into a little windfall, if you must know, so you're safe for quite a while.' She got her bag out, intending to show him the wad of notes Talbin had given her for the information about her mother and Jez. She'd taken the money with her by mistake the previous night, because her friend had turned up to give her a lift and had been nagging her to hurry up. But once she'd discovered what she'd done, she'd been really careful not to leave her bag unwatched. She scrabbled through the contents, but couldn't find the roll of notes. Panicking, she tipped everything out on the table. A few coins rolled here and there, but there was no sign of the notes.

'You didn't take it with you to a club! Oh, Andi.'

She burst into tears. 'I forgot I had it until I got there. How am I going to live now?'

'Social security.'

She grabbed some kitchen roll to wipe her eyes, but the tears still kept coming.

'Oh, hell, don't!'

Ross put his arms round her and held her close till the sobs died down. She wiped her nose and eyes, then sat by the table while he made her another coffee to replace the cold one.

'Why are you doing this to yourself?' he asked.

She couldn't think of an answer.

'Do the drugs make you happy?'

She stared at him blankly then shook her head. 'They just, you know, make things fun.'

'For how long?'

'A few hours.'

'Can't you find your fun another way?'

'Yeah, like you do, staring at someone else's computer all day then coming home to stare at your own computer all night. You're a fine one to talk. That's not a life.'

He stepped back. 'Well, I can see it's no use talking to you, but you know how I feel about the drugs now and if I see any funny business going on here, I'll leave at once. I mean that, Andi.'

When he'd gone upstairs she wished she hadn't been so rude to him. He was a nice guy, and he'd only been trying to help. He'd held her to comfort her just like her dad used to do.

Tears rolled down her cheeks as she thought of her dad. She wanted him back. So badly. He'd have known what she should do, though he'd have told her off for taking drugs. He'd *always* helped her out. Her mother didn't care about anything except her stupid writing.

But whatever anyone said, Andi couldn't bear the thought of going on social security and having to accept boring jobs if they were offered.

Who could have taken her money? She'd been careful, only left her handbag with her friend while she danced.

Surely Mandy hadn't taken it?

She froze, trying to work out whether this was possible. Mandy was a new friend. She didn't know her all that well, but they'd gone out together a few times and had a good time.

She looked at the clock. Mandy worked in a café. She'd go straight round to ask her what had happened to the money. She scrabbled through the loose change and tears threatened again. She didn't even have enough for her fare and a cup of coffee.

She'd have to pawn something. She'd done it once before when she was short of money. No biggie. You just paid what you owed the next week and got whatever it was back again.

Only she'd not have a wage to pay with now.

She had to get her money back, whatever it took.

⋆ ⋆ ⋆

Jez rang Sophie before he went to sleep, smiling as he put the phone down after a chat that had gone on for longer than he'd intended. She'd been yawning in the end and so had he, but he hadn't wanted to put the phone down.

He slept better than he had for a long time and woke to the sound of children's laughter and a voice hushing them. Putting on his dressing gown, he wandered into the living area, to find Jane helping Ryan drink some fruit juice while Hayley ate some pieces of apple. The child looked at him warily then at Jane, as if for reassurance.

'Say good morning to your granddad. Where

are your manners today? He won't want to kiss you if you don't smile at him.'

Hayley obligingly smiled and presented her cheek, which Jez kissed with great pleasure. Would he ever get blasé about this gift of family? He didn't think so.

Ryan then insisted on being kissed as well, clutching Jez's arm with a sticky hand and laughing when Jez, remembering a childhood game, walked his fingers up the child's arm to tickle his neck.

Fat gurgles of laughter rewarded him and when he saw Jane nodding approval, he felt emotion well up and had to blink his eyes.

'Can we order a proper breakfast now, Mr Winter?'

'Jez. No one on my team calls me Mr Winter. I'm sorry. I should have told you last night that you can order anything you want from room service.'

'I looked for a menu, but couldn't find one. What do they serve here?'

'Anything you ask for. When you pay this much for a hotel room, *they* fit in with you, not the other way round.'

'Goodness. If it's so expensive, we'd better hope that house of yours won't be long. Shall I order something for you at the same time?'

'I don't usually bother with breakfast.'

'Then you ought to. Everyone needs a proper start to the day. I'll order boiled eggs with soldiers for the children, and how about the same for you? That way they'll see you eating and make less fuss about finishing theirs.'

Amusement welled in him. 'All right.'

There was a knock on the door and they heard Craig come out of his room near the entrance. 'I'll get it,' he called.

'Do you really need a bodyguard all the time?' Jane asked with a frown.

'Sadly, yes. They still haven't caught the guy who attacked me.' He fingered his face.

'Eh, I don't know what the world's coming to.'

★   ★   ★

On the floor below Tom woke with a start, remembering where he was and surprised to see he'd slept till eight o'clock. He got out of bed and had a quick shower, worried that the children might be disturbing Jez.

When he tried to get the lift to the top floor, it wouldn't work and went straight down to the ground floor. The doors didn't open for a minute or two and he was just beginning to wonder if it was malfunctioning when they slid back to show a concierge waiting for him.

'Where were you trying to go, sir?'

'To the penthouse suite, to my father's, Jez Winter.'

'I'll just ring through and check that it's all right, shall I?'

Donna, who had just entered the hotel, hurried across the foyer to join them. 'I can vouch for Tom and take him up. Perhaps you'd arrange for him to have a key card issued?'

'Only Mr Channing can do that.'

'OK. I'll speak to Kevin about it.' She turned

191

to Tom. 'Did you sleep well? Good. I'm sorry you have to stay on a different floor and face all these restrictions when you want to see your children, but we can't be too careful of Jez.'

'My father's had a hard year, hasn't he?'

'A hard few years, reading between the lines. His second wife sounds to have been a prime bitch-woman.'

'How long have you been with him?'

'Just a few months, but Kevin's been with him for ever. They knew each other as lads, I think. Ah, here we are.'

She let them into the suite with her key card and they heard voices from the living area, then Hayley's high-pitched giggles.

'Doesn't sound as if they're missing me,' Tom said.

In the living area they found Jez on the floor, being a 'horsey' and giving Hayley a ride, with Ryan grinning widely as he held tight to Jane's hand and waited for his turn. Both children were dressed and looked rosy, as if they'd just had a bath.

Ryan suddenly noticed his father and set off running across the room, yelling, 'Daddy! Daddy!' at the top of his voice.

Tom swung him up in his arms, then did the same to Hayley, grinning at Jez. 'I see they've been making use of you already. I warn you, Hayley loves playing horses.'

Jez stood up, grinning ruefully and rubbing his bad leg. 'Not sure I wasn't a bit over-enthusiastic with that. How did you sleep?'

'I had trouble dropping off, but then slept very

soundly. How did the kids sleep, Jane?'

'Like logs. Didn't stir till seven o'clock, by which time I was up and ready for them.'

He turned to Jez, not wanting him to feel left out. 'And you?'

'Better than for a long time. Have you had breakfast? There's food set out and you've just time to grab some before the lawyer arrives. We need to make sure we can keep these two rascals here.'

It was clear to Tom as the morning passed that Jez was used to being at the centre of activity. He never seemed to raise his voice, but he was the one people turned to for instructions and when he wanted to make himself heard, they listened. He seemed perfectly at ease having people round all the time. Tom wasn't sure he'd like that.

In the end they all drove out to see the house, the lawyer included, as he wanted to check on the accommodation provided for Tom, the nanny and the children.

The main house was full of new furniture wrapped in plastic, old furniture covered in sheets and workmen installing some extra kitchen equipment under the watchful eye of a security guard. Jane approved their accommodation unreservedly, going pink with pleasure when she found that she'd have her own flat and saw how well-appointed it was.

'Though you'll have to tell security if you're expecting visitors,' Donna warned her. 'Do you know anyone in the south?'

'My niece lives in London. It'll be lovely to catch up with her again.'

193

'We'll have to arrange a deputy nanny for your time off.' Donna got out the stylus and made a note on her personal organizer.

'Will there be guards on duty all the time?' Tom asked, seeing yet another man in security uniform passing the window.

'Yes. With so many people coming and going, we thought it better to hire extra people. After everything's finished, we'll just have one person on duty inside the house and we'll rely mainly on the security system, which, if I know Kevin, will be state of the art.'

'Can I see it?' Tom asked. 'I'm pretty good with electronics and I'd love to know what they're setting up here.'

'Of course. Just arrange it with Kevin next time you see him.'

The lawyer left as soon as he'd approved the accommodation. He warned Tom, however, that the children's mother would be entitled to access and if necessary they would have to offer to pay her fares to London.

That didn't please Tom, because he knew Gail's erratic behaviour would unsettle the children and might embarrass his father. He was sure she would rev up her campaign to force him to come back to her once she found out he was living in luxury with Jez.

* * *

Andi managed to pawn her CD player and used the Underground to visit her friend at work. When Mandy saw her coming she ducked into the back of the café so Andi shoved her way behind the counter.

The manager tried to push her out again, but she said through gritted teeth, 'If you don't let me see Mandy, I'll call the police because some of my money went missing when she was looking after my handbag.'

'I'll take you round the back myself,' he said, 'but if you cause any trouble, it'll be *me* who calls the police.'

Only Mandy was no longer there.

'She left in a hurry,' one of the kitchen hands said with a snigger. 'Not like her. She doesn't usually do anything in a hurry.'

'Have you any idea where I can find her?' Andi asked.

The guy hesitated, then said, 'At that club, the Four Keys. She's getting in a bit deep there, if you ask me. It's not a nice place.'

'Thanks.'

Andi made her way to the club and hammered on the back door. When she explained why she was there, they let her inside, but took her to one of the deputy managers, a sleazy guy she'd met before. She was beginning to feel a bit uneasy now, and was surprised how shabby it all looked by daylight.

He folded his arms and leaned against the door. 'You're not going anywhere till you tell me why you're so keen to see Mandy.'

She explained.

He looked her up and down. 'You were a fool to bring so much money with you. And not only have you just missed her, but she's paid off rather a large debt she owed us. I'm sorry if it was your money she was using, but we've got it now and we're keeping it. You'll be joining a long line of people if you're trying to get anything back from her.'

Andi could feel tears threatening. 'But what am I going to do?'

He pursed his lips, looking her up and down in a way that made her feel undressed.

'I feel a bit guilty about the money. How about you come and work here?'

'Doing what?'

'Hostess work.'

'Oh, no!'

He leaned forward on the desk. 'It's legit. We don't allow prostitutes in here. The police don't like it. You'd have to be nice to the customers, but you don't have to have sex with them.'

She hesitated, then asked, 'How much would I earn?'

He named a sum which was twice as much as she'd earned in her other job.

'That's — not bad.'

'You'll be working long hours. Oh, and you'll have to dress in the clothes we provide.'

'I'm not going topless for anyone.'

He sighed and rolled his eyes towards the ceiling. 'Have I asked her to go topless?' he asked it.

She still felt uneasy about working here, but could see no alternative, so accepted his offer. He rang someone and a woman took her away and found her a skimpy outfit which only just covered her breasts and showed a lot of leg. It was a good thing she had a decent figure but even so she didn't like the idea of walking around dressed like that. Still, think of the money, she told herself. You only need to work here for a short time, just till you find something better.

She was feeling marginally more cheerful as she made her way home. She didn't want to go to the police about the money because they'd ask all sorts of awkward questions, she was sure, and it might come out that she'd been taking drugs.

Ross was making his lunch. 'Did you get your money back?'

'No, but I got a job.'

'That's good. Doing what?'

When she explained he looked at her in disgust. 'They'll have you on the game before you're through.'

'They will not! I'm just being a hostess.'

'Softly, softly, catchee monkey,' he said as he took his sandwiches across to the table. 'You're a bloody idiot, Andi.'

'What else am I going to do?'

'Get a proper job, like the rest of us. Sign on till then.' He got out a book, ignoring her.

She didn't feel hungry, so went up to her bedroom to have a lie down because she was feeling a bit washed out. She'd better go easy on that stuff from now on. No wonder Mandy had given her a freebie. She'd been too spaced out to notice that her money had gone.

★   ★   ★

197

Sophie was up in her bedroom when she saw the group of people wandering round the garden next door. Jez and entourage, she thought with a wry smile. There were two small children and a tall young man who looked so like Jez he must be the long-lost son.

She wished she could see more of her own grandchildren, wished she wasn't at odds with Andi. Oh dear, she was turning into a moaning Minnie — even if she was only moaning to herself.

The phone rang and she picked it up. Her agent.

'How's the book coming along?'

'Quite well. I've had a few interruptions but I'm more or less on schedule.'

'We should have lunch soon. There are a few things we need to discuss. Do you have your diary handy?'

'I'll just nip down to my office and fish it out.'

She knew he'd have good news for her. It was his way. Ring up and arrange lunch then spring a lovely surprise on her, an extra sale or an increase in the advance money to be paid for her next book. When they'd arranged a day, she sat down at the computer. Soon the old magic took hold and she forgot the rest of the world, only realizing the phone must have rung when she stopped for the day and saw the flashing light.

Jez. Her heart did a little skip of joy as she rang him back and enjoyed nearly an hour of conversation.

'We're pulling out all the stops to move in next door as soon as we can,' he said as they tried for the third time to say goodbye. 'Soon I'll be able to nip across the garden to visit you. We'll not have any privacy if you come to see me here at the moment.'

* * *

That night a new melody floated into his mind and he stopped his conversation with Tom to listen to it, eyes closed. But he was jerked out of it by a hand on his arm.

'Are you all right, Dad? *Dad!*'

He blinked at his son and smiled but couldn't concentrate. 'Just thought of a new melody. I've got to get it down. Hell, I can't wait to move in and get my music gear set up properly again. Where did I put my guitar? And I'm sure I had something to write with . . . '

Tom watched in wonderment as his father sat down in the other half of the room and totally forgot about him. He heard bits and pieces of the new tune, but not enough to show what it was like. He wondered if one day his father would let him play with him. He wasn't a bad guitarist, not in his father's league, but until he met Gail he'd played at his mother's church sometimes, and jammed with some other guys at uni.

He'd not understood why his mother was so against him playing the guitar or taking an interest in music until the truth came out about who his father was.

As Jez showed no signs of stopping, Tom decided to get an early night. He went to find

Jane, who was sitting reading in her bedroom, and looked in on the kids, who were sleeping peacefully.

Craig materialized before he could even try to open the entrance door to the suite and he sighed at the security precautions.

'We'll have your key card fixed by tomorrow,' he said as he took Tom to his room.

'You'd think I could go down one floor by the fire stairs,' Tom grumbled.

'They're closely guarded too. You'd be surprised at the famous people who've stayed here, and some not so famous but very rich. It's one of the most secure hotels in London.'

★ ★ ★

In Lancashire Gail got ready to go to church with her mother-in-law, amused at what a naive fool Mary Prichard was, so cocooned from the real world that she didn't know which way was up. Her mother-in-law moved from home to church to shops, associated only with family and friends she'd known for years, and didn't even watch the TV news because she said it focused on the wrong things, death and disaster.

Although she was longing for a drink, Gail didn't dare take even one mouthful of wine. The drink could wait, her marriage couldn't. Why hadn't Tom told her he was Jez Winter's son? Why hadn't he done something about it earlier?

When the Prichards' car drew up at the gate, Gail fixed a smile to her face and went out to join them.

The service wasn't as boring as she'd expected because the music was great. Then there was a session where a couple of new members were 'called' and staggered to the front to confess their sins and be accepted into her church. Gail studied that carefully, because she might have to do it to convince people she'd reformed. She'd rather not, though. The mere thought of doing it made her want to laugh hysterically, so she called up an image of Tom, swanning around in a luxury hotel, and that did the trick, took away all desire to laugh.

It was nice not to have to look after the children. It had been a mistake to have the second one. Two were ten times the trouble of one. But it had kept Tom with her and that was the main thing. Now that he was rich, they could hire someone to look after Hayley and Ryan.

The singing restarted, a song she knew because Tom sang it sometimes. She liked it when he sang to her and had been sorry when she realized she'd smashed his guitar, terrified too because he'd looked like he was going to thump her. Thinking of that made more tears come to her eyes.

When Mary pressed a clean handkerchief into her hand, she accepted it with a sniff and wiped her eyes, taking care not to smudge her make-up. Afterwards she told her mother-in-law she'd been crying at the memory of Tom playing his guitar but that didn't seem to go down well.

What had Jez Winter ever seen in boring old Mary Prichard?

When she got home Gail opened one of the

bottles of wine she'd hidden away and gulped a whole glass down. It had been very wearing being nice to a fool. She'd earned this.

Some time later she was surprised to find that she'd drunk the whole bottle without noticing it. But she didn't let herself open a second one, much as she'd have liked to, because she had to be up early the following morning. Mary was coming round to help her clean the house. What fun that would be!

'Damn you, Tom Prichard!' she said as she made her way up to bed. 'I'll pay you back for this one day.'

She dreamed of being in London, going to parties, drinking champagne by the bucketful and buying lots of new clothes.

11

The *In Depth* article had helped give Sophie her privacy back but Jez's preparations for moving in next door drew the media's attention back to her.

She watched what was going on sometimes from her bedroom window, a little ashamed of herself for using a pair of binoculars to get a better view but unable to resist. She was amazed by the speed with which things moved and by the number of uniformed security men keeping an eye on operations. That brought home to her how seriously Kevin took the threat to his employer's life.

Jez phoned her every lunchtime and evening, and though they talked of meeting again, he said Kevin had advised him not to do anything to increase the press's interest in her.

'It'll only be another day or two before we move in.' Jez's voice was like dark velvet, beautiful when he spoke as well as when he sang. 'Then we'll be able to use the gate without anyone seeing us.'

'Good. I'll make you a welcome-to-the-house cake and come for a guided tour.'

'A chocolate cake? That's my favourite so far.'

She laughed. 'All right, you're on.'

'How's the story going?'

'Really well.'

'Tell me what it's about.'

'If you don't mind, I won't. I'm a bit superstitious about revealing my stories to anyone before they're complete. How's the new song going?'

'As well as can be expected when I'm not able to lock myself away in my studio and play it properly.'

'It must be very frustrating.'

'Tell me about it. Look, I have a message from Kevin: you might try going to the shops tomorrow, to see if they leave you in peace. He thinks they will. But keep a careful watch behind you and note who parks nearby or follows you anywhere. Get the number of the car if you can.'

'I'll do that.'

The following day she made a quick trip down to the local shops. She did wonder whether a car was following her, and it parked nearby in the shoppers' car park, but whoever was inside it didn't follow or pester her. Since its windows were heavily tinted she couldn't see the driver. She took note of the number on principle.

She wondered if Talbin was simply biding his time, if he guessed about her and Jez or knew about the new gate between the two properties. The security system would show if anyone even tried to open that gate.

Could she be happy with such a watchful, limited life? She didn't know. But she wanted to be with Jez, get to know him better, see if they worked as a couple. She was missing being with him, even though she'd only seen him a few times. Talking on the phone wasn't the same, though she did enjoy their daily conversations.

How quickly her need for him had grown!

She kept telling herself the attraction could fade as quickly, especially on his side, but that did nothing to damp down her feelings.

Anyway, she didn't want to dampen them down. She felt fully alive again, for the first time in years.

But there was one obstacle still to be got over, one secret she had to tell him about, something that could only be said face to face, because she had to see how he reacted.

Would it matter to a man used to such beautiful women?

★　★　★

'We can move in tomorrow, Jez, if you don't mind workmen coming and going still,' Donna announced when she returned to the hotel to report the day's progress. 'I think we've even got a housekeeper lined up.' She grinned. 'Actually the housekeeper is a he, gay and very camp. But he has a wonderful sense of humour and brilliant references.'

'Sounds OK to me.' Jez beamed at her. 'How on earth did you get things done so quickly?'

'Tom helped me quite a bit, actually, and you've paid through the nose for rapid service. There's just one other thing we need to do today. We need beds for the children and I don't know much about that sort of thing, I must confess. I wondered if Jane could come to the shops with me this afternoon, and Tom, could you watch the children?'

He nodded. 'No worries.'

'I'll help you look after them,' Jez said at once.

'No playing horsies, though!' Donna warned. 'The physio said it wasn't good for you.'

Jez pulled a face at her. 'All right, Mummy dear.'

Hayley came across to lean casually against him. 'Will you play me a song on your guitar today, like Daddy does?'

Jez stilled and looked at his son. 'You play the guitar? Why didn't you say?'

Tom shrugged. 'I'm not in your league, but I do play reasonably. I learned at Mum's church. They have some great music there.'

'Gospel?'

'Yeah. A few black people joined the congregation when I was in my teens and they made a huge difference. You should hear the choir sing 'Just A Closer Walk With Thee'. There's a woman who leads the singing and she's top. She pours her heart and soul into it, makes me shiver sometimes, it's so good.'

'Gospel can be wonderful. You couldn't get much better training in feeling what music's about. What happened to your guitar? Didn't you think of bringing it with you?'

Tom hesitated.

'Mummy broke it,' Hayley said. 'Daddy cried when he threw it away.'

Jez saw Tom's flush of embarrassment and his heart went out to his son. Imagine having your only musical instrument destroyed! 'I've got a spare here. You can use that.'

'Are you sure?'

'Of course.' The way his son's face lit up meant that however good or bad Tom was at playing, he loved it, and that delighted Jez.

As soon as Donna and Jane had left, he fetched the guitar for Tom.

'It's a Martin.'

'Yes. They make great guitars.' Jez watched how his son handled the instrument and saw it was with the hands of a lover.

Tom strummed a few chords and listened with his head on one side, then adjusted one string before strumming again and nodding in satisfaction. 'This is a wonderful guitar, Jez. If this is your spare, what's your main guitar like?'

'I'll get it.' Jez walked back into his bedroom and came out, holding another guitar for his son's inspection.

Tom put the Martin down and took the new one from Jez, whistling softly as he saw the make and tried a few chords. 'A Gibson. Of course.'

'Yes. It has a particularly sweet tone. It's my favourite acoustic guitar.' He took it back. 'You can keep that one, if you like.'

Tom stiffened. 'Even I know it must have cost a fortune. I'm *not* trying to wheedle expensive presents out of you.'

Jez sighed. 'Your expression was just like your mother's when you said that. I know you're not trying to con me, Tom. But I can't think of anything that'll make me happier than to give my son a guitar, something I'd have done when you were much younger if I'd been allowed. I totally understand how you must miss having your own guitar and I'm sure you'll enjoy playing this one, so stop being so bloody stiff-necked.'

Tom's voice was gruff. 'Thanks, then. I'm not in your league as a musician, though, so don't expect too much.'

'The only league I want you to be in is the one for music lovers. Do you know 'He's Got The Whole World In His Hands'?'

Tom nodded. 'They played it a lot at church.'

'Let's give it a go, then.'

Jez took care not to watch Tom as they played, because his son was clearly nervous. He sang the tune, but could hear that his son was playing well, better than he'd expected.

Almost immediately Hayley began dancing, showing a good sense of rhythm and clapping in time to the music. Ryan clapped his hands any old how, not managing to make a real clapping sound, and jigged about less expertly beside her.

'Daddy sing too!' she insisted when they'd finished the first verse.

'Go on!' Jez urged. 'This isn't an exam.'

Hesitantly at first, then with more confidence, Tom joined in, and once he'd forgotten to be nervous his voice gathered power. Jez nearly stopped singing in surprise, because it was a good voice and the training in his mother's church had given Tom the 'gospel' touch. His passion for the music poured forth freely as he sang.

Making no comment, Jez led the way into another song, an old one of his own. At the end of the verse, he deliberately played the chords, leaving Tom to improvise, which he did without seeming to realize he'd been guided into it. And he produced a very creditable guitar solo, slightly different from the one that had been recorded. That further gladdened Jez's heart.

After a while Tom urged, 'You sing the melody now!' then he put in the harmonies.

When they'd finished Jez bowed his head, so moved was he. Looking up, he saw his son's anxious expression and said quickly, 'You're good, really good. Surely you know that?'

Tom blushed and let out a sigh of relief. 'You looked as if you were upset.'

'I was moved to tears because my son, my only son, has inherited my musical ability.'

'I'm OK. I don't make mistakes with the chords or anything, and I can hit the right note, but I'm not in your league.'

'You're more than competent.' Jez left it at that for now, realizing that his son was embarrassed and not used to receiving compliments about his music. He turned the attention to Hayley instead. 'Even my granddaughter was up dancing — *and* in time to the music.'

'She loves to dance and sing.' Tom lowered his voice, 'Trouble is, Gail always said my playing gave her a headache, so we could only do it when she was out. All *she* wanted was to keep them quiet.'

Hayley began tugging Jez's arm. 'Play some more, Granddad! Play 'Dancing Queen'.'

'It's one of her favourites,' Tom said apologetically. 'She's a real Abba fan.'

'I like their music too. It's brilliantly arranged, with memorable melodies and rich harmonies.' Jez struck up the well-known tune, his son joining in, and Hayley started dancing again, head wagging, arms waving.

When it was over, Jez said wonderingly, 'I've seen TV children's shows where the littlies are up and dancing, but I've never been involved in it before. It's marvellous to see them enjoying the music.' He looked back at his son. 'You will accept the guitar, won't you? I know it's going to a good home and my only condition is that you'll play with me.'

Tom blew his nose and picked the instrument up again, saying gruffly, 'Any time you can stand it.'

Jez hid his puzzlement at this remark. His son played well, had a great voice and a perfect sense of rhythm. Why did he seem to think he was no good?

Was it his wife who'd done that to him or his mother? Whoever it was had been cruel. Denying someone who had the gift access to music was cruel. His son's wife went even further down in Jez's estimation, and so did Mary.

What could Tom do in the music industry with a little encouragement? It would be interesting to find out.

He smiled as another thought occurred to him. At the very least, this session had signalled which of Jez's enterprises Tom might be most suited to; his record company. It never hurt to know about what went on in the industry. It wasn't a big company and it was very picky about what it produced, but it was well respected.

★   ★   ★

210

That night was the first time Andi worked at the club. She'd said she had things to do, couldn't start straight away, feeling jittery about it. She'd nearly not turned up, but shortage of money had driven her to it.

First of all, they insisted on her taking another name and put a label on her left breast saying 'Chiffon — Hostess'. What sort of name was that, Chiffon? Feeling very underdressed, she wandered out into the bar area. It didn't feel as friendly tonight, for some reason, and her job meant she had to dance with anyone who asked her, which meant some horrible men, old ones as well as young. Some eyed her as if she was naked and pawed her, laughing when she batted their hands away from her breasts and told them to stop.

She wanted to run away but didn't dare, because the manager kept strolling past. Each time he stopped to watch her, occasionally signalling to smile more. By the end of the evening her face was aching with the effort of keeping the smile there.

When the club closed, one obnoxious man asked to go home with her and wouldn't take no for an answer, holding tight to her arm and trying to drag her towards the door. To her relief, the manager came to her rescue, pacifying the customer but holding on to her so that she couldn't get away.

He turned to her and asked in a low voice, 'Sure you don't want to take him up on his offer?'

'Definitely not.'

'You could earn three times as much money for an extra half-hour's work. And I could find you a safe place to entertain him.'

She glared at him. 'I'd never, ever do that sort of thing and if it's expected, then I quit.'

He shrugged. 'Your loss. And it's not expected, as I told you, so no need to get your knickers in a twist. It's merely an optional extra. Now, would you like a hit to celebrate your first evening's work? It's on the house tonight.'

'No, thank you. I'm so tired all I want to do is go home and sleep. Can you call me a taxi, please?'

'You're a foolish girl. Some of the other hostesses earn a hell of a lot more than you have.' As she opened her mouth, he held up one hand to stop her speaking. 'OK, OK. I'll call you a taxi. Staff use the back entrance.'

All she could think of on the way home was that Ross was right, and they did want her to go into prostitution. The mere thought of that made her feel sick.

Perhaps she should throw herself on her mother's mercy?

No, she couldn't, definitely couldn't *bear* to do that. Look at how she'd lost it that time and attacked her mum, who had been furious, and with reason. What would her dad have said to that sort of behaviour? He'd have been really upset with her. And she was ashamed of it, herself.

No, she had to get out of this mess on her own, so she'd give the nightclub work one more try, see if they'd got the message about what she was available for, and eke out the money she earned there very carefully.

If they continued to press her to do other things, she'd quit. Definitely. There had to be other jobs she could do.

She cried when she was in bed. Nothing was going right. Nothing!

★　★　★

The next day Sophie stood at the bedroom window, watching Jez move into the new house. Vans had been coming and going for several days, some bringing workmen, others bringing furniture. A big pantechnicon had disgorged one bed after another. How many people were sleeping there, for heaven's sake?

To her surprise, her daughter-in-law turned up that morning with the children, which was very unusual. Sophie bit back her annoyance at being disturbed during her writing time. 'Come in. How lovely to see you.'

Kerry gave one of her frozen imitations of a smile. 'We were passing by, so I thought we'd call in. William's been worried about you, but you look fine to me. After all, you're not young any more, so it's to be expected you'd get tired more easily.'

Why did her daughter-in-law's comments always seem to be putting her down, Sophie wondered as she led the way into the kitchen. 'Would you like something to drink? And a piece of my home-made cake, maybe?'

'Jordan would like milk or water. I don't

believe in giving children drinks full of chemicals. The baby's just been fed. And I'd like a cup of herbal tea, if you have any.' She saw the cake sitting under its transparent cover on the breakfast bar and licked her lips involuntarily. 'Um — what sort of cake is it?'

'All-organic, with dried fruit and walnuts, very little sugar or fat,' Sophie said promptly. It wasn't organic and it contained both butter and sugar, but Kerry wasn't to know that.

'Perhaps just a small piece for Jordan, then, and one for me.'

Sophie got out the plates.

'Has *he* moved in next door yet?'

She wondered if this was the purpose of the visit. 'Who?'

Kerry's eyes narrowed. 'You know who. Jez Winter.'

'I don't know whether he's moved in or not.'

'But you're friendly with him. Surely he's told you?' She took one of her nibbling, rodent-like bites, then added, 'William said you and Winter were together. The man can't have dumped you so quickly, surely?'

Kerry had no idea how rude she was, Sophie told herself, biting her tongue for the millionth time. How William put up with a wife like that, she'd never understand. 'My social life is my own business.'

'But we're your family. And actually, I quite like his music. I'd love to meet him.'

Sophie shuddered mentally at the mere thought of that and vowed to avoid it at all costs until she was more sure of what was going on between herself and Jez.

'You're not going deaf, are you? People your age sometimes start losing their hearing.'

'You didn't ask any questions but as it happens, I don't feel the need to introduce my friends to my family, any more than you introduce *your* friends to me.'

'It's not at all the same. *My* friends aren't famous.'

To Sophie's relief, the baby started to cry lustily and Kerry first tried rocking the stroller, then picked up the baby, who obliged by a loud burp and spat a mouthful of regurgitated milk down her mother's front.

'She's always doing that!' Kerry gave her little daughter a dirty look, thrust the baby into Sophie's hands and rushed to wipe herself down. 'Jordan was much easier to look after. I'm not having any more children.'

Sophie wondered what she was supposed to say to that and could think of nothing. She jiggled the baby, who, to give Kerry her due, looked rosy and well-cared for. But Jordan always seemed subdued for a two-year-old, and no doubt this little one would be nagged into submission too as soon as she was old enough to understand English.

'I must say I think you're being very mean, keeping Jez Winter to yourself,' Kerry grumbled.

'He's not a parcel to be passed round.'

'You do say some strange things. I hope you don't write like that. I must get round to reading one of your books one day, when I'm not so busy, though they're probably meant for older

215

women.' Kerry looked at the clock. 'Well, I suppose I'd better be going.'

'It was lovely to see the children, but I'm afraid mornings are my best working time, so could you make it the afternoon next time you visit?' She'd asked the same thing dozens of times before, to no avail.

Kerry flapped one hand. 'Oh, family don't count.'

Sophie deliberately blocked her path. 'Yes, they do. I'm a working woman, not a lady of leisure. If you come in the morning again, I'll not answer the door.'

The frost around Kerry went colder by several degrees.

When she'd waved goodbye to little Jordan and checked that the gate had closed properly, Sophie went into her meditation room with a groan of frustration and it was a while before she calmed down again enough to write.

12

Even though he was feeling better by the day, Jez was weary by the time they'd moved in. But once people stopped asking him things, he couldn't resist wandering down to his studio. It was full of boxes, sound equipment, his keyboard and the rest of his guitars, newly out of storage, and his computer, which had music-recording software on it. Everything needed unpacking and setting up, and he was looking forward to doing that . . . but not today.

Tom peered round the door. 'Donna said you'd be in here. Hey, this is going to make a fantastic studio.' He walked to the window and back, whistling softly as he saw the make of keyboard, then went over to his father. 'You look tired. Why don't you go and have a lie down?'

'I seem to have spent the past few months lying down.' Jez was unable to keep the sharp edge from his voice. 'What I want to do — *need* to do — is make music. It's inside my head and aching to be let out. But all this has to be set up first.' He waved one hand at the jumble surrounding him.

Tom went to look at the computer and its various attachments. 'I could set it up for you, if you like. I promise I'd not damage anything. I'm pretty good with computers.'

Jez frowned. Normally he didn't allow anyone else to touch his music computer, but somehow

Tom was different. Not only was he his son, but he was young enough to understand computers properly, instead of learning about them step by painful step. 'All right. That'd be a big help. I've got the leads labelled.' He went across to whisper his password in his son's ear. 'Keep that to yourself. You're the only other person in the world who knows it.'

Tom went slightly pink and tried unsuccessfully to hide his pleasure.

Jez retreated to his bedroom, sighing in relief to find that someone had made up his bed. At the sound of footsteps he turned to see Donna bringing in a tray.

'We thought you should have something to eat before you lie down. It's — '

'I'm not hungry and — Is that Sophie's chocolate cake?'

'Yes. She delivered it to the gate and Kevin OK'd it to come inside.'

Jez broke off a piece of the generous slice and ate it slowly, closing his eyes in bliss. 'If she wasn't a novelist, she'd be a famous cook, I'm sure. And this is without wheat flour, you know. She's going to write a cookery book for people with food problems one day.'

Donna smiled and backed towards the door. 'Yeah. You've told me that a few times. I'll buy a copy when she does. I tasted the crumbs and my diet went straight out of the window. We're all going to have a slice now. Have a good rest, Jez.'

He ate the cake slowly and with relish, thought about ringing to thank Sophie then decided to lie down for a few minutes first. When he woke, it was two hours later and the house seemed very still.

He got out of the bed, doing stretching exercises automatically to get both sides of his body in balance as he went across to the window. The removal men had taken their mammoth boxes on wheels away and the gardens were no longer full of Lowryesque figures hauling furniture and boxes around. From here he could see the front gates and gardens, but not Sophie's house. He went into a bedroom at the other side of this wing. That was better! He could see the rear of her house from here.

What was she doing now? Writing? He glanced at his watch. It was late afternoon. Maybe she'd stopped for the day. On that thought he went back to his bedroom, fumbled through his pockets for his mobile phone, and rang her.

'Are you working?'

'Only on business stuff. I've finished my story-telling for the day.'

'Can I come over?'

'I thought you were only going to visit me after dark.'

'The gate's well hidden by the trees on both sides. I'm sure no one will be able to see me.'

'I'd love you to come over.'

'I'll be there in two minutes.' Then common sense reasserted itself. 'No, it'll be a bit longer. I'd better find Kevin to escort me.'

He sighed as he ended the call. No point in hiring minders if you didn't use their services. He still remembered the lunatic holding a knife to his throat, slashing at him, so that he thought he'd be killed. He still woke up in the night with a start because he'd relieved it in a nightmare. No one could understand why the man had stopped where he did, but he had, thank goodness. It'd been left to a car windscreen to do more damage a month afterwards, thanks to a drunken driver and a slippery road.

When would the need for such caution end? What if they never caught the fellow and Jez spent his whole life looking over his shoulder? That thought made him furious sometimes.

★　★　★

The phone call lifted Sophie's spirits immediately. She rushed upstairs to make sure she looked all right, changed the clothes she'd been sitting around in all day and ran a brush through her hair. After hesitating over the perfume bottle, she shook her head. Too obvious.

Downstairs, she checked that the living room and kitchen were tidy then waited in the room that looked out towards the gate, noticing with pleasure that the two chestnut trees on either side of the wall were just coming into bloom, with a few of the lovely white flowers showing here and there, like shy candles nestled against the towering mass of green. Last year she'd let the two lads in the rear house have some of the conkers and had kept a couple in a dish near her computer for a while, fingering their glossy brown sheen when she stopped to think about the next scene. They should have called the street Horse Chestnut Lane, really, but it'd not have sounded as nice.

The gate opened and Jez came through into her garden, leaving Kevin standing in the opening in the dappled shadow of the trees. Sophie hurried to open the door.

As she closed it behind the two of them, her breath caught in her throat at the sight of the naked hunger on Jez's face. She didn't wait for him to kiss her, but put her arms round his neck and kissed him.

It was like setting a match to a fire. Her reaction to his touch was so fierce that the world vanished and there seemed only the two of them, kissing, caressing — *No!*

It was a major effort to step back, but before they went any further, she had to tell him. She didn't want him finding out in the middle of making love. When — if — they made love, she wanted it to be perfect.

She'd been dreading this moment, though.

'Come into the kitchen, Jez.'

He put out one hand to bar her way. 'Why did you stop me? You were responding, enjoying it as much as I was.'

'Because there's something I have to tell you first before we go any further. Let's go into the living room.'

She would have walked ahead, but he took her hand and laced his fingers in hers. She could feel her hand trembling in his and saw him look down at it, then at her.

What would he think when she told him? Would he find her unattractive, draw back, not want to touch her?

Tom was pleased he'd been able to help his father set up the studio and computer, would have loved to stay and play with it, but he had to check that his children were all right. When he went across to the cottage, he found them playing quietly on the floor with a couple of their favourite toys. Jane had unpacked all their clothes and made up the beds already.

She smiled round. 'It's a lovely little house, though why I say little when it's bigger than my house back home, I don't know.'

'How's your flat?'

'Great. Come and see it.' She turned to pick Ryan up, but Tom took him from her and tossed his son in the air, making him laugh. It was wonderful not to have to keep the kids quiet all the time and they were looking rosier and plumper already, thanks to Jane's care and the good food they were eating.

The flat had one bedroom with a bathroom, a sitting room and a small kitchen. Jane smoothed the blue-flowered duvet cover with a proprietorial hand. 'Lovely, isn't it? Everything's brand new, you can tell that. I don't know how Donna managed to do it all so quickly.'

'How about a cup of tea? I'm parched.'

'You and your cups of tea! It's a wonder you don't squelch when you walk.'

'Have you talked to that new housekeeper about food for Ryan and Hayley?'

'Oh, yes. He's a lovely man, even if he is . . . you know. He and his friend are going to

222

cook everyone's evening meal, if we want, and
supply food for you and me to get our own
breakfasts and lunches. I have to order what we
need from him twice a week. It's almost like a
village here, isn't it?'

'Except for the security. You won't forget to
lock up when you go over to the big house, will
you?'

'Of course not. I've learned our number off by
heart. Now, you put that kettle on and we'll
christen these new mugs of mine. I think there's
cartons of juice for the children.'

★   ★   ★

Sophie stared down into her cup of peppermint
tea. On the big armchair at right angles to hers
Jez sat very still, not pushing her to begin. And
that was a good thing, because she didn't know
where to start. But it had to be done, so she put
the cup down untasted and hunted desperately
for the right words.

'After Bill died, I fell ill myself. Cancer.' She
took a deep breath and said it, 'Breast cancer.'
Her hand had gone up to touch her right breast
before she knew it. 'I had to have a mastectomy.
I've — been clear for three years now and
— things look good, but . . . ' The words just
wouldn't come out.

His voice was so gentle, she could have wept.

'But you think I might not want you because
of that.'

She nodded and peeped quickly at his face.
She'd been so terrified of seeing revulsion there,

but instead she saw love, saw it so clearly that she gulped and nearly broke down.

'Did you think that would make a difference to me?'

She shrugged. 'I can't tell. Some people reacted in unexpected ways when I was diagnosed, even vanished from my social scene entirely. Others — especially my two best friends — stood by me. They were wonderful.'

'Do you have a prosthesis? Is that why you're so — nervous?'

'No. I had a breast reconstruction. I wasn't sure whether to bother, didn't think I'd ever want to make love again. After Bill died, I couldn't see myself finding another man. But in the end I had the reconstruction done for myself, so that I'd look — more normal. So that I'd feel right.' He started to speak but she held up one hand. 'Let me finish before I run out of courage.'

She took another deep breath and went on with her explanation. 'They did it by back flap. The surgeon removed and redirected muscles and blood vessels from my back to make a new breast mound. So there's a scar on my back, which shows more than the scar in front, actually. It's quite a major operation and it took about two months before I was feeling myself again, but . . . it looks pretty good. They even added an artificial nipple later. Only . . . it doesn't work like a real breast, hasn't the same feeling.'

As he reached out to take her hand, she searched his face again and found only tenderness there. When a tear escaped her, he moved to wipe it away with a fingertip. 'Oh, Sophie, it's *you* I love, and this is part of you. No one's perfect. I'm not unscathed myself. I've got scars on my face and worse ones on my body. I still have nightmares sometimes about the intruder, still feel that knife at my throat.'

He tugged her towards him and she went willingly, letting him pull her on to his lap, nestling against him.

They didn't say anything for a while, didn't need to. It was enough to sit quietly, letting their breaths mingle, sharing the warmth of their bodies.

'If it's confession time,' he said at last, 'then I have to remind you that I'm a very bad risk and you'd be a fool to take up with me, but I'm hoping desperately that you will.'

She studied his face, dear to her already. 'And if I do want to take up with you . . . ?'

'Then we'll face the world together and let the press say what it will. If things go well between us, I'll ask you to stay with me, marry me.'

She gave him a quick hug. 'You may not want me to. I'm not easy to live with. Andi pointed that out only recently. I vanish into my office and I'm absent-minded when a story is pouring out. I really need my solitude and I'd hate to live in anyone's pocket, even the man I love.'

He chuckled, a rich, deep sound. 'That's perfect.'

She looked at him in puzzlement.

'I was going to tell you the same thing. Only it's a studio I vanish into, not an office, and I make a lot of noise there.'

Pulling her towards him, he kissed her again, but didn't take the embrace any further. He must have seen that she was still anxious about what she'd told him because he said quietly, 'When we make love for the first time, I want it to be perfect. Not a hurried coupling, after which we separate for the night and I creep furtively across the garden.' He smiled ruefully. 'It won't be easy to wait, because I want you very much, but I think you still need to take this slowly. Am I right?'

She nodded and raised his hand to her lips. 'I do need that. It's happened so quickly between us.'

'But we're officially an item now?'

'We are.'

'And you'll let me tell you that I love you?'

Her breath caught in her throat as she looked at him. 'I'll be upset if you don't, because I love you, too.'

'That's wonderful.'

They talked quietly, honestly, and they enjoyed silences too, fleeting touches, kisses. She felt young again, as if she'd reached the end of a long, dark tunnel and moved into the sunshine. And she'd never seen that look of utter content on his face before. It made her feel good that she could put it there.

She went to get them a snack, just cheese and fruit and nuts, and they picked at the platter as they chatted.

Happiness was welling up inside her. This quiet time seemed to bind them together more than anything else could. And the fact that he'd understood she wasn't ready for passion yet gave her more hope than anything. How could you make a good relationship if you didn't sense the other person's most important needs and feelings?

When the clock chimed ten, Jez eased away from her. 'You look as tired as I feel. I'd better ring Kevin to come and get me.'

They walked to the back door hand in hand, and blew kisses to one another as Jez turned at the gate to look back at her.

She went to bed still wrapped in a warm cloud of happiness, such as she hadn't felt for years.

*   *   *

Andi felt uneasy as she got ready for work. Twice she stopped what she was doing to stare into space. Should she go to the club or not? She hated it there.

Only what choice did she have? She needed money to live. And she'd not enjoyed her previous job, either. Maybe most people were like that, hating their jobs, but doing them because you had to earn a living. Her mother was so lucky.

That made her stop to think again and brought tears to her eyes. No, her mother hadn't been lucky. She'd lost her husband, then had to go through the terrors of breast cancer without his support. And Andi hadn't been much use, either, she realized that now. She'd been too young, too lost in her own grief for her father.

227

She'd never apologized for that lack of support, should have done.

When she was more settled financially, she was going to try to get on better terms with her mother. But an apology would hardly be credible if she went cap in hand begging at the same time. She had to learn to stand on her own feet first.

As she entered the club, her heart sank. Instinctively she pulled her coat closely round herself to cover the revealing garments she was wearing. Then she straightened her spine and went through into the staff room. *Just do it*, she told herself.

The first person she saw as she walked out into the club was the man who'd hassled her the night before. She stopped dead as she saw him moving towards her and tried to slip through the crowd to one side.

The manager was there immediately. 'You've a customer and he's a good one here. See that you're nice to him tonight.'

'Please. Let one of the other girls look after him. I don't like him.'

'He doesn't want one of the other girls and what you like or don't like doesn't matter. We're paying you to smile and be nice to the sort of people who find it hard to pull their own chicks.' For a moment his hand tightened on her arm. It hurt and he could see that, but he smiled and kept up the pressure.

When the customer came up to them, also smiling, the manager let go in such a way that he pushed her towards the man.

'Chiffon! Lovely to see you again.'

'Nice to see you, too.'

'My name's Eric.'

'Eric.' Numbly she let him buy her a drink, then danced with him. When another guy came up to ask her to dance, she was relieved, but Eric put his arm round her shoulders.

'She's with me.'

The other man shrugged and moved off. She somehow dredged up another smile. Well, she hoped it looked as if she was smiling. She felt like a circus clown. Maybe she should have painted on a smile with lipstick?

The evening seemed interminable but at least she didn't have to search for things to say because Eric talked about himself non-stop. He didn't ask much about her, except to make sure she wasn't married or in a relationship.

She stopped drinking alcohol, frightened of losing control of herself, and drank fruit juice instead.

Just after midnight, the room started to spin round her and before she could cry out, everything blurred and faded.

* * *

Someone was whimpering. Andi could hear it quite clearly. Whoever it was sounded really upset.

'Can you hear me? Open your eyes if you can hear me.'

She tried to but couldn't. The whimpering started again.

229

The voice boomed out above her head but the words were meaningless. 'She's well out of it. Better call the police.'

A little later she managed to half-open her eyes. There were lights flashing and someone else was bending over her. Where was she? It was so cold and damp, she couldn't stop shivering.

'She's opened her eyes. What's your name, love? Tell us your name.'

She tried to form the words, but they came out sounding as if she was drunk. 'Andi . . . Carr.'

'Well, Andi, we're going to get you to hospital. You were unconscious, so we need to check you out.'

'Where . . . What . . . ?' It was too hard to speak, so she closed her eyes again.

When she opened them, she was in a bed, with curtains drawn round her. She panicked and tried to sit up but couldn't. Only then did she realize she was the one who kept whimpering.

The curtain moved and a nurse came in. 'So you're awake again. How do you feel?'

It wasn't as hard to speak this time, but she still sounded drunk. 'Dopey.'

'What's your name? Your address?'

She listened patiently as Andi stumbled out the information, then patted her arm. 'Can you give me a sample?'

Andi nodded but when the nurse brought a commode, she protested, 'I don't need that. I can go in the toilets.'

'We need to test your urine. We think you may have been drugged.'

It was a moment before Andi could speak. 'I can't — remember anything.'

'That's the effect of some drugs.'

'I didn't — take anything. Not a thing. I was working — at the club.'

'Let's do the test, shall we? Good girl.' She covered the container and straightened the bedcovers. 'They want to talk to you now.'

This time when the curtain opened it was a police officer who came in. As the nurse carried away the sample, the newcomer took the seat next to Andi.

'The nurse says you're starting to make sense.'

Andi looked at her. 'I can't remember anything. How did I get here?' That terrified her.

The woman's face was tight, as if she was holding back anger. 'No, you won't remember. We think you've been doped with something like Rohypnol. The test will show if we're right but you've got all the classic symptoms. Look, I'm sorry if this upsets you, but we need to take you to the Rape Unit to find out whether anyone assaulted you. We suspect they did, but we want to make sure. Is that all right?'

Andi tried to think, but her head seemed full of cotton wool. In the end it was her companion's obvious concern for her that convinced her to agree. 'Yes, but could you — call my mother? Could she meet us there?'

'Good idea. Give me her number.'

'It's unlisted. You won't pass it on to anyone?'

'No. It's quite safe with me.' She took it down and gave the piece of paper to someone outside. 'Do you want to get dressed now? We've found some clothes for you. We've had to take yours away for examination.'

Andi let herself be helped to dress in paper clothing, then sat in a wheelchair wrapped in a blanket as they pushed her out to a car. She felt numb, disoriented, as if this was happening to someone else and she was just watching.

Would her mother come? Yes, of course she would. She had to. Andi couldn't bear it if she didn't.

13

Sophie jerked awake as the phone rang. She fumbled for it in the darkness and nearly knocked it off the bedside table. Eventually she managed to put it to her ear. 'Yes?'

'Mrs Carr? Police here. Sergeant Milson.'

'If this is a joke — '

'It isn't. Your daughter's in trouble and needs you.'

Suddenly Sophie felt very wide awake. 'What's wrong?'

'She was found unconscious in an alley. She may have been assaulted. She asked us to contact you.'

'Tell me where to come.' Sophie switched on the bedside light and jotted down the address.

'Just one more thing, Mrs Carr. It's the Rape Unit you're coming to.'

'*Andi's been raped?*'

'We think so. We're still doing tests. Oh, and can you bring some clothes for your daughter?'

'Yes. I'm on my way.' She got dressed any old how, then found some clothes stet. Grabbing her handbag, she switched off the security system that guarded the rest of the house while she was asleep in the main bedroom and went out to the garage. It had been built for three cars but had only ever housed one. Her footsteps echoed as she crossed the floor and she kept glancing round uneasily, even though she knew no one could possibly have got in without triggering the alarm system.

She switched on the security system again, then set off through the night, terrified of what she'd find.

What had they *done* to her daughter?

★　★　★

Andi had seen what happened in rape units on TV shows — who hadn't? But it felt different when it was happening to you.

Two women were waiting for her, and they introduced themselves as a doctor and a special police officer attached to the unit. They were kindness itself but she still kept crying, couldn't seem to stop. She wanted her mother.

When the phone rang, she stopped talking to listen.

The police officer put it down. 'Your mother's on her way.'

'Thank goodness! Oh, thank goodness!'

'Do you want to wait for her before we do anything?'

Andi nodded, only half understanding what they were saying. Time seemed to tick along very slowly. She kept looking at the clock and finding only two minutes had passed, then looking again with the same result.

When the door opened, she rushed across to fling herself into her mother's arms, alternately weeping and trying to thank her.

In the end she managed to calm down and sat on a sofa with her mother's arm round her shoulders, trying to make sense of what the other two women were saying to her. But she couldn't seem to concentrate.

In the end her mother cradled her face in one hand and said slowly and clearly, 'Andi, darling, will you let the doctor examine you? If someone has hurt you, we want to catch them, don't we? Stop them doing it to anyone else. Let them examine you now.'

She nodded. 'You won't go away?'

'Of course not. I'll be waiting right here when you return, I promise.'

Andi hated the thought of the examination, almost changed her mind as she followed the doctor into the next room, then suddenly the thought of Eric jumped into her mind. The last thing she remembered was sitting having a drink with him.

She paused at the door. 'Eric.'

The policewoman looked at her questioningly.

'There was a customer at the club called Eric and they made me dance with him and have drinks with him all night. He was horrible. The way he kept touching me, looking at me, made me shiver.'

'They?'

'At the club. I'm a hostess, just go there to dance and talk to people. I'm *not* a prostitute. I don't go with men after work.'

The policewoman took down the details. 'I'll just pass this on before we go any further. We'll see if we can get any CCTV footage before the person realises what's happened. If you remember anything else, let me know.'

The doctor was very gentle but at her touch Andi started sobbing again, she didn't know why.

'Do you want me to stop?'

'No. Just get it over with.' She dug her fingers into the palms of her hands and started counting the cracks in the ceiling.

'There, that's finished. You can have a shower now.'

But she had to find out. 'Did they do it? Rape me?'

'Yes.'

She shuddered and felt like vomiting, but when the doctor again suggested a shower, she couldn't get the rest of the paper clothes off quickly enough. She stayed under the hot water for a long time, didn't want to come out, but in the end the doctor coaxed her out and showed her the clothes her mother had brought.

It was wonderful to be covered up again, covered from head to toe. She'd never complain about her mother's taste in clothes as long as she lived.

In the waiting room, she went to sit close to her mother again. When Sophie took her hand, that simple act brought another rush of tears because Andi felt so dirty, in spite of the shower.

Her mother squeezed the hand. 'Try to answer their questions, darling. We want to catch him, don't we? Stop him doing this to other women?'

So she did her best, because that was the only thing she was certain of, that she wanted him caught. It had to be that horrible Eric person,

236

just had to. Who else could it have been?

When the questioning was over, Andi turned to her mother. 'Can I come home with you? Just for a few days. I'll be very quiet, won't disturb you — ' She began weeping again. She hadn't cried like this since her dad died.

'Of course you can come home with me. I was going to suggest it.'

★   ★   ★

Sophie let Andi choose which bedroom she wanted, because they'd told her to give her daughter as much power as possible, even over tiny details. She made sure there were plenty of towels in the en suite, not knowing what else to say or do to help.

In the end she ran out of things to fuss about and a huge yawn overtook her. 'Will you be all right? Do you want me to stay with you?'

Andi gave her a wan smile. 'I'm tired. I don't think that horrible stuff has worn off yet. All I want to do now is sleep.'

'I'll leave you, then. Remember, I'm just across the corridor if you need me.' She went across to the door.

'Mum.'

'Yes?'

'Thank you.'

She had to go back then and smooth the hair back from Andi's forehead so that she could plant a kiss there, as she had done when she was a small child. Same straight, heavy hair as her own, but the forehead beneath it was flushed and the eyes swollen from weeping.

Her daughter's arms came up round her neck. 'I'm sorry.'

'What for?'

'Being awful to you. I was going to come and tell you but I couldn't do that and ask you for money at the same time, could I? That's why I was trying to earn as much as I could. I wasn't going to keep working at that horrible place.'

'I wish you had come to me.'

'So do I.'

'Well, we'll focus on moving on, making a good life for you. I'll help in every way I can.'

'Is that what you did, when you got cancer, focused on moving on? Is that how you got better?'

'Yes. I took one day at a time and did the best I could with it. It's easier to cope with one day when things overwhelm you.' She hugged her daughter again. 'I do love you, you know.' She watched Andi snuggle down and smile at her, a real smile this time.

'I don't know how you put up with me, but I'm glad you do.'

'You're my daughter. Nothing you do can take that bond away. You're part of me.'

Sophie went to bed but couldn't sleep, kept listening in case Andi needed her, wondering if they'd catch the rapist, praying the tests for sexually transmitted diseases and pregnancy would prove negative, though you had a long wait for some of the results.

A couple of times, as night moved towards dawn, she thought of Jez and warmth filled her briefly at how happy he'd made her feel. But that soon slid away into the distance, because for the moment she had to save all her energy for helping her daughter.

This wasn't going to be allowed to ruin Andi's life, whatever it took to help her through it.

★ ★ ★

Jez woke feeling happy, even before he remembered why. Then he stretched lazily. Should he ring Sophie straight away to wish her good morning? Why not?

But her phone rang and rang, then the call was picked up by the answering system, and a cool voice that sounded like a relative of Sophie, not the woman herself, asked him to leave her a message.

'Jez here. Just wanted to say good morning.' He hesitated then added, 'And to tell you I love you.'

★ ★ ★

The phone woke Sophie but she didn't want to speak to anyone. She lay there, listening, but could hear nothing, so went to check on Andi.

The other bedroom was empty. She ran downstairs, closing her eyes in relief when she found her daughter sitting in the kitchen, cradling a mug of hot chocolate with her hands. It had always been a family comfort drink.

'Good morning, darling.'

Andi's smile was so bleak Sophie could have

239

wept, but that wouldn't do any good, so she went to make herself a drink and joined her daughter at the table.

'Did you sleep?'

'Yes, but it was full of nightmares — no, not exactly nightmares, just anxieties and swirling darkness. I feel as if I've got a bad hangover this morning.'

'Shall I get you a paracetamol?'

'Yes, please.'

Sophie got out the tablets and passed the packet to Andi, who sat staring at it as if she didn't know what to do with it, then sucked in a sudden breath and pushed a couple of tablets out, going to the sink to get a glass of water. She stood there afterwards for a long time with the empty glass in her hand before setting it down carefully.

'Would you like something to eat?'

'Not yet.' Again, a pause before she added, 'Thanks.'

'Do you want to go and see my doctor? Or a counsellor?'

'No, I don't think so. The doctor I saw last night was very thorough. I — don't want to see anyone really, just stay here quietly. Is that all right?' Andi stared at Sophie, eyes bright with tears. 'I can't believe it happened.'

'The police were pretty definite.'

'But I can't remember a thing. You'd think I'd remember *something*, wouldn't you? And how can they prosecute anyone if I don't remember what happened, let alone who did it?'

'I don't know. Would you mind if I got myself

240

something to eat? You know what I'm like in the mornings.'

A ghost of a smile passed across Andi's face. 'Hungry. Are you still as bad?'

'Yes.'

'You're sure you don't mind me staying here for a bit?'

'I think you should stay for longer than a bit. It's going to have an effect and you should be with someone who cares about you till you've recovered.' She hesitated, then said the other thing. 'I know you've been taking drugs. I wondered if you needed help to get them out of your system?'

'I really didn't use them very often, just let you think I did. It was only when I went out at weekends.' She shuddered. 'I'm never going clubbing again. Or using stuff.'

'What *are* you going to do?'

'What do you mean?'

'You have no job. If you're not going out with your friends, you'll need something to fill your time. I discovered when I was ill that nothing is worse than sitting brooding.'

'I'll think of something. Not today, though.'

'If you like, I can teach you to meditate. Or you can go to classes to learn. That helped me more than anything.'

'Maybe. Can I just — chill out for a while, though?' She gave another of her bleak smiles. 'I know you've got the old Protestant work ethic, but I need to get my head together first.'

'Do what seems right. Listen to your own body.'

Andi looked down. 'Thanks for lending me some clothes. Maybe later, when you've finished writing, we could go and get my things?'

'Of course. But we'll go whenever you say, now if you like. I want you to feel comfortable and those are not really your style. The writing can wait.'

Andi nodded.

Her daughter seemed like a limp, two-dimensional version of herself. Sophie didn't know what to do for the best, whether to hover nearby, or leave Andi in peace.

She'd found books to help her through the cancer, but she doubted there were any manuals for the mothers of young women who'd been raped. She felt so helpless, so angry.

★ ★ ★

Gail heard the knocking on the front door and rolled over in bed with a groan. She didn't want to see anyone.

The letterbox flap rattled and a voice echoed up from the hall. 'Gail? Are you there? Are you all right?'

Her mother-in-law!

She jumped out of bed and stared at herself in the mirror, shocked at how puffy her face was, but quickly dismissed the image. No one got up looking lovely. She'd not bothered to undress last night, thank goodness, but she'd had a few drinks of cheap plonk and her head was thumping.

'Coming!' She dragged a brush through her

242

hair, flushing the toilet as she passed the bathroom to give herself an excuse for not answering immediately.

Opening the door she forced a smile. 'Mary. How are you? Come in.'

'You took a long time to answer.'

'I was using the toilet.'

Without asking permission, Mary walked through into the kitchen, stopping in the doorway so that Gail had to peep over her shoulder to see anything. How had the place got in such a mess with only her in the house?

Mary walked forward, eyes flicking here and there. 'This is no way to live.'

Gail saw the empty bottle under the table at the same time as Mary did, but wasn't quick enough to nudge it out of sight with her foot.

Mary held it up. 'I thought you'd stopped drinking.'

'It was just a couple of glasses.'

'The bottle's empty.'

Gail had no answer to that. There was another empty bottle up in her bedroom as well. It never seemed possible in the mornings that she'd drunk two whole bottles, but at night the wine slipped down easily, making all her troubles go away. She went to put the kettle on. She could never think properly till she'd had a cup of strong coffee.

Mary began clearing up, banging the plates down on the draining board and scraping the debris together.

'Don't! I'll do that.'

But it was too late. Her damned mother-in-law

had opened the waste bin and seen the other empty bottles Gail had meant to take out to the dustbin.

Mary straightened up again, her expression thunderous. 'You've been lying to me.'

Gail began to weep, forcing sobs out.

'And you can stop pretending to cry. There are no tears coming out of your eyes.'

'I can't help drinking. I get lonely. I'm no good at living on my own. It's your son's fault. He shouldn't have left me.'

'Were you drinking this much when the children were here?'

Gail tried to lie, but with that disapproving gaze on her, the words just wouldn't come out convincingly.

Mary took a step backwards, lips so tightly pressed together they vanished into a thin, puckered line. 'When you decide that you really want to change your ways, you know where to find me.'

'Wait!'

But the old hag had gone before Gail could stop her. Groaning, she sank down at the table. Lifting her cup of coffee up with two hands, because they were shaking, she tried to think what to do.

But she couldn't come up with anything.

What she needed was a hair of the dog. Only because this was a crisis. She never usually drank so early. There must be another bottle somewhere. She searched the kitchen, pulling things out of cupboards and leaving them scattered across the floor, checking all her old hiding places, but finding nothing.

'Have to go and buy some more, then,' she muttered. 'I need something to help me through. I'll give up drinking later, after Tom comes back. He'll help me. He'll have money then from his rich daddy.' She was talking to herself again. She had to stop that.

Picking up her handbag, she hunted for her car keys, then went out. She hit one of the gateposts when backing out. The car parking space was too narrow, always had been.

The man at the off-licence frowned at her as she dumped a six-bottle container of the special-offer wine on the counter. 'Should you be driving, love?'

'Mind your own bloody business.' She slapped her credit card down and scribbled her signature.

She tried to manage on only one bottle that day, she really did, but it was so lonely on her own and the day seemed to go on for ever. It was Tom's fault, all of it, and she was going to make him sorry he'd left her.

And if she had to do that through the children, upset them a bit, well, they'd benefit in the long run.

Tom definitely wasn't going to leave her behind when he started living the high life.

14

Tom's mobile rang and his heart sank when he saw it was his mother. But he might as well face her now as worry about what she wanted, so he sat down on the nearest chair. 'Hi, Mum.'

'I thought you'd have rung me before now, Tom.'

'We've been flat out.'

'Too busy for a short phone call to your parents to say you were all right?'

'I was going to ring this evening. We're in Jez's house now, you know. The kids and I have a cottage in the grounds. It's great. And Jane has a flat leading off it. They put a door through into my house specially so that she can look after the kids if I'm not there.'

'Jane?'

'Jane Burtill. You know, our old neighbour. She's working as our nanny now. She often used to look after the kids when Gail was — '

'Drunk.'

'Yes. Drunk.'

'I went round to your *old* house this morning at nearly eleven o'clock and found your wife still in bed. She'd drunk a whole bottle of wine the evening before! *A whole bottle!* And there were other empty bottles in the rubbish bin.'

'That was an abstemious night, then, because these days she usually drinks two bottles.'

Silence, then. 'I didn't know it was so bad.'

'I tried to tell you, but you wouldn't believe me.'

'She needs help, Tom.'

'I know, but you can't force someone to dry out. Don't you think I've tried? Jez offered to pay for her to go into one of those fancy drug-rehabilitation places, but she wouldn't.'

'She's confused, really misses you. And she's desperate to get back together.'

'Mum, Gail thinks I'm rich now and what she really wants is her share of the good life. She only cares for herself, you know. She doesn't even care for the kids. Did she even ask about them?' There was no answer. 'No, I thought not.'

He heard how his voice had risen and took a deep breath before saying more quietly, 'And whatever Gail says or does, I'm not taking her back. If it hadn't been for the kids, I'd not have stayed with her this long.'

'How are the children?'

'Rosy again, clean, well fed. They can sing and dance without anyone slapping them.'

'She didn't do that!'

'She did. Anything to keep them quiet when her head was aching from the booze. Hayley learned to hide from her, and to hide Ryan.'

As the silence continued, he said, 'Look, I'll ring you in a couple of days, but I have to go and help Jez set up his studio now. He's giving me so much that I want to do something in return. See you soon.'

He switched off the phone before she could protest, then sat with his head in his hands, torn every which way.

'Are you all right?'

He turned to see Donna looking at him anxiously. He couldn't speak, only shake his head.

She came to sit next to him. 'Anything I can do to help?'

He found his voice. 'No. Not really.' But it was a comfort that Donna had offered.

She stood up. 'If I can ever help . . . I mean that.'

'Thanks.' He watched her leave, trim and smartly dressed. Intelligence and purpose shone from her eyes — and beautiful eyes they were too, dark brown with thick lashes. Why hadn't he waited till he could meet someone like her? Why had he let Gail trap him into marriage while he was at university? She'd barely waited for him to graduate before getting pregnant.

He'd never be free of her now, even if he didn't live with her. He'd have to pay maintenance and he knew he'd worry about what she'd do to herself. But that didn't mean he intended to sponge off his father. He'd accept help at the moment, for the children's sake, but he'd pay Jez back eventually.

On that thought he went into the studio. There was a lot to set up and check still, but he understood this sort of thing and Jez clearly didn't, had only learned how to use the equipment once it was all connected.

★　★　★

It was good to save Jez the cost of someone to set it all up, and anyway, Tom was enjoying the task.

248

State of the art, this equipment was. Wonderful sounds you could get from it.

⋆ ⋆ ⋆

Jez rang Sophie again at lunchtime, and to his relief she picked up the phone. 'You must have started work early. I tried to phone you this morning. Didn't you get my message?'

'Yes. But I have a — a family crisis on my hands.'

'Anything I can help with?'

'No. But I might not be able to see you for a few days. It's Andi. I'll call you when things have settled down a bit. Have to go now.'

He stared at the buzzing phone in surprise. She'd sounded so unlike herself, so tight and upset.

Craig came in. 'Kevin rang. Says to give him a bell at home. Important.'

'OK.' Jez picked up the phone again.

'Thought you'd like to know this,' Kevin said. 'Sophie's daughter was raped last night and found unconscious in an alley.'

Jez closed his eyes. No wonder Sophie had sounded distant.

'You still there?'

'Mmm. Do the police know who did it?'

'No.'

'How did you find out?'

'You'd asked me to keep an eye on Andi, remember? The guy I had tailing her lost her in the club where she was working — a really sleazy place, that, don't know what she was thinking of. When he gave up waiting around for her it was

249

about two o'clock. There was a queue for taxis so he set off walking, passed a crime scene and saw an ambulance. He stopped out of curiosity and recognized Andi as they took her away.'

'Got any friends in the force who could slip you some more information?'

'Not in that area. They're very close-mouthed about what they're doing, and rightly so. Anyway, just thought you should know.'

'Thanks.' Jez put the phone down. He wanted to help, but couldn't think of anything to do except leave Sophie alone with her daughter.

He wandered along to the studio and pitched in to work with Tom. How would he feel if someone had assaulted his son? Gutted. Absolutely gutted.

'You seem a bit upset, Dad.'

He gave Tom the bare bones of it.

A short time later Tom told him about Mary's phone call. 'I'm worried Gail will get custody of the children.'

'We'll make sure she doesn't. Sometimes money can help.' Mostly it just bought *things*, but this was important.

★   ★   ★

Sophie spent the day with her daughter, who alternated between tears, silence and snapping. Andi was still furious that she couldn't remember anything.

'I'm sorry I stopped you writing,' she said at teatime, but she didn't sound sorry, she sounded aggressive.

'I wouldn't leave you when you need me.'

Andi looked at her as if she'd never seen her before, then shook her head as if puzzled and continued to pick at her food.

Afterwards, in desperation, Sophie suggested they try some meditation. 'It got me through some bad times, brought peace to my soul.'

'I don't know how. And anyway, I'm not into that touchy-feely stuff.'

'Give it a try. I can teach you.'

'You've never even invited me into that room before. I've seen it, but you've never shared it with me. You don't share much with other people.'

Sophie closed her eyes and counted to twenty, then asked mildly, 'Should I have invited you in? Would you have wanted to use it?'

A shrug, then Andi got up to stare out of the window. 'I've not known what I wanted. I feel . . . '

Sophie held her breath, sure that it was important to get Andi to talk about her feelings. What came out didn't surprise her, but she was glad it was out in the open.

Andi swung round and went to stare at the bookcase. 'I feel as if I've been lost for years.'

'Ever since your father died.'

She swung round. 'Yes. Do you still miss Dad?'

'Of course I do.'

'But you're seeing Jez Winter. How can you?'

'The two things aren't mutually exclusive. Bill and I always said we'd want the other to find someone else if one of us died.'

'But no one can replace Dad, *no one*. Especially a man who's been into drugs and probably still is.'

'Jez isn't into drugs now. He doesn't even drink alcohol.'

'That's what he tells you.'

Sophie prayed for patience. 'Come and see how it feels in my meditation room. I like to think I've made stone tapes there.'

'What do you mean?'

'That tranquillity has soaked into the walls.' She led the way and pointed to the floor. 'Sit on the rug, that's what it's for.'

Andi sat down and ran her fingers over the quilted patterns and textures, watching the patterns of coloured light coming in through the stained-glass window play over her fingers as they moved slowly with the sun. She looked up at the window and her voice was gentler. 'That's so beautiful.'

'I fell in love with it on sight.'

'Maybe it'd be nice if I just sat here on my own for a while. You're right. It does feel peaceful in here. I'm grateful for your help and company, but what I'd really like is to be alone.'

'I'll be in my office if you need me.' Sophie hesitated in the doorway, but Andi had closed her eyes and for the first time that day was looking as if she was finding some measure of peace.

It was very hard dealing with someone who snarled at you as if you were the enemy, then clung to you as if you were a life raft, then turned away again.

She thought of Jez, wondering what he was doing, wishing he was here to lean on, just a little. She could stand on her own feet, she'd proved that, but sometimes it was good to have a helping hand. Only, with the way her daughter was feeling, Jez was the last person Sophie could call on. She didn't dare call on her friends, either, because Andi was always scornful of them, seeming jealous of their long friendship.

One day at a time. She closed her eyes and slid into a short meditation, focusing on a flower she had in her office vase. It had been one of the most beautiful roses she'd ever seen, dark red with a rich perfume. But it was fading now. It was a reminder that everything passes, good and bad.

★   ★   ★

The next morning Donna came storming into the eating area. 'He's done it again.'

Jez pushed his scrambled eggs aside, surprised at her vehemence. 'Who's done what?'

She slapped a newspaper down on the table. 'That Talbin creature. He's been muckraking. This time it's Sophie's daughter. He's using her now to get at you and her mother. As if she hasn't enough to bear without him splashing the news all over the papers that she's been raped. He's even got a photo of her being wheeled off to hospital, not a good photo, so not his. He must have bought it from some bystander.'

Jez grabbed it and scanned the page. 'Oh, hell! I wonder if Sophie knows.'

253

'I think someone had better warn her. Want me to go and do it?'

'No, I will.'

He didn't wait for Kevin, but snatched up the newspaper cutting and walked through the gardens. The sunny day seemed to mock the darkness that was marring Sophie's life, the bad news he was taking to her. But it was better if she knew, he was sure of that.

★   ★   ★

Sophie heard someone knocking on the back door and frowned. No one used that door except Jez and he hadn't rung to check it was all right to come and see her. If he had, she'd have stopped him.

She went to see who it was, feeling foolish as she detoured to peer through the window first. It was Jez. Her heart lifted to see him, then she heard footsteps and turned to see Andi.

'I don't want to see anyone, Mum.'

'Jez has just popped over from next door. You go back to what you were doing and I'll see what he wants.'

'Does he do this often?'

'He visits me sometimes, yes.'

'I bet he does!'

'I don't like your tone.'

'And I don't like to think my mum is screwing around with someone like him.'

'That's unfair.' Sophie pushed past her and opened the door, hoping her anger at her daughter wasn't showing.

254

Jez looked from her face to her daughter's. 'I know you'd rather not see me, but it's important — and it's about you, Andi, so can you please stay?'

'Come in. Would you like a coffee? And some cake?'

'If it's not too much trouble.'

In the kitchen she saw him move towards his usual seat but there was a half-full mug of coffee there, so he moved to another.

Scowling at him, Andi slumped on to the stool and picked up the mug.

'It's a sultana cake today,' Sophie said to fill the heavy silence.

'If it's as good as your other cakes, I can't wait to taste it.'

She made him a mug of coffee and cut a slice of cake. 'Would you like a piece, Andi?' But her daughter shook her head and continued to scowl at them.

'What's the problem, Jez?' Sophie slid into a place next to him and resisted the temptation to take hold of his hand.

'This. I'm sorry to be the bearer of bad news, but we thought you should know.'

She read it, exclaiming in disgust at the veiled innuendos about Andi, her work at the club, and the 'possible assault' that had happened. The next article asked pointedly whether today's revealing fashions were inciting violence against young women and invited readers to contact the paper and give their views. She looked at her daughter. 'It's about the attack on you.'

'What?' Andi read the article, burst into tears

255

and ran out. Her footsteps pounded on the stairs and the door to her bedroom slammed hard enough to rattle the nearby windows.

'Is he allowed to write that sort of thing about a case that's still under investigation?' Sophie asked.

Jez picked up the paper, smoothing it out. 'He treads on thin ice at times, but he usually stays just the right side of the law. It's better to ignore him than sue. He thrives on attention and writes more articles about that. I did sue him once and win, and he's never forgiven me for it, which is why he hounds me, I think. I'm sorry. I didn't mean to bring this sort of thing down on you. Or on Andi when she's so vulnerable.'

'Did you know what had happened to her?'

'In broad terms. One of Kevin's men walked past as they were taking her away in an ambulance. Kevin keeps an eye on everyone connected to me, you see, so the man knew who Andi was.'

'Oh.' She let Jez take her hand, then gave in to temptation and leaned against him with a sigh.

'Has it been bad?'

'Very. She's dreadfully upset, as you'd expect, tearful one minute, snapping at me the next. She'd been drugged and can't remember anything. That makes it worse, somehow. They not only violated her body, but her mind.'

'She needs professional help.'

'I know. I'm going to find someone. But I'm not sure Andi will take up the offer of help.'

'Let me find someone for you. It's something I *can* do for you.' He cupped her face in his hand and kissed her. Not a long kiss, not at all passionate, the sort of kiss her husband would have given her if she were in trouble, exactly the sort of kiss she needed just now.

'Can't keep your hands off one another, can you?'

They swung round to see Andi standing in the doorway, glaring at them. Neither had heard her come downstairs again.

'Your mother's upset,' Jez said mildly. 'If you can't see the difference between a supportive kiss and a passionate one — '

'I don't want to see you two kissing at all! It's gross. I get raped and *she* carries on, business as usual, sex on demand.'

She turned and ran out again.

Sophie bent her head, but Jez saw the tear that escaped. 'I see what you mean about mood swings. That must be hard on you.'

'Not nearly as hard as it is on her.'

'Why the hell was she working in that place? Couldn't you have stopped her?'

'I didn't know. And even if I had, she'd not have listened to me. She never does. She'd lost her job and needed money. I'd offered to pay her rent but told her to go on social security for her living expenses. I thought it'd make her find a job more quickly. She seems to think she has a right to my money and a life of luxury, but she's twenty-four, Jez, not fourteen, and should be standing on her own feet. Besides . . . she's not easy to live with. I need peace to do my writing . . . and to keep my body balanced.' She was sure that stress wouldn't help her ongoing efforts to stay free of cancer.

'She must have loved her father deeply to resent you finding anyone else.'

'Yes, she did. She resents my work as well. I spent a lot of my spare time writing when she was a teenager, so she and her father did things together while I stayed home. She blames me for that.'

'It's hard, isn't it?'

'What?'

'The creative urge. Damned if you do, damned if you don't.' He kissed her cheek and stood up. 'I'll find out about counselling or whatever is best and phone you.'

'Thanks.' She watched him walk towards the door. 'Don't you need to ring Kevin first to escort you back?'

'I was very brave today and came across all on my own.'

'You shouldn't take risks.'

'It's daylight. I'd see anyone lurking. Don't forget that. If there's anything I can do to help, anything at all . . . '

'I know. I love you, Jez. I'll try to talk to Andi about us, try to make her understand.' Though she didn't feel she had much hope of succeeding.

When she'd seen Jez out and watched him safely through the gate, Sophie went upstairs.

Her daughter was standing by her bedroom window, staring out at the horse chestnut tree. She turned, biting her lower lip. 'I'm sorry. I don't know why I acted like that.'

'Because you're upset. But I wish you hadn't sounded off at Jez. He doesn't deserve that. He came across to help.'

'Why did you tell him about me? I asked you not to tell your friends.'

'I didn't tell him. One of his men passed by as you were being carried into the ambulance. The security staff know all the people Jez deals with, you see, me and my family included.'

'Oh. Sorry. I thought you'd told him.' She fiddled with the curtain. 'You're in love with him, aren't you?'

'I think so. It's early days yet, though.'

'I hate to think of you replacing Dad.'

'Life moves on, darling. And I've not exactly rushed into another relationship, have I? It's nearly five years since Bill died.'

'I suppose.'

'What would you like to do tomorrow? I wondered if you'd enjoy a drive out into the country or we could go down to Brighton and walk along the beach.' She looked out of the window. 'Weather permitting.'

'I don't want to go anywhere. Besides, the police said they'd be in touch. They haven't much to go on, have they? I can't see them making an arrest. I bet it was that Eric creature who did it and he's going to get away with it.' She shuddered and began to sob again. 'Sorry. Sorry. I can't keep it together. I'm being awful to you and you're trying to help me. Please don't get mad at me.'

Sophie took her in her arms. 'It's early days yet, darling. We'll get through this together.'

'But life will never be the same, will it? I'll always wonder what he did to me.'

'Life brings bad things as well as good. You

259

can't avoid that, have to take the rough with the smooth.'

'Grandma used to say that, didn't she?'

'Yes. And it used to make me angry, so I'd better stop saying it to you. Come down and have a piece of cake. You hardly ate a thing for breakfast.'

It was a relief when Andi said she wanted to sit in the meditation room again.

Sophie went outside and picked another flower, putting it in her office. She thought she saw a flash out of the corner of her eye, as if someone had just taken a photo of her, but she must have been mistaken, because you couldn't see this part of the garden from the street, and anyway there was no one around. The couple who lived in the next house worked long hours and their sons would still be at school.

* * *

Jez got home after a pleasant stroll through his overgrown gardens and found Tom in the studio, chatting animatedly to Donna and demonstrating something electronic. When Jez looked round, he saw the whole family there. The children were sitting in one corner, under Jane's watchful eye, playing very gently with a tambourine and a triangle, instruments he'd bought out of nostalgia for the times he'd played them as a child.

He stopped in the doorway to feast his eyes on this wonderfully normal scene, then Hayley caught sight of him and screeched in pleasure, dropping the tambourine and rushing across to him.

'Play for us, G'anddad.'

She tugged him towards the guitar and Jane, who'd stood up ready to intervene, studied his face and stayed where she was.

He winked at the nanny then went to get his guitar, the little girl standing right beside him, jigging about impatiently.

'What shall I play, Hayley?'

''Dancing Queen'.'

'It's her favourite,' Tom said apologetically. 'She asks for it again and again. I'm sorry if you don't like it.'

'I'm happy to play for her.' He checked that the guitar was in tune. 'I can see I'll have to write some dancing songs for this young lady, once I find out if she really can dance.'

'I can, G'anddad, I can!'

Ryan trailed across to join them, a little shyer than his sister.

Jez played some Abba tunes, but didn't know the other children's songs Hayley asked for. 'I'll have to learn some new tunes, I see.'

'Daddy can play them.'

He offered the guitar to Tom, who flushed. 'You don't need to indulge her to this extent. This is your best guitar.'

'It's here to be played, not put in a display case. And I'm enjoying the jam session. Play it for her!'

So Tom played a few tunes and sang, nervously at first, then he forgot his audience and lost himself in the music, while his children

261

jigged about happily nearby.

'Come and get your teas now, children,' Jane said after a while. 'Your granddad's tired.'

Both children protested but somehow she had them out of the room within minutes and without any tears.

'She's brilliant with them,' Tom said, putting the guitar back carefully on its stand.

'I'll just go and finish my work for the day,' Donna said.

Jez went over to the door with her. 'Before you go, I want you to do something for me.' He explained in a low voice about Andi and the need for counselling.

'I'll get on to it straight away,' Donna said.

'Poor Andi,' Tom said.

'Um — there's some good news too.'

'Oh?'

'I'm — er — in love with Sophie Carr, and she with me. Her daughter seemed revolted by that. I hope you don't mind.'

'I'm thrilled for you. And don't let the daughter stop you getting together with Sophie. I hope you'll both be very happy.'

'It's early days and I don't have a good track record with women, but I do love Sophie.' He was surprised how deep, and yet how gentle the love was, as well as how powerful.

Maybe this time . . .

15

Gail wandered outside for a breath of fresh air and stopped to frown at the crumpled wing of the car. How had that happened? Had she hit something or had someone hit her in a car park? It happened.

Well, the car was the least of her worries. A crumpled wing wasn't going to stop her driving, after all.

She glanced towards the next house, empty now. That old bitch had certainly done well out of their break-up. It wasn't fair. Tom's mother said Jane was living in London now with him and the children. Gail had always longed to live in London and move away from this dump of a town.

She turned to go back inside, intending to get a glass of wine, just a small one to lift her spirits. She'd have to go and buy some more tomorrow. It was amazing how quickly the bottles got used up.

But a car drew up outside her house as she was going inside and she saw the pastor from her mother-in-law's church getting out of it.

Oh, hell! Not him again! He'd come round yesterday as well, only she'd been in bed and once she'd peeped out and seen who it was, she hadn't answered the door. Still, it wouldn't hurt to keep on his good side, just in case she needed support in her custody application. Good thing she'd not had a drink yet.

'Good afternoon, Gail.'

She hated his smarmy smile and his oily voice but smiled back. 'Nice to see you again, Elliott.'

'May I come in and talk to you?'

'I suppose so.' He came into her living room and sat down, grimacing as he lifted some clothes off the armchair. Well, what did he expect, turning up without warning — a house beautiful?

'Should we start with a prayer?'

She bent her head and let him waffle on, wondering what he really wanted today.

When he'd finished, he leaned forward, hands clasped. 'Mary came to see me. She was very upset.'

'She upset me, too.'

'Oh? How did she do that?'

'The way she talked to me, as if I was worthless.'

'She said you'd been drinking. Perhaps you mistook what she was saying.'

Gail shrugged. 'I know what I heard. Anyway, if her stupid son would only come back, and bring Hayley and Ryan, I'd not *need* to drink.'

'You must miss your children very much.'

'What? Oh, yes. Yes, I do.' She snatched a tissue from the box and dabbed at her eyes, and either he had worse eyesight than Mary or he didn't think of looking to see whether she was producing tears or not.

'Have you contacted your husband since he went to London?'

She bent her head, still hiding behind the

tissue, surprised to realize she hadn't even thought of ringing him. How stupid was that? She had his mobile number. 'I daren't,' she admitted and that at least wasn't a lie.

'Shall I ring him for you?'

She sniffed and dabbed, thinking this through. 'Would you?'

'Of course. I'll do anything I can to help.'

She went to fetch a phone and dialled Tom's number then held the phone out to Elliott. 'You speak to him first. He hangs up on me.'

Well, he might hang up if she spoke to him. She wouldn't put anything past him lately.

★ ★ ★

Tom looked at his mobile to see who was ringing. Gail. Should he answer it or not? He'd better. If he didn't, she'd not stop ringing till she got through to him. 'Hello?'

'This is Elliott, the pastor at your mother's church.'

'My mother's all right, isn't she?'

'Your mother's fine, if rather troubled in spirit. It's your wife I'm worried about — we're all worried about Gail. She's here with me now, but she's been afraid to ring you. Would you speak to her, listen to her?'

'My lawyer said I should avoid arguments.'

'She doesn't want to argue with you, just ask how you are. And she's really worried about the children.'

Tom was about to give a sharp response to that but had second thoughts. He didn't want

265

to say or do anything they could twist round in a court of law. 'Of course I'll speak to her.'

There was a rustling sound and Gail said, 'Tom?' in a breathless voice, which meant she was putting on her bewildered, girlish act. It didn't fool him any more, but it still fooled other people sometimes.

'What do you want, Gail?'

'I want you to come back to me. Oh, Tom. Please come back!'

'You know I'm not going to do that.'

'I could join you in London. Do you realize I don't even know where my children are! I miss them, want them back.'

'Why? So you can neglect them again?'

'I wasn't well. Everyone has an off day or two.'

'You can't come here, Gail, and I'm not coming back to the north till the hearing. The children are happy and well cared for, and they're staying where they are.'

'Hearing?'

'The custody hearing. Surely you got the letter? It was sent registered post, so you must have signed for it or we'd have heard.'

She racked her brain but had no memory of it. 'I've not seen it.'

'Put Elliott on again, will you.'

'Why?'

'I need to ask him something.' Tom waited, then when Elliott took the phone, he said without preamble, 'She's been served with papers for a custody hearing next week. They were definitely delivered and she signed for them. Can you find out what she's done with

266

them and make sure she turns up?'

He switched off the phone and left it off.

* * *

Sophie picked up the phone, ready to put it down again if it was someone she didn't want to speak to, though how a stranger would get this number, she didn't know.

'Peter Shane here.'

'Oh, hi, Peter.'

'Have you a minute?'

'Yes.'

'You've seen the newspaper article about your daughter? Right. Could you tell me how Talbin found out about the incident?'

'We don't know.'

'Is it true that she was raped?'

'Sadly, yes.'

'That's terrible. I'm so sorry. Look, I know it's not a good time, but can I come and talk to you — and to her, if she can stand it? It could be useful in my exposé of Talbin. I've found out some rather interesting things.'

'I'll ask Andi and ring you back if — '

'Ask Andi what?'

She swung round to her daughter. 'Hold on, Peter.' She explained rapidly.

Andi stared at her. 'What's he like?'

'Peter's really nice and has a good reputation. I trust him.'

'Tell him to come round, then. He might as well. Everyone knows about me now. We should put up a sign in the front garden.'

267

★　★　★

Peter arrived within the hour. He was carrying two bunches of flowers, gave one to Sophie, the other to Andi. 'It seems to me you both need a bit of TLC.'

Andi stared down at hers and started to cry.

He stared at Sophie in dismay, then turned back to the younger woman. 'I'm sorry. I didn't mean to upset you.'

She gulped and cradled the flowers against her chest. 'It's OK. I cry all the time at the moment. I just — can't remember the last time anyone bought me flowers. They're lovely.'

'We'll make this quick, if you like.'

He questioned Andi gently, pausing when emotion over-whelmed her, and noting down her answers in shorthand.

'I've not seen anyone using that for a while,' Sophie said.

'Not everyone wants me to use a voice recorder and I didn't think Andi would today. Am I right?'

She nodded.

'That's all I needed to ask, but I wanted to see you in person. It helps me to understand the whole picture. If I want to use any of this in an article, I'll OK it with you first, I promise. All right?'

'Yes. I think I'll go and rest now.'

But Sophie noticed that Andi went towards the meditation room, not her bedroom.

'It must be hard on you,' Peter said quietly.

'The hardest thing is to feel so helpless.'

'Could you do me another favour? I need to speak to Jez Winter, but that PA of his won't let me. Says he's busy at the moment. Could you have a word with him and ask him to speak to me?'

'What is it about?'

'The attack on him. I may have turned something up. I wasn't sure whether to tell his PA about that. It's fairly confidential stuff.'

She hesitated, then said, 'I could phone him now, if you like. There's a gate between our gardens. If he's not doing anything, he might nip across. No one would see you two meeting then.'

Peter nodded slowly and smiled. 'He's the one you care about, isn't he? Your voice goes softer when you say his name.'

She didn't pretend to misunderstand him. 'Could be. It's early days, though. I'll go and ring him from my office. I won't be long.'

★   ★   ★

The phone rang and when Donna saw the number of the caller, she beckoned to Jez. 'It's Sophie.'

He couldn't stop himself smiling as he snatched it up. While she was looking after her daughter, he treasured every contact with her. 'Hi, there.'

'Hi, Jez. Look, I've got Peter Shane here. He's still working on his exposé of Talbin. He'd like to speak to you. You could nip through the gardens and come here, then no one would see you meeting him.'

'You're sure it's worth it?'

'I don't know what his information is, but I trust him not to waste our time.'

'I'll have to bring Kevin and Donna. They manage that side of my affairs.'

'That's all right.'

'We'll come straight away.' He welcomed any excuse to see her again, hadn't felt like this since he was a teenager.

He realized he was standing smiling at nothing and forced himself to get moving.

★　★　★

Peter waited in the living room. Across the internal courtyard he could see a shadowy figure in a room with a stained-glass window, Andi presumably. What was she doing? Sitting on the floor? Her whole body was drooping, poor thing.

He heard voices and turned round as the others came in.

Jez went to sit with Sophie, smiling at her so warmly she blushed. Tom watched them with a smile. Kevin's face was expressionless and he sat with arms folded, giving nothing away. Donna was alert, as always, her eyes going from one person to the other as if assessing their feelings.

'Is this private or can anyone join in?'

Everyone turned round.

Andi raised her chin defiantly.

'You're welcome to join us, darling. Come and sit down.' Sophie gestured to the couch, but Andi walked across to a chair standing on its own and took that.

Peter summed up his research and then went on to talk about Jez's intruder. 'Did it ever occur to you that the attack on you might have been a set-up?'

Kevin leaned forward, as if to hear better.

'It felt real enough with a knife held at my throat and my face slashed,' Jez said, shuddering. 'I still have nightmares about it.'

'Why do you say that, Shane?' Kevin asked.

'I've read and re-read all the newspaper reports of the incident, and the press statements your people put out. What I can't find out is what made the intruder stop and leave. I mean, he had the upper hand, wasn't doing it for gain. Do you know, Jez?'

He frowned, then slowly shook his head. 'No, I don't. One minute he was there, threatening to kill me, the next I was sprawled on the floor, the door was open and I heard footsteps running away.'

'Did you try to go after him?'

'No way. I locked myself in my bathroom, held a towel to my face and called the police on my mobile.'

'Did they find any clue as to who he was?'

'No. But he said he'd be back one day to finish what he'd started.' Jez shuddered and Sophie reached out without thinking to take his hand. Across the room Andi was staring at him sympathetically.

Kevin cleared his throat. 'What's your point, Shane?'

'I'm wondering whether Talbin isn't creating his own news stories. There are a couple of others in the past year or two that he's been the one to scoop and no one else has had even a sniff of.'

'Have you discussed this with the police?'

'Not yet. I've nothing to go on, really, just gut instinct. But I've been a journo for over twenty years, and I've learned to trust my instincts. How did he find out about Andi, come to that?'

There was silence in the room, then she asked, 'Do you think he set up *my* attack?'

'Shouldn't think he'd take that risk for someone he didn't know or care about. But he might have known you were working as a hostess and hoped to get some mileage out of that. He could have paid someone at the club to let him know if anything interesting happened to you. If so, who knew enough to do that?'

'I probably deserved all I got, working at a place like that.' She tried to laugh but it sounded more like a sob.

'No one deserves that sort of treatment,' Peter said quietly.

Andi shook her head blindly and huddled down in her chair, avoiding everyone's eyes.

He exchanged sad glances with Sophie, then looked round the room and got back to business. 'I can keep you informed of anything I find out. Perhaps you'd do the same for me?'

'Do that. And do you have a card, some number where I can contact you directly?' Kevin asked.

Peter fumbled in his inner pocket and fished out a business card. 'This is a private number, not for public consumption.' He stood up. 'I'll leave now. Look, I wanted to bring you flowers, Sophie and Andi, because you're the sort of women men do that to, but they made a good cover for my visit as well, too. Will you walk with me to the door, Sophie, to lend credibility to that?'

When they got there, he smiled at her, wishing she was looking at him the way she'd looked at Jez. 'Could you come outside and be seen saying goodbye? Maybe even kiss my cheek? Just in case there's someone watching?'

'Of course.' She stood waving as he drove off.

He turned his mind firmly to Talbin. He was determined to find out what was going on.

★ ★ ★

'Why don't you and Andi come across with us?' Jez asked. 'You can see the progress, Sophie, and you've never even seen the house, Andi. My housekeeper makes little snacks for this time of day. He's as camp as they come and a wonderful cook. So's his partner, who's working on the garden.'

'Yes, do come!' Tom urged. 'You can meet my children.'

Sophie looked questioningly at Andi. It would certainly be a relief to get out of this house for a while. If her own meditating had made 'stone tapes' in one room, her daughter's pain was filling the rest of the house with a distinctly depressed atmosphere. She saw Andi's scowl lighten just a little at the mention of children and was pleased that she was interested enough to

273

ask how old they were.

'Hayley's four, almost five, and Ryan's two.' Tom gave them all an embarrassed smile. 'Of course *I* think they're great kids.'

'They are,' Jez said at once.

Andi hesitated. 'Well . . . why not? Is that all right with you, Mum?'

Sophie nodded, hoping no one had noticed her sigh of relief but Jez winked at her and she knew he'd picked up on her feelings. Again.

Kevin led the way, stopping to lock the gate behind them. Donna and Tom went on ahead, chatting to Andi.

Jez and Sophie let Kevin overtake them.

'I'm missing you,' he said.

'It's only been a day or two.'

'Nonetheless.' He took her hand and she let him, but pulled hers away before they joined the others at the door, not wanting to upset Andi.

Jez showed them round the main areas, unable to conceal his pride in the various period features: the high ceilings, moulded plasterwork cornices, the old-fashioned fireplaces with carved wooden surrounds and the row of leadlights at the top of the windows. 'There's a lot to do to get the place in shape, but I'm looking forward to it. I've never lived in an older house before and this one has such character.'

'You've made a lot of progress already,' Sophie said. 'It's feeling more like a home.'

'Donna has to take the credit for that.'

When they got to the studio, he waved his son forward. 'I'll let Tom explain the equipment, because he's the one who set it up. I know how to use it but he really understands how it works.'

As they walked back into the hall, Tom suggested taking Andi across to meet his children.

Donna said she'd go across too, because she wanted to check that everything was to Jane's satisfaction.

Sophie watched her daughter leave, worrying that Andi would have one of her flare-ups of misery or anger and say something she shouldn't.

'Donna will keep an eye on her,' Jez said quietly. 'Come here and let me hold you.'

Since Kevin had disappeared once they entered the house, they were alone. She moved closer and put her arms round Jez's neck, resting her head against his cheek. It felt so good to be close to him that she sighed in pleasure.

'I could get very used to this,' he murmured into her hair.

'Me, too.' Every time she was alone with him, she felt so 'right'.

Sometimes you just had to trust your instincts, whether your children approved of your choices or not.

*　★　*

Tom led the way into his cottage, calling out to let Jane know it was him. Andi followed, wondering why she was doing this. But she did like children and she'd do almost anything to stop herself thinking about *that*.

There were giggles and Hayley came running down the stairs. She'd gained so much momentum by the time she realized her father

275

wasn't alone that trying to stop made her lose her balance and start falling.

Andi was nearest and managed to catch her, while Tom made sure Ryan got down the stairs safely. They exchanged relieved smiles.

The feel of the small body in her arms brought back memories of happier times. For several years Andi had earned money by babysitting a neighbour's children, but it hadn't felt like work because she loved littlies and they usually seemed to behave for her.

Her mother had suggested she go into childcare as a career, but her father had said it didn't pay well and was a waste of a good brain. She'd enrolled in a university course mainly to please him. In the end he'd died before she finished the first year and she'd been too upset to study, or even think about taking her exams. She still didn't regret trying to please him, but maybe here was an idea for her future, looking after children.

'Are you all right?'

She smiled at Tom. 'Yes. I was just remembering how I used to babysit when I was a teenager.'

'I'm not a baby!' Hayley protested at once.

Andi bent down again to help her straighten her clothes. 'I can see that. But they call it babysitting even when it's looking after ten-year-olds. You must be — what — six?' She added a year, knowing how young children cared about looking older.

Hayley beamed at her. 'I'm nearly five.'

'Goodness, you're tall for your age.'

276

'Like my daddy.'

Tom winked at Andi then shepherded them into the sitting room and Jane offered to make some coffee.

The hour they spent playing with the children was the happiest Andi had spent since she'd woken up in hospital.

As she walked back home with her mother, accompanied by Kevin, she said thoughtfully, 'I'd forgotten how much I like being with small children.'

'You always were better than me at dealing with them.'

It was a small thing, but it felt good to have her mother admit her daughter was better at something than her, because really, Andi knew she'd made a mess of her life. Big time. For a moment, tears threatened again, but she sniffed them away.

'I'll go and have a lie down now, I think. I feel really washed out still.'

Her mother gave her a quick hug and she hesitated, then hugged her mother back. 'You still wear the same perfume. I remember it from when I was a child.'

⋆　⋆　⋆

William rang that evening. 'How's Andi?'

'Ask her yourself.' Sophie passed the phone to her daughter, mouthing *William* as she did so.

Andi pulled a face at the phone. 'Hi, Willi.'

Sophie couldn't help smiling. Her son hated anyone shortening his name, especially to Willi

— which of course had made his sister do it quite often.

The two of them chatted for a few moments, more amicably than usual, then Andi passed the phone back to her mother.

William had his fussy tone. 'Mum, Kerry's worried about Andi. She wants to come round and see her tomorrow some time. Is that all right?'

Knowing how much the two young women disliked one another, Sophie said at once, 'No. We're not having visitors at the moment.'

'Kerry's not a *visitor*, she's family.'

'Even so.'

'She needn't stay long.'

'William, did you hear me say no? We do not want any visitors, even family. Your sister needs peace and quiet to recover. Now, I really have to get back to work.'

She put the phone down without waiting for his answer and saw Andi smiling at her. 'What's so amusing?'

'The way you put your foot down with William. I'm glad you did. Kerry is the last person I want to talk to.' Andi's smile faded. 'But I bet she turns up tomorrow anyway.'

'If she does, we'll pretend we're not at home. She can't force us to open the door, after all.'

* * *

Maybe there was still some hope for the future, Andi thought as she went to bed that night. Other women got over being raped. So could she. Only, other women could remember what had happened. She couldn't and her imagination painted new horrors every time she tried to sleep. She was most worried of all that whoever it was had taken photos of her, photos that one day other people would see.

Stop that, she told herself. *Don't go there.*

She woke in the middle of the night with her throat feeling raw and realized she'd been screaming. Since she'd had to leave a lamp switched on, she could see her mother kneeling by her bed.

'Oh, darling!'

'I thought I was getting over it,' she sobbed against her mother's beautiful purple dressing gown.

'You are. But you'll be having mood swings for a while yet, I should think.'

'Why don't they *catch* him?'

'I don't know.'

'I'm sure it'd be easier to get over it if he'd been arrested. Then I'd know he'd be punished, at least, that he wouldn't come after me to gloat, or attack me again.'

'Shh now. You're safe here. I'll sit with you for a while and you can let yourself drift off to sleep.'

Andi didn't manage to sleep but she could see her mother trying to stifle yawns, so pretended to doze off.

After the door had clicked shut she lay for ages, wide awake, trying to keep the horrible thoughts at bay, glad of the lamp, longing for morning. Things never seemed quite as bad in daylight. Or when you were playing with little children. Strange, that.

16

The following day Donna rang up with the name of a counsellor who was very highly thought of and might be able to help Andi. She hesitated then asked, 'You don't think Andi would like a part-time job, do you? Is she up to it yet? You must say if she isn't.'

'Doing what?'

'Stand-in nanny so that Jane can have a few hours off to meet her niece tomorrow. Tom's doing some work for Jez, so it'd be a big help.'

'Why not ask her yourself?' Sophie passed the phone to her daughter and went into her office.

Andi came to find her a few minutes later, looking a little brighter. 'I said yes.'

'Great. They're lovely kids.'

'It feels strange to think of earning money by babysitting again. But Donna is offering a lot more money than I used to earn. They're lovely kids and being with them makes me feel better.' She stared down at the floor, avoiding her mother's eyes. 'It's a real step in moving on, don't you think, doing this?'

'Yes. And it hurts to move on, but you can't wallow in misery for ever — though it's very early days for you yet. I felt a bit like that after your father died. Each new thing I did hurt, because Bill wasn't there to do them with me, and yet I didn't intend to wither away because I was on my own.'

Andi was silent for a few moments, thinking this over, then gave a faint smile. 'I don't intend to wither away either. I'll look after Hayley and Ryan really carefully, I promise you.'

'Of course you will. And Tom will be next door in the big house if you need to ask about anything.'

'Donna said if things went well, she'd like me to look after them regularly, to give Jane a break, and she knows some other people who'd offer me occasional days of work here and there. That'd be another step forward, wouldn't it? And I'd be earning my own money.'

'Definitely good stuff.'

⋆ ⋆ ⋆

Late the following morning, Sophie waved goodbye to Andi as she went through the gate into the next garden, anticipating a blissful few hours writing in peace. She found it hard to write with other people nearby, needed space and quiet to fill with her imaginary characters.

She hoped Jez would have a good day, trying out his new studio. And that Andi would enjoy looking after the children.

Now, where had she stopped in her story . . . The real world faded from round her and the imaginary world took its place.

⋆ ⋆ ⋆

Andi listened carefully to Jane's instructions, with Hayley holding her hand and jigging about in excitement.

'I'll look after them really carefully,' she promised.

As they got lunch ready, Jane chatted quietly. 'We've not really got into routines here yet, but we're starting to. We don't eat any junk food, for a start. They've had far too much of that in their short lives.'

Andi knew Jane was studying her carefully, but that didn't worry her. She always felt confident with children.

After lunch, Jane got ready, kissed each child and kissed Andi's cheek too, which felt nice, then set off.

Tom popped across in the middle of the afternoon to check that things were all right and smiled to see his daughter cuddled up to Andi, who was telling her a story. 'Not got a cuddle for your daddy?' he demanded, pretending to be upset when Hayley didn't run towards him. 'I'll cry if you don't. Boo hoo!'

'You're only pretending to cry,' Hayley said at once.

'How do you know that?'

'Because your mouth goes wiggly when you pretend.'

He roared with laughter and tossed her in the air. 'There's no fooling you, is there, young lady?'

'How's the studio going?' Andi asked as he set the giggling child down.

Tom's face lit up. 'It's magic. They've checked it all out and I got most things right when I set it up. Jez is using it now and do you know what? He's offered to get me trained to be a sound

282

engineer if I want. *If I want!* I'd kill for a job like that. I love music.'

'What's your favourite kind of music?'

They were off immediately into a discussion which revealed that they had fairly similar tastes.

When he left, Andi smiled. It had all been so normal, just as if she'd been talking to Ross, or another friend. What pleased her most was that Tom knew what had happened to her and hadn't been revolted by it, something which had been worrying her. And he'd left his children in her care. It felt good to be trusted.

When she went home, Craig walked through the gardens with her to let her through the gate, but she had to hammer on the front door to rouse her mother, who was lost in her writing as usual.

'You're hopeless, Mum. You'd better give me a key and tell me the pass number of the security system or I could be standing out there for hours.'

'Sorry. I'll just have to finish this scene while I can see it in my mind.'

It usually irritated Andi the way her mother could forget the real world when she was lost in a story, but today, for some strange reason, it made her smile. Her mother's absent-mindedness was yet another proof that the world hadn't changed that much.

She went to look in the fridge and see if there was anything for tea. Salad, as usual. It was surprising how curvaceous her mother was when she ate enough salad to be stick-thin. It wasn't always true that people were fatter because they pigged out on food.

Andi was glad she took after her father's side of the family. They were tall and lean and though he'd eaten heartily, he'd never put any weight on. Poor Dad. He'd not lived to a decent old age. Being the same body type was OK, but she hoped she didn't take after him for heart attacks.

She seemed to be seeing the world differently since *it* happened.

She'd ask her mum to go with her to pick up some stuff from her old place tomorrow, assuming she would let her stay here for a while. She didn't think she'd feel safe anywhere else after dark.

In the meantime, she'd see if there were any DVDs she fancied. Or maybe read a book. Her mum had hundreds.

It felt good to have nothing pressing to do, good that her mother wasn't fussing over her. And she'd enjoyed playing with the children. From what Hayley had let slip their mother had never played with them, only yelled at them to be quiet. How awful was that!

★   ★   ★

Three days later, on the Monday, Tom was scheduled to attend the hearing about the custody of his children. The lawyer had decided that Jane should go as well, both to prove he had someone sensible to look after the children and to give evidence, if necessary, about Gail's drinking.

Donna booked them early morning flights to

Manchester and arranged for Andi to come over for the whole day, promising to stay nearby in case she was needed.

'I don't think I shall be, though,' she told Tom. 'I watched Andi carefully when she was with the kids before and they were really happy with her. Jane says the same. And they're going over for a dancing session with Jez in the afternoon, so honestly, you don't need to worry.'

Tom wasn't worrying about the children but about the hearing, but he didn't tell her that. His stomach was churning when he got up and he couldn't face breakfast. He didn't know what he'd do if they granted custody to Gail.

The lawyer joined them at the airport, the flight was smooth and another big black limo was waiting for them in Manchester.

Gail was already in the waiting room, ready for the hearing. She was well turned out, for once, and was flanked by his mother, the pastor and someone who looked like a lawyer. She stood up and would have rushed across to him, but Tom stepped back instinctively. He didn't want her touching him.

Elliott pulled her back and said something to her. She subsided with a huff of anger, scowling at Tom.

As he'd feared, Gail was on her best behaviour, playing the upset mother and sobbing delicately into a handkerchief. He'd bet there weren't really any tears. She admitted that she'd been drinking but insisted she wasn't doing so now. Losing her children had taught her a hard lesson.

Tom answered the questions truthfully, guided by his lawyer, and then Jane took the stand. For a moment, Gail's face contorted with anger and the look she gave their neighbour would have curdled milk.

Jane radiated common sense and decency as she answered the questions, revealing that she'd had to help out regularly because she'd found Gail drunk or because the children were being neglected.

'Is there anyone else who can bear this out?'

Tom looked at his mother. She tried to avoid his eyes, wriggling uncomfortably in her seat. Tom whispered to his lawyer.

'Mrs Prichard, I wonder if you've ever seen your daughter-in-law drunk?'

Mary hesitated, then nodded.

'Please speak more loudly. Have you seen her drunk and how often?'

'Yes, I have. Several times.'

'When was the most recent one?'

'A few days ago.'

It was her testimony which set the seal on the decision. When it was announced that Tom would be given custody, Gail stood up.

'Please sit down, Mrs Prichard.'

'No, I won't. Call this justice? I don't even know where my children are!' she yelled. 'He's not even given me their address in London. That's not *fair*.'

The judge wrote something down and looked across at Tom's lawyer. 'Please make sure Mrs Prichard has the address of her children.'

'Yes, your honour.'

'Now kindly sit down, Mrs Prichard.'

Her lawyer tugged at her arm but she shook him off. Forgetting her upset-mother act completely, she began shouting abuse at Tom, using language that made his mother blush scarlet. Gail shoved the lawyer away so roughly when he tried to make her sit down that she knocked him off his chair. She then lunged across the room towards Tom, hands outstretched, fingers curled into claws as if ready to strike.

Elliott ran to grab her and her lawyer scrambled to his feet to help him, but they had to drag her out of the room forcibly. She fought and shrieked the whole way.

'I think she's cooked her own goose there,' Tom's lawyer whispered with a smug expression.

'Do we have to give her our address?'

'I'm afraid so.'

'Isn't it enough that she's got my phone number? If she wants to come down to see the kids, she can phone and we can meet somewhere else.'

'If the judge says give her your address, that's what you have to do.'

Tom sighed. He was relieved by the main decision, but he hated to see Gail make such a fool of herself, hated the way she looked these days. She was nothing like the slender, laughing girl he'd married.

Outside there was no sign of her, but his mother was waiting to speak to him. He went across to hug her and she leaned against him for a minute.

'Are you going to stay in London?'

'Yes. Jez has offered me a job *and* the cottage to live in.'

'I'm glad for you, but I'll miss you and the children. What sort of job?'

He hesitated but couldn't very well refuse to tell her. 'Working in his recording studio.'

Her lips grew tight. 'I might have known he'd drag you into his way of life.'

'You know I've always loved music.'

'It's a Godless lifestyle.'

'Please, Mum, don't start on that.'

She breathed deeply, then took out a handkerchief and blew her nose. 'I don't know where you're living, either.'

'I'll give you the address. Here, I'll write it down. Perhaps you and Dad can come and visit one weekend? I know it's a long way, but you could make a little holiday of it, stay in a hotel, see a show.'

'You know I don't approve of theatrical performances,' she said, lips pinching together. 'But we may come and see the children, if that's all right.'

'Of course it is.' But she wasn't as good with the children as Jane was, didn't seem able to relax, was always trying to tell them about religion. As if they understood at that age! He wondered what she'd been like when she was younger, to attract a man like Jez. She would still be an attractive woman if she took more care with her appearance, but that too had changed and she now wore dull clothes and a very plain hairstyle.

He didn't feel like chatting on the way back to London and was grateful that Jane was sitting between him and the lawyer on the plane.

He'd won custody, so he should be feeling happy. Right? And he was relieved. Very. But it was no pleasure to see Gail destroying herself like that. He'd bet she'd gone straight home to have a drink and was cursing him this very minute.

★   ★   ★

When Elliott dropped Gail at her home, he and Mary offered to stay with her for a while.

'No, thanks. I'll be fine.'

'But will you?' he asked, giving her one of his earnest looks. 'I'm worried that you'll start drinking again.'

'I won't.'

'Promise me.'

'I promise. Really.'

She meant it too.

It was alcohol which had broken up her marriage so if she stopped drinking, surely Tom would return to her?

She lasted two hours and then had one little drink.

She woke the next morning on the floor in the living room.

★   ★   ★

Jez really enjoyed his sessions with his two grandchildren. When they came across to see

289

him that afternoon, he looked up from the keyboard with a smile. But his question was for Andi, who was looking a bit wan. 'Hey, how's it going?'

'OK.'

Hayley came to stand right next to him. 'Ryan had a sleep so me and Andi lied down too, because we hafta play quietly when he's having a nap. We did games with our fingers. I've been good all day, G'anddad, like Daddy said.'

'Wow, how about that? And I've been learning to play some new songs for you. Will you sing them for me?'

He chose two Wiggles songs and soon had the children up and dancing. When they pulled Andi up to join them, she resisted at first then danced along with them.

Jez's heart was breaking for her, because although she was making an effort for the children's sake, she looked very unhappy when she wasn't dealing with them.

No young woman should have to face what she had. It sickened him to his soul to think about it. He'd ask Kevin if it was possible to find out more than the police could if money was no object.

* * *

When the phone rang, Sophie let it, not wanting to be interrupted. Then she remembered Andi and picked it up in case her daughter needed help. But it was Jez.

'Just thought you should know that Andi's

290

doing fine with the kids. They came over to spend some time with me and then went back to get their tea. I wondered if you were still working?'

'I'm winding down. I've just got to finish polishing this scene.'

'How about having dinner with me over here, then you and Andi can walk back together later?'

'I'd love that.'

'I'll come and meet you at the gate. Give me a ring when you're ready.'

She couldn't settle down to writing again, but it didn't matter. She made notes about the next scene, then saved her work and backed it up carefully.

Wanting to look good, she went up to change, choosing one of her favourite skirts, in swirling shades of dusky violet, and wearing it today with a plain matching top. Andi would have pulled a face at the outfit and told her it wasn't in fashion — or she would have done before the rape — but Sophie had stopped caring about fashion when she got cancer. Now, what she cared about most was wearing colours that pleased her and made her feel happy when she looked at them, in fabrics which felt soft to the touch.

She rang Jez to say she was ready and stayed on the phone to him until he said he was coming through the gate now. As she was closing the door, she wondered if she heard a sound. She stopped to listen, but couldn't hear anything. It was probably one of the neighbours. There were signs of movement in the nearby houses, with people home from work or school, and even as

291

she watched, one garage door rolled up and a car reversed out of it.

She didn't see a lot of her neighbours, though they waved as they passed or stopped to talk about the weather once in a while.

'You shouldn't come to stand outside until we get here, Sophie,' Kevin chided in his deep voice.

'I was enjoying the fresh air.' She lifted her face to the sky, where the sun was sliding down towards the horizon. 'Look at how long the shadows are at this time of the evening. I'm glad they left some of those horse chestnut trees when they built this development. These two are magnificent.'

Jez took her hand and they went back through the gate. Once they were near the house, Kevin vanished and Jez took her to sit at an outdoor table on the other side of the house. There was a gas outdoor heater to keep them warm and a bottle of champagne was standing in a silvery wine cooler, another bottle in a second cooler.

'Shall we?' he asked.

'You don't need to open a bottle of champagne for me. I'll share yours.'

'You'll have proper champagne tonight. It's more appropriate. Truly, it doesn't worry me.'

'Why is it appropriate? Are we celebrating something?'

'Meeting one another, I hope.'

'That seems an excellent reason to celebrate.' She accepted a glass, clinked it against his and sipped, enjoying the astringent taste and the feel of bubbles in her mouth. 'What time is Tom due back?'

'About nine o'clock, I think. Gives us a few hours together, for once. The housekeeper's left a casserole and some salads. I explained about you and wheat, and he said he could thicken the casserole with potato flour. Do you want to eat now or a little later?'

'Later. It's nice to relax with a friend.'

But as they raised their glasses to one another again, the air was suddenly charged with that strange electricity that seems to hum around two people who want one another. She realized her hand was shaking slightly as she put the glass down. And she could find no reason to deny the feelings inside her.

But she was still nervous of making love to him. Jez had said he didn't mind the scarring, but what if he did? What if he found the idea of her reconstructed breast repellent?

'What put that look on your face?' he asked, setting his own glass down.

'Just thinking.'

'You looked frightened for a few moments.'

'I was. Jez, I haven't made love to anyone since Bill died, and . . . '

'Do you want to set the demons at rest, or wait a little longer?'

'I want you so much and . . . I want to feel a woman again.'

He put special stoppers in the bottles, then pulled her to her feet. 'Let me take you to my bedroom, after which — ' he grinned wickedly — 'we'll play show and tell.'

She couldn't help shivering a little as they reached his room, but his kisses and caresses made her forget her worries, and all she could think of was the joy of being with someone you loved, someone who wanted to give you pleasure, someone who reacted to your lightest touch . . .

After they'd made love, she lay nestled against him.

'You felt very much like a woman to me,' he murmured.

'A woman in love.' She gave in to the temptation to stroke his face, loving the lean angles of it, the long narrow nose, the still abundant hair, which had been tied back when they started making love, but was now tickling her face. 'You're going grey, do you know that?'

'I do. They wanted me to dye it for the last cover photo, but I wouldn't. If my fans can't count the years, journalists can, and I think it'd look silly to pretend I'm still thirty.'

'It suits you.'

'You've hardly any grey in your hair, just a thread of silver here and there.'

'My family don't go grey, but the colour does fade a little. Mine was as bright as Andi's when I was younger.' She pulled his face closer to kiss his cheek. 'Thank you.'

'For what?'

'Making me feel good about my body again.'

He gave her the grin of a triumphant, post-coital male. 'Any time. But if we're going to eat our meal before Tom gets back, I think we should get dressed now. Do you want a shower?'

They showered together, dressed in a leisurely way and wandered down to the kitchen hand in

294

hand to get their meal.

She loved him so much.

★ ★ ★

Andi stared at her as they went into the house. 'You look different tonight — glowing.'

'Do I?'

'Oh, no! You've had sex with him tonight, haven't you?'

Sophie could feel herself blushing. 'None of your business.'

'No. I suppose not.'

She couldn't help asking, 'Does it show so clearly? How embarrassing!'

'Only to me, because I know you.'

Her daughter was still radiating disapproval, so Sophie tried to explain. 'I've not made love to anyone since the cancer. It made me feel — whole again — still a woman. He didn't mind the scars at all.' Had kissed them, actually.

Andi looked at her in shock. 'I never thought of that. How you must feel. I've never thought of you, have I? Only of myself. What sort of horrible person am I?' She began to cry.

Sophie sighed for the loss of her happy mood, but pulled her daughter into her arms and let her weep. When Andi had stopped, she said firmly, 'You're going to see this counsellor. You can't go on berating yourself like this.'

'It'll do no good.'

'You might at least try, if only to please me.'

'Oh, very well.'

'And try to understand about me and Jez, too.'

295

Andi turned and went up to her bedroom without answering that one, but something about the stiffness of her spine said that she still hadn't forgiven her mother for taking a lover, not really.

As if you could stop yourself falling in love, Sophie thought as she went to get a mug of hot chocolate. As if you should even try. She took it up to bed with her, leaving the door open in case Andi had another nightmare.

17

Sophie rang Jez first thing in the morning, giving in to an urge to speak to him. She could hear the smile in his voice when he realized it was her.

'Hi, gorgeous!'

'Just wanted to say good morning to you. I didn't wake you, did I?'

'No. I was lying there thinking about you, wishing you were here with me.'

'I'm the same.'

'How did it go with Andi last night?'

'She guessed — about us, what we'd been doing.'

'And you were embarrassed.'

'Well — yes.'

He chuckled. 'It's nothing to be ashamed of.'

'She's not used to the idea of us being in love. Her father was so special to her, she can't understand how I could ever look at someone else.'

'He must have been a great guy.'

'He was.'

'I suppose you'll be writing all day, no chance of having lunch with me?'

'No, sorry. I have to take Andi to pick up some of her things from the house she's been living in.'

'Is she moving back there or staying with you permanently?'

'Staying with me for the time being, but I'll keep paying her rent — in case.'

'You won't let her being there come between us?'

'No more than necessary. At the moment, she has nightmares every night, wakes screaming. I can't leave her to face that alone, just as you have to help Tom.'

'I understand that, even if I don't like it.'

'She's promised to see the counsellor Donna found for us. I'm going to ring and make an appointment today.'

'Let Donna do that. I'm sure she'll get an earlier appointment than you could.'

'I can't impose.'

'She'll be pleased to help. She hates the thought of what happened, just as we all do.'

When Sophie went downstairs, she found Andi sitting in the kitchen holding a mug of tea, looking exhausted. 'Have you been up long?'

'A couple of hours. I'm having trouble staying asleep.'

'You should have called me.'

'I'm already disturbing your nights too often.'

'A mother's privilege.' That won a tired smile, at least.

'Who were you ringing?'

'Jez.'

'Oh.'

Sophie went to get breakfast, not elaborating. When she sneaked a glance, her daughter was frowning into her cup. Andi didn't say anything else for a while.

★ ★ ★

Gail had run out of wine again. This time, she'd better buy more than six measly bottles, she decided. And go to a supermarket further away from home, where no one would recognize her. She definitely didn't want to bump into her mother-in-law. She'd better buy some food while she was at it. Just a few bits and pieces. She hadn't felt all that hungry lately.

She set off in the early afternoon, hoping the roads wouldn't be as crowded. She didn't want any more accidents. Someone had bashed in the wing of her car, though she couldn't remember the incident. Tom would go spare when he saw it.

The road was clear, so she didn't bother to slow down as she turned into the supermarket car park, but another car seemed to appear out of nowhere and smashed into her. She screamed and then something hit her on the head. The next thing she knew, she was lying on the grass near her car. Lights were flashing and a policeman was standing nearby.

'She's conscious,' someone said. 'And she's been very lucky, doesn't seem to have broken anything, just a tap on the head. Better take her to hospital for a check-up though, just in case.'

The policeman knelt beside her. 'Would you blow into this, please, madam?'

Gail looked at the tube in horror and closed her eyes.

'She's lost consciousness again,' he called.

Someone else knelt, took her pulse and opened her eye forcibly. 'I don't think so. She's just closing her eyes. Open your eyes, please, madam.'

She didn't dare.

Silence, then the policeman said, 'I'd better come with you, make sure they take a blood sample and check for alcohol. Her breath definitely smells of booze. Here, take her handbag with you. I've got her details now. We don't want anyone stealing her things. I'll follow you.'

Gail kept her eyes closed all the way to the hospital, refusing to speak or respond to them in any way.

They took her to a cubicle, she could see that through her eyelashes if she opened her eyes a tiny bit. But she didn't admit she was awake, the mere thought of doing that and having to answer questions filled her with panic.

'A doctor will be along in a minute,' the same voice said. 'But I'm pretty sure she's conscious.'

When the footsteps had gone away, Gail half-opened her eyes and took a cautious look round. She was alone in a curtained cubicle, but someone was standing outside it, someone with black, highly polished shoes and dark-blue trousers that showed underneath the knee-high curtain.

Tears leaked out of her eyes but she didn't risk moving to brush them away. What was she going to do now?

The shoes moved away, she heard the person walk a few steps and come back. After a minute he did the same again, going further this time, as if he couldn't bear to stand still.

Gail saw her handbag sitting on a chair next to the bed. Her shoes were on the floor under it.

Careful to make no noise, she slid off the bed, picked up her shoes and bag and waited till the feet started walking away from her again. A quick glance outside showed that there was a bend in the corridor in the opposite direction. She'd run away the next time he walked down the corridor.

The policeman came to stand outside the cubicle for a minute or two. She kept willing him to start moving again. Why didn't he start pacing up and down again? She needed to get away.

'Ah, there you are, Doctor!' he called.

Quickly she put her things back and lay down on the bed. Only just in time.

The doctor came in, accompanied by a nurse, checked her out and said, 'We know you're awake, Mrs Prichard.'

'Head hurts,' she muttered. 'Lights hurt my eyes.'

Someone held her eyelid open again and shone a light into her eyes.

'Doesn't look as if she's got concussion, but you can't always tell. Her speech is slurred.'

'That could be because she's been drinking. Could you take a blood sample, please, Doctor?'

Gail forced herself not to protest or move as someone stuck a needle in her arm.

'I'll go and arrange her admission, just for a few hours, to make sure she's all right. She's got bruising on her forehead, so something must have whacked her.'

When everything was silent, Gail peeped again. The policeman had resumed his pacing.

She got off the bed and picked up her things. When he started to walk away down the corridor, she slipped out of the cubicle and ran in the opposite direction in her stockinged feet, heart thudding, expecting to hear shouts behind her.

★ ★ ★

Just before teatime there was a knock on Mary's door and when she opened it she found two policewomen on the doorstep. She looked at them in sheer terror.

'May we come inside, Mrs Prichard?'

'What's happened? My husband — ?'

'This is not to do with him. It's about Gail Prichard. She's your daughter-in-law, I believe?'

'Yes.' She led the way inside, shuddering with relief. If anything happened to Brian, she didn't know what she'd do. 'Please sit down.'

'We're trying to locate Gail. She's not at home but one of the neighbours gave us your address and as you don't live far away, we thought we'd just pop round. Have you seen her today?'

'No. I saw her yesterday at the custody hearing, but not today. Why?'

'She's had a car accident.'

'Oh, no! She wasn't hurt, was she?'

'Fortunately no one was hurt, but blood tests showed she'd been drinking.'

'Gail does drink too much.'

'She was taken to hospital, but she ran away and we don't know where she is now. We're hoping you can help us.'

'No. No, I can't, I'm afraid. She didn't come here. Oh, I wish she had!' Mary sagged back in her chair, one hand pressed against her chest.

'Are you all right, Mrs Prichard?'

'Yes. Just — shocked. Heart pounding. Could you pass me my handbag, please?' She sprayed under her tongue and waited a moment or two until her heart slowed down a little. 'It'll be because of the hearing.' She explained how Gail had lost custody of the children the day before.

'Do you have a phone number and address for your son?'

Mary went to find the information Tom had given her.

As the officers were leaving, one gave her a card. 'You *will* let us know if your daughter-in-law contacts you? Our number's here.'

'Yes. Of course. That poor girl needs help, though, not punishment.'

'She can't receive either unless we find her.'

Once the door had closed behind them, Mary picked up the phone and rang her son.

⋆　⋆　⋆

Tom listened in horror. When the call ended, he couldn't think what to do next, didn't realize he'd been standing with it still in his hand in the middle of the room until Donna came across to him.

'Tom? Are you all right? Is there some bad news?'

He blinked and her anxious face came into focus. 'It's Gail. She's had a car accident. She'd

303

been drinking, was well over the limit, apparently. Only she ran away from the hospital and no one knows where she is now. The police are looking for her.'

'Oh, no!'

'She went off her trolley in court, abusing me and cursing. If she could have got to me, she'd have clawed my eyes out, I'm sure. I can't believe how she's changed lately. She used to hate drunken drivers, we both did.' He looked at Donna again. 'I don't know what to do.'

She gave him a quick hug and he held on to her for a few moments, burying his head in her shoulder, relieved when she didn't push him away.

'I'm so sorry, Tom.' She pulled away. 'We'd better tell Jez and Kevin.'

'Give me a minute, will you?'

'Of course. Shall I get you a cup of coffee?'

'Tea would be better. Do you mind?'

'No, of course not.'

He watched her walk briskly away and couldn't help making the inevitable comparison between her and his wife. Hugging Donna had been — unsettling, had woken feelings inside him. She was, after all, a very attractive woman, and it had been a long time.

Don't think about it! he told himself.

At least, not yet. Not till he'd got his life sorted out, then maybe . . .

When Donna came back, she brought a cup for herself and sat with him, not annoying him with chatter, not expecting anything, just being there. When he'd finished, he put the empty mug down reluctantly. 'I'd better go and tell Jez now.'

'And Kevin. I'll send him to join you. Is there any chance she'll come after the kids?'

'It'll be me she comes after. Gail would never hurt the kids, but she's not much interested in them. It's like a fortress here, though, and she's not the brightest button in the universe. She'd never find a way in.'

Jez listened to his son's tale with a sinking feeling. Something else to complicate Tom's life. He looked at Kevin. 'The kids will be safe here, won't they?'

'Oh, yes,' his chief of security said confidently. 'It'd take someone with a lot of skill to break in, and even then there are hidden giveaways that would alert us. We've got the whole surveillance system up and running now. It's state-of-the-art. But just in case, I suggest you tell Jane to keep the children within the grounds. I know they like the park down the road, but for the moment they should stay close.'

Tom nodded. 'I will. I'd better go and tell her now.'

He walked slowly, enjoying the warmth of the sun on his skin. He was worrying about nothing. Kevin knew what he was talking about. Only . . . the worries wouldn't go away.

★   ★   ★

Donna rang Andi up with another job offer. 'Hope this isn't asking too much, and you must say if it is, but a friend of mine has a big ball tonight, her husband's annual company bash,

305

and her babysitter has let her down. I said I'd ask you if you'd mind looking after her children. They're eight and ten, really nice kids, won't give you any trouble, but it'll be an all-night job. She'll send a taxi for you and send you home in one as well tomorrow morning. She'll pay well.'

'How much?'

Donna told her.

'Seems a fair rate to me. I'm happy to do it.'

'She'll make sure she has her mobile with her, so you can always ring her if there's a problem.'

Andi felt happier as she got ready to go out. She was leaving early so that she could meet the kids before their parents left. It felt good to be earning money. She went to find her mother and twirled round. 'Do I look like a modern Mary Poppins?'

'No, but you look extremely neat and tidy. Very sensible not to tart yourself up.'

Andi shuddered. 'I don't think I'll ever want to tart myself up or try to look sexy again.'

'Oh, darling.'

'It's all right. I'm not going to cry all over you again. Now, I'll go and keep an eye open for the taxi.'

Soon she was gone and Sophie breathed a sigh of relief. When the phone rang, she wasn't surprised that it was Jez.

'All alone, my pretty lady?' he teased. 'Would you be receiving gentlemen callers tonight?'

'Only one gentleman. And — ' she took a deep breath, feeling a little shy — 'I'm offering bed and breakfast as well as dinner. If the gentleman in question is interested.'

'He is.'

After they'd ended the call, she smiled. It had taken courage for her to ask him to stay the night. Things had moved on so fast between them she alternated between feeling blissfully happy and worrying that it couldn't last.

★ ★ ★

Kevin looked up as Jez came into the security area.

'I'm spending the night next door.'

'Are you sure that's wise? Wouldn't it be better to bring her across here?'

'She does have a security system there, you know.'

'Make sure she sets it, then. We don't want anyone getting at you.'

'A person can be too cautious. It's months since that sod held a knife to my throat. I don't intend to spend the rest of my life cowering indoors.'

'You must be feeling a lot better to start rebelling,' Kevin teased.

Jez grinned at him and clapped him on the shoulder. 'I am. Much better. There's nothing like happiness for making you feel good. Now, I'll just go and pack a few things and I'm off.'

They walked through the grounds together and Kevin walked right up to the back door with him.

'There's really no need to cling like a limpet.'

'I prefer to make sure you're safe. That's what you pay me for.'

The door opened and Jez stepped inside.

Kevin smiled grimly as he walked away. It was being ultra-cautious escorting Jez next door, but he still felt guilty that someone had got through their old security system and terrorized him. Trouble was, there was no such thing as a perfect system. Whenever people had an input into running something, systems could go wrong.

He swung round, thinking he'd heard a rustling in the foliage, but a bird flew out, so he carried on, locking the wooden gate carefully behind him.

★　★　★

Jez pulled Sophie into his arms. 'I can't believe we have the whole night together.'

'Isn't it wonderful?'

Her eyes were shining with love, there was no other word for it. When they went into the kitchen, she had a meal almost ready to be served.

'We're getting to feel like an old married couple,' he teased.

'It does feel comfortable being together,' she admitted.

'Yes. And you never seem to be in a bad mood. Do you ever get grumpy?'

'I'm not a moody person. Are you?'

He frowned, trying to work it out. 'I don't think so. Not nowadays, anyway. In fact, if we could just sort out the person threatening my life, and settle Tom's affairs, I'd be extremely happy.' He told her about Gail's accident and disappearance.

'That's dreadful. Do you think she'll be coming after the children?'

'Who knows? I've never met the woman, so I'm no judge. Tom says she'd never hurt them, but from the sounds of it, she's fixated on getting him back and may try to use them to do that. And people don't always think or act rationally when they're under the influence.' He stared into space for a moment or two, then his smile returned. 'Let's change the subject. We don't want to spend the evening talking about other people's problems.'

'What do we want to spend the evening doing, apart from eating?' She went to check something in a slow cooker.

He followed and peered into it. 'That smells wonderful. I'm getting very fond of home cooking.'

'Do you want a taste?' She offered him the spoon.

He forced himself to concentrate on the food, taking it slowly off the spoon and savouring it. 'Delicious.'

When they sat down to eat, it felt like the scene from an old movie he'd seen, where both characters were feeding each other more than food.

'Tom Jones,' she said suddenly.

'Yes. I was just thinking about that scene.' It was an effort to raise his fork to his mouth.

She smiled, such a smug smile he asked what was amusing her.

'I don't think I've ever had this effect on anyone before.'

He didn't ask about her husband. Comparisons with other relationships were not a good thing. He'd learned that the hard way. 'It's a wonderful effect,' he said simply and held her gaze as he slowly lifted his fork again and moved his mouth around the piece of meat.

She breathed deeply and looked down at the food. 'I don't think anyone's ever had so strong an effect on me, either. I'd rather take things slowly tonight, though. If you don't mind.'

He could do that, of course he could. But it wasn't his choice. You couldn't drag your lady love up to bed by the hair, though, could you? But those cavemen had a point.

After the meal, he helped her clear up then they went to sit in the living room. With the indoor lamps turned low, some skilful outdoor lighting made a fairyland of the courtyard, which distracted him nicely. 'Who designed your outdoor lighting?'

'Me.'

'It's beautiful. Will you do mine?'

'When I'm in between books. I save jobs like that for when I'm thinking of a new story. Gentle physical work seems to spark off ideas.'

He put his arm round her. 'Tell me more about yourself. I want to know everything. What your childhood was like, what your favourite food is, what your plans are for the future, why you became a writer . . . Every single thing.'

'If you'll do the same.'

'Of course.' He had to kiss her cheek, it looked so soft. This wasn't just about passion and wanting her in bed. He wanted her in his life.

Permanently. The words popped out before he could stop himself.

'Will you marry me, Sophie?'

'*What?*'

He slid off the couch and went down on one knee. Taking her hand, he said it again, because he wanted so much for it to happen. 'Will you marry me?'

The hand trembled in his. He looked at it, then at her and raised it to his lips before sitting on the sofa again. 'Have I upset you?'

'No. I'm just — astonished.'

'I am too. I didn't plan to ask you, it just slipped out. But it's what I want. Desperately.'

'Don't you think we should try living together for a while first?'

'If you prefer it, we can do that, but I'd prefer to get married.' He guessed what she must be thinking. 'Whatever it is between you and me feels so different from the other times, so gentle and right and wonderful, that I want the world to know you're mine. And I want us to be together all the time.' He waited.

She gave him a long look, as if searching his very soul, then she took his hands in hers and echoed his gesture by kissing them gently, one after the other. 'Yes, I will marry you, Jez.'

He hugged her close, letting out a long breath of sheer happiness, then he whirled her to her feet and danced her round the house. 'This is one time when I'm sorry I've given up drinking, because we ought to be toasting our future in the very best champagne.'

'Sparkling apple juice will do just as well.'

'In champagne glasses?'

'Of course.'

He raised his glass to her. 'I love you.'

She raised hers and clinked it against his. 'I love you too, Jez. So very much.'

'I'm hoping you'll teach me to do the marriage thing right this time.'

'Be sure of it.'

★ ★ ★

Andi came home the next morning looking pleased with herself but with dark circles under her eyes that said she still wasn't sleeping properly.

Sophie had sent Jez home early, because she wanted to break the news about their deepening relationship to her daughter on her own. She was terrified Andi might say something to upset him when she found out.

'How did it go, darling?'

'Easy-peasy, Mum. They were lovely children and I really enjoyed playing with them, talking to them. Children are so uncomplicated. They want me to babysit tonight as well. It's their anniversary.'

'That's marvellous. Well done.'

She looked at her mother, then stared harder. 'I suppose *he* spent the night here.'

'Yes. I had a wonderful time.' Sophie couldn't stop herself from smiling.

Andi's tone became sharper. 'I'd better move out as soon as I can, then, and leave you two lovebirds alone.'

'Oh, darling, please don't spoil it for me.'

They frowned at one another across the kitchen, then Andi's shoulders sagged. 'I just can't seem to get my head around it — you finding another guy, that is.'

'Please try. It's so important to me.'

'You'll be telling me next that you're going to marry him.' She gaped in shock as her mother's face went crimson. 'Already?'

Sophie nodded. 'When someone is right, you just know. Well, I do. It was exactly the same with your father. Please be happy for me — for us.'

Andi saw how her mother's face was soft with love and made a big effort not to spoil that, though she wasn't sure she trusted Jez Winter not to hurt such a gentle person.

She gave her mother a hug, hiding her face in Sophie's shoulder so that she wouldn't betray the contradictory feelings that were tearing her apart. There was resentment, jealousy and yet a wish that her mother really would be happy with Jez. Then she remembered. 'What about the breast-cancer thing?'

'He doesn't care, except for my well-being of course. And he knows that I've not yet reached my five-year anniversary, that it could happen again. But nothing's ever guaranteed in life, is it?'

Her face went sad in that special way she had when she was thinking of Andi's father. 'You won't — forget Dad?'

'Of course not. After all our years together, Bill's an integral part of who I am now.'

'But you've accepted Jez's proposal, haven't you?'
'Oh, yes.'

313

Andi sought for something to lighten the moment and suddenly thought of William and Kerry's reaction to this news. She couldn't help grinning. 'Can I be there when you tell my dear brother?'

'I was going to phone him.'

'Can I listen in?'

'Why?'

'Because he and Kerry will be furious. They're already grudging every penny you spend because you'll have less to leave to them. The thought of you having a husband and your money being out of their control will drive them absolutely crazy.'

'My money's never been controlled by William.'

'I know. But that's not for lack of trying on his part. He's always on at you to spend less — don't tell me he isn't, I've heard him — and he freaked out when you bought this big house.'

'You can't know that.'

'Oh, can't I! I've heard him sounding off to Kerry about it and I've also overheard my dear sister-in-law wondering what you'll be worth when you die and consoling him with the thought that the house will be increasing in value.'

'You have?'

''Fraid so.'

'But he's earning enough to support them in comfort. He doesn't *need* my money.'

'He'll never earn enough money to suit Kerry. She's a greedy bitch and you got her hopes up when you developed breast cancer.'

Sophie sighed. 'I've tried to like her.'

'I tried too at first. I don't any more, so you don't need to pretend when you're talking to me.'

'But she's still family.'

'Well, she doesn't feel like it. She hasn't tried to like us or even to get to know us properly. All *she* wants to do is control people. She and Willi are a matched pair where that's concerned. So . . . you'll let me listen in when you tell them, won't you? Pretty please? It'll so cheer me up.'

Sophie laughed. 'All right. But I'm not telling them yet. I'm too happy and I don't want anything to spoil it. I'll — um, keep you updated on our plans. Oh, and I nearly forgot. Donna got you an appointment with that counsellor this afternoon. Do you want me to go with you?'

'No, thanks.' Andi held up one hand. 'I'm grateful, I really am, but I'll do that myself. And I'll pay my own taxi fares, too, though I'll have to let you pay for the sessions, I'm afraid.'

'I'm happy to. It's so important.'

Andi went to put her things away, then walked to her bedroom window, feeling restless. She'd been out overnight and come back safely, but she'd felt a bit wobbly and nervous sitting alone in the back of the taxi going there. How dumb was that? It was a good thing she was seeing the counsellor today. She didn't want to feel like this for ever, because that would mean *he* had won.

She hadn't told her mother, but since it had happened, she felt afraid every time it grew dark.

She couldn't help it, just — couldn't. No amount of reasoning with herself lessened the fear.

And she was never going into a club again as long as she lived. Never, ever.

18

Gail hitched a ride down to London, or rather three rides. She smiled and chatted to the various drivers, letting one of them buy her a cup of coffee at a motorway services, and trying to hide it when she got shaky with the need for a drink.

The final driver dropped her near a tube station and she went to study the map on the wall to work out how to get to the address where Tom had her children locked away from her. She didn't know what she was going to do when she got there, only that she had to find him and take her children back.

He'd know how to deal with the police for her. That rich father of his could hire a fancy lawyer to get her off this silly charge. She'd hardly had anything to drink. Their tests must have been wrong.

The most important thing now was to find a way to convince Tom that she'd changed, would give up the drinking and look after the children better.

'Can I help you, madam?'

She swung round, saw someone in uniform and nearly freaked out, then realized it was a railway uniform, not police, and nodded towards the map. 'I've never been to London before so I don't know how to use the tube. I need to get to this address.' She held out the scrap of paper.

'You've got posh friends if they live there.' He fished a map of the Underground out of his pocket. 'Keep this for future reference. Now, you take this line, change here and then get off and ask again when you arrive at this station.'

She nodded, repeated what he'd said and let him show her how to buy a ticket. Before she went to look for the platform, she slipped into the Ladies'. A glance in the mirror made her stop dead, horrified. She looked terrible! Her clothing was crumpled, the remains of her make-up were smeared round her eyes and as for her hair, it was a greasy tangle. She went back outside again and found a store selling cheap T-shirts, bought herself a new one and went back into the Ladies' to change and do something about her hair.

Only then did she go to find a train. She leaned back with a sigh of relief as she sat down, keeping a careful eye on the stations they passed through until they got to the one where she had to change.

She got lost again, but a motherly woman showed her where to go and there wasn't long to wait for the next train.

By the time Gail got out of the station, it was getting late.

She found an off-licence and asked directions, then gave in to temptation and bought a bottle of whisky, just to give her confidence a boost, and a packet of mints to hide the smell of alcohol. She chose whisky because she didn't really like the taste. It would be fatal to her plans to get drunk, but a sip or two would help calm her nerves.

Outside, she opened the bottle with shaking hands and pulled a face at the first mouthful, but she liked the warmth as it went down and soon she began to feel more relaxed.

It was only a mile or so, the man at the off-licence had said, so she walked, taking her time, looking at the increasingly large houses with envy.

When she got to Chestnut Lane, she was amazed at how huge some of the houses were. Talk about mansions! How unfair was that? Tom and the children living in a place like this while she was on her own in a tiny semi just down the road from an industrial estate. 'Well, no more, Tom Prichard!' she muttered. 'You're going to do your duty by me from now on. I'm your *wife*.'

A passer-by slowed down to stare at her strangely and she made a rude sign, laughing loudly when he jerked away in shock and hurried off.

She stopped to pop another mint into her mouth. You couldn't be too careful.

Jez Winter's house was the largest in the street and was protected by high old-fashioned walls, topped with broken glass. Heavy metal gates barred the drive. There was a sign on the wall; THESE PREMISES ARE UNDER SECURITY SUR-VEILLANCE. PLEASE RING FOR ADMITTANCE.

Well, no one was going to keep her out, because they might not let her even see Tom. She'd have to take care how she got in, couldn't afford to mess it up. It might be her last chance to set things right with him.

She walked on past the house, stopping to

study the garden of the one next door, a smaller place, but still much larger than any house she'd ever lived in. It too had a high wall in front, but a modern brick one and no broken glass on top. There was an iron gate with a security sign on it and a buzzer. How the hell was she going to get inside if they were all like this?

As if in answer to her prayers, a taxi came along and stopped at the gates. She moved casually past then stopped. The driver wound down his window and pressed the buzzer, speaking to someone at the house.

Gail crept nearer, hiding behind a huge tree growing at the edge of the footpath.

A minute later the gate started to slide back and the taxi moved slowly forward. Bending low, she ran after it into the garden and dived into some nearby bushes, breaking branches and making a loud rustling, cracking sound. She lay still, waiting to see if anyone had noticed her, but the taxi stopped at the front door, someone got in and then it drove away.

No one came looking for an intruder. Ignoring the branches poking into her, she lay back and laughed softly to herself.

I'm too clever for you, Tom Prichard! What a surprise you're going to get!

★ ★ ★

Tom felt anxious all day. He couldn't concentrate on anything, kept wondering what Gail was doing, where she was now. And then he'd have to check on the children again.

He noticed that Jez looked particularly happy, but didn't ask, because he couldn't stop thinking about Gail. He might not want to be married to her, but he didn't want her to come to any harm, and she'd not only had a car accident but was in trouble with the police. What would she do next? Surely she'd not harm herself?

His mother rang up in the evening to ask if there was any news but he had to tell her no.

'She'll be coming to see you, Tom. I'm sure of it.'

'Why do you say that?'

'Because every time we were with her, she talked about you, was sure you'd get back together, blamed her drinking on you, for leaving her.'

'Well, we both know that's not true. She started drinking while she was with me and it built up for years.'

'Why did she drink so heavily, though? There must be some reason.'

'How do I know why some people drink and others don't? I was too busy earning a living, getting all the overtime I could so that Gail wouldn't spend us into debt.'

'You must have some idea of the reason why, Tom. Perhaps you didn't love her enough. You should pray for guidance. The Lord will tell you what to do if you listen carefully.'

He sighed as he put the phone down. His mother's faith was a wonderful thing for her, made her very happy, but he didn't share it.

Jane, who was giving the children their supper, looked across the room at him in concern. 'Not more bad news?'

He shook his head, looking meaningfully at the children. 'Tell you later.'

When they were in bed, Jane didn't go to her own flat, but came to join him. 'Tell me to mind my own business, if you like, and I will. Or talk to me and I'll listen. I don't give advice unless people ask for it.'

He bowed his head and asked without looking at her. 'Do you think I drove Gail to drink?'

'Definitely not.'

He looked up in surprise, she sounded so certain.

'Some people seem hell-bent on destroying themselves, Tom love. That's their fault, though they usually blame others. I didn't drive my husband to drink, and as far as I could see you were a good husband and father, a good provider too. Gail is a weak reed. Some people just are. We help them if we can, but we mustn't let them destroy us — especially, in this case, your children.'

'I didn't love Gail, though.'

'Did you love her when you married her?'

'Yes. Or I thought I did. But later, when she started drinking, when she got herself pregnant on purpose to keep me with her, it killed something in me. I couldn't even touch her any more.' He hesitated. 'My mother thinks I should go back to Gail and try to help her.'

'Your wife is an adult. She has to take responsibility for her own actions. No one can force alcoholics to give up the booze or keep them away from it, if they're determined to keep on drinking. They have to want to do that themselves.'

He thought of Jez, who smilingly refused a drink, and yet who admitted to having used not only alcohol, but drugs of all sorts. Jez had given it up. Could Gail? He doubted it. 'I can't bear to put the children in her care again. She wouldn't mean to hurt them, but it's a wonder she hasn't already done so. If you hadn't been next door, they'd often have gone hungry, because I couldn't be there all the time and earn a living. But I'd still help her if I could only think what to do.'

'I can't tell you what to do, Tom. And don't let anyone else try to tell you, either. Do what feels right to you. Hopefully, you have a long lifetime ahead of you. Choose carefully what you do with it, who you spend it with.'

He smiled at her, feeling comforted by their chat, inconclusive as it had been. 'Go and have the rest you deserve now, Jane. And thank you for listening. It helped a lot.'

She got up and came across to kiss his cheek. 'You're a good lad.'

The warmth left by her lips seemed to linger for a while. His mother wasn't one for casual kissing and cuddling, but he'd seen Jane hug the kids, kiss them, laugh with them. Andi did it too. Kids needed to be shown they were loved. His two were always coming to touch him and cuddle up to him. He loved that.

★ ★ ★

Gail found out there was a security system round this house by accidentally tripping a sensor and

323

switching on an outside light. She threw herself behind a tall clump of flowers and lay very still. She saw someone come to a window and peer out, so mewed like a cat. She'd always been good at that and grinned as the person went away from the window. Lying looking up at the darkening sky, she purred softly to herself.

When the moon rose, she prowled round the garden, keeping away from the house itself. To her disappointment the walls round the side of Jez Winter's house had broken glass all along the tops just like the front ones, and the gate between the two houses might look old-fashioned but it had a fancy modern electronic lock on the wall beside it, lit up so you could see which button to press.

The only hope she could see of getting into the next garden was by climbing the big tree that overhung the wall, but she wasn't sure she could manage that. And it'd be hard to do it in the dark, far too risky. Anyway it had started to rain now, just a gentle misting rain, but it'd make the tree slippery.

She was starting to get damp and didn't want to catch her death of cold by spending the night in soaking clothes, so looked round for shelter. Surely there must be a garden shed in a posh place like this?

When she found a summer house, it seemed a sign that fate was on her side. She went to shelter inside with a sigh of relief just as the rain began to pound down heavily on the roof. She only wondered if the place was security wired after she'd gone inside.

She stood near the door for ages, waiting to see if anyone came out of the house, ready to run away if they did. But no one appeared. In the end she lay down on one of the sun loungers stored there, because she was feeling tired.

She woke up shivering with cold, squinted at her watch in the moonlight and gasped in shock to find it was one o'clock in the morning. She'd better stay here all night, but she was so cold. Taking the cushions off the other chairs, she draped them over herself. It helped to keep her a bit warmer. Not enough, though.

In the end she had a little drink and that warmed her properly.

'You wait, Tom Bloody Prichard,' she muttered. 'I'll pay you back for this. It's all *your* fault.'

⋆ ⋆ ⋆

Jez woke early, feeling more like his old self than he had for a long time. A catchy little tune popped into his head as he lay feeling relaxed and happy. He'd composed a few lately, a sign that he was truly better, surely?

Getting up, he stretched lazily then slipped into his dressing gown. It had rained during the night and the garden looked fresh in the early morning sunlight. As he stood by the window, a bird hopped on to the sill and another one followed. 'One Little Birdie,' he muttered. 'That's it!'

He went straight down to the studio to fiddle with the melody line on the keyboard. When he was satisfied he switched on his computer and keyed in the melody to the music program, seeing the music writing itself across the screen. A damned sight more convenient than writing it down by hand. He created a file and saved it.

Now he had to find some words, and flesh out the first of the simple songs he wanted to write for his grandchildren. He opened his word-processing program and —

'Have you had your coffee and biscuits yet?'

'What?' He turned round to see Donna standing in the doorway, hands on hips.

'You haven't had anything, have you? If you had, there'd be mugs and plates lying around.'

He leaned back, smiling, suddenly aware that he was extremely thirsty. 'No, I haven't.'

'It's eight o'clock.'

He looked at his keyboard with regret. 'I've been up since six. Didn't notice how time was passing.'

'You know your doctor said you should have a snack early on, even if you don't feel like it. I'll fetch you something.' She went to the kitchen.

He went back to working on the lyrics, which meant modifying the melody a little and . . . Something was waved to and fro under his nose and he snapped into awareness to see what she'd brought: coffee and a couple of biscuits.

He sipped the coffee, realized it wasn't too hot and took a mouthful. 'I'm writing a song for the children. Want to hear it? The lyrics are still a bit uncertain, but I've got the chorus.'

He played a cheerful little introduction, then sang:

One little birdie in a tree,
Two little birdies, then there's three.
Three little birdies then there's four,
Hop-hop-hopping to my door.

She listened, moving her head in time to the music without realizing what she was doing until he pointed it out gleefully.

'It's really cute, Jez, such a catchy tune. Hayley and Ryan will love it. I can just see them dancing to it, hopping like birds.'

'I love playing for them, making them happy.'

'You look happy yourself today.'

He nodded. 'I am. I can't tell you why yet, but I will soon.'

'Sophie?'

'Yes.'

'Good. About time you found yourself a real woman. I really like her. She's so sane and reasonable, yet she still does her own thing.'

'Good morning.'

She turned round. 'Oh, hello, Tom. Come and listen to what your father's written. I must get on with my work.'

Jez passed Tom the guitar, sang the new tune and within minutes the two of them were laughing together. Soon, they were discussing the second verse, three little squirrels this time. Tom suggested an improvement and they worked happily together.

His son didn't realize how good he was musically, Jez thought. Tom might be inexperienced but he had a feel for music that was inborn. You either had it or you didn't.

Jez intended to see that Tom got a chance to use his musical skills — and not just as a sound engineer. But he'd let things develop naturally.

★　★　★

In the middle of the morning Jane took the children out for a walk round the garden. Usually they'd walk down the street to the local park, which had a playground with swings. They loved to play out of doors, something their mother hadn't let them do very often.

She found an old bench and sat down, encouraging them to hop and skip along the paths nearby, which had been laid out around a group of overgrown flowerbeds and bushes that had gone feral.

She turned her face up to the sun for a minute or two, enjoying its warmth.

★　★　★

Jez rang Sophie when he'd finished working on the song and she invited him over for a late lunch.

'I can't seem to settle to work today. I'm too excited,' she confessed. 'Andi's gone out to see the counsellor again.'

'I'm hoping to persuade you to come out and choose an engagement ring with me this afternoon. Will you?'

'We'll see. There's no hurry.'

'*I* want to hurry.'

'I'm beginning to feel as if I've got on an

express train and it's running away with me.'

'I wouldn't mind running away with you. I'll come over straight away.'

He turned to ring through to security and ask for an escort, then shook his head. What harm could possibly come to him in his own garden? He wasn't even stepping out on to the street.

He strolled through the grounds, stopping to chat to Jane for a minute or two and promising to play for the children later in the afternoon, then went through the gate that led to Sophie's, closing it carefully behind him.

$$\star \quad \star \quad \star$$

Gail was watching from her hiding place and saw Jez Winter come through the gate. He was so like Tom, older of course, but with the same narrow features and laughing eyes.

And before the gate closed, she also caught a glimpse of her children playing in the garden next door. Fate was still on her side. She'd never have as good a chance to snatch them.

She waited till the door of the house had shut behind Jez and some fat woman with a stupid grin on her face, then ran across to the tree, heart pounding. There was a garden bench under it and if she stood on the back of it, she could reach the lower branches, just.

Good thing she was wearing jeans. Puffing and panting, she got herself into the tree, clambered slowly from one branch to the next, getting on to one that hung over the next garden. She'd loved climbing trees when she was a child, though it had got her into trouble because she'd torn and dirtied her clothes. She wasn't enjoying it now, though, and had slipped at one stage and nearly fallen.

From here she could see the children a short distance away, playing and calling out to Jane. Good. Keep making a noise, brats. I don't want that old bitch to hear me.

Feeling a bit light-headed, she edged along to where the branch hung across a branch of the next-door tree. The one she was on swayed to and fro under her as it grew narrower. Suddenly the one she wanted to get to seemed too frail to hold her weight. How did you tell?

She wished that she hadn't had a nip of whisky, then tossed her head and told herself this was the only chance she'd get. She'd never fallen out of a tree yet, and even if she did, it wasn't far to the ground.

She nearly lost her balance as she transferred to the other tree, and grazed the side of her hand quite badly, scrabbling to stay on the new branch. It was a wonder Jane didn't hear her.

Gail clung to the branch for a minute or two, till her heart stopped pounding. No time to waste. She needed to snatch the children while they were in the garden because she'd never get into the house, she was sure.

The kids were playing some sort of hopping game along the paths and Jane was sitting watching them. Anger surged up in Gail and without thinking it through, she picked up a piece of fallen branch and crept up behind her old neighbour. She waited till the children were out of sight behind a mess of dead plants and hit Jane's head as hard as she could.

The old woman was knocked sideways on the bench with the force of the blow and she didn't stir.

For a moment, Gail felt afraid at what she'd done. What if she'd killed her? Then she saw Jane's chest rising and falling and let out her breath in a whoosh of relief. No, just knocked her out, and serve her bloody well right.

'Mummy!'

She turned and scooped Hayley up in her arms, smacking a kiss on her cheek. 'Hello, love. Give Mummy a kiss, then.'

Hayley pecked her cheek and by that time Ryan was holding up his arms. Emotion surged through her. How dare Tom take her children away from her! She was the one who'd had them, not him. She loved them and they loved her.

'Why is Jane lying down with her eyes closed?' Hayley asked.

'Because we're going to play hide and seek. Shh. Let's creep away. Don't make any noise or she'll hear where we go.' Holding a child by each hand she led the way towards the rear of the big house, not sure what she'd find there, but knowing there was no way she could get two small children up the tree and back over the wall.

And luck was still running her way, because there, behind the house, was a big delivery van with its doors open, showing stacks of boxes inside.

'We'll hide in the van,' Gail whispered and ran

across to it, scooping up each child in turn and making them crouch down behind a pile of boxes. She knelt down with them, putting one finger to her lips. 'Isn't this fun?'

Hayley looked at her as if unsure.

A man came out and closed the van's rear doors, then got into the driver's seat and started up the engine. Gail watched him through a small glass window, feeling gleeful. It was so easy. She was really looking forward to ringing Tom and telling him she had the children, giving him orders about what to do.

She climbed safely down.

The van stopped again after a short time and the man opened the rear doors to lift out a box. He was staring at them as if they were aliens with two heads.

'What the hell — ! Sorry,' she said, standing up. 'Me and the kids wanted to see if we could do it, get into a van and sneak a lift. We've not hurt anything.'

'I should call the police.'

Her heart began to thud at the mere thought, but she kept a smile on her face. 'They'd just tell you not to waste their time. We've not stolen or damaged anything. You can check.'

'If I wasn't in a hurry, I'd call them anyway.' He stared round at the boxes and parcels suspiciously, blocking her way out until he'd checked them.

'Want to wee-wee,' Ryan said suddenly, clutching himself.

'He'd better not do it here!' The man hauled Gail out of the van by the arm, then lifted the two children down. 'Now get the hell out of my sight before I change my mind.'

She went and helped Ryan to wee in a park near some shops, then decided to phone Tom straight away. She made her voice harsh, knowing the children were frightened of her when she spoke like that. 'Go and sit on that bench, you two. *Stay there and do not make any noise.*'

They did as she'd told them, huddling up to one another in a way that always made her feel like a monster.

She dialled Tom's mobile, tapping her foot impatiently as she waited for him to answer.

* * *

Tom saw who was calling and answered the phone quickly. 'Gail! Where the hell are you?'

'Wouldn't you like to know?'

He could hear that she'd been drinking, not a lot, but enough to slur her speech.

'My mother rang. She says you had an accident and ran away from the police.'

'She's an interfering bitch. It was just a little misunderstanding. All sorted now.'

'It can't be. The police are still looking for you.'

'More to the point, have *you* looked for the children lately?'

His blood ran cold. 'What do you mean?'

'Think they're safe behind those big walls with broken glass on the top, do you? Well, I got in easily enough and I got the kids out too.'

'I don't believe you.'

'Go and look for them. I'll call back in half an hour and tell you what I want you to do.'

'Gail, don't — ' He looked at the buzzing phone, stuffed it in his pocket and ran across to the cottage. No sign of Jane or the children there. He saw Craig crossing the yard and yelled out, 'Have you seen Jane?'

Craig turned round and Tom's face must have shown how anxious he was because Craig ran across to join him.

'What's the matter, mate?'

Tom explained.

'I saw Jane taking the kids to play in the back garden. They've played there before. I'll show you.'

He led the way, exclaiming in shock at the sight of the still figure on the bench and kneeling beside her. 'She's been hit on the head.'

Tom knew at once who'd done it. 'I'll call for an ambulance. Where's Jez?'

'In his studio.'

'He told me he was going to visit Sophie. Didn't he call for an escort?'

'No.'

Tom held up one hand to stop him speaking. 'Hello. Yes, we need an ambulance. An old woman's been attacked, hit over the head, I think. She's unconscious.' He gave them the address.

'Better not move her,' Craig said. 'She's breathing OK, but you don't know if the blow injured her neck or spine. I'll run back and tell someone to open the gates for the ambulance,

334

then I'll try to find Jez. You'll be all right on your own here, won't you?'

Tom nodded. 'My wife's ringing back in half an hour. I wasn't thinking. I should have asked for the police as well as the ambulance.'

'I'll call Kevin.' Craig got his mobile out and keyed in a number, speaking into the phone as he ran through the garden.

Tom looked down at Jane, feeling sick at the sight of the poor woman. Gail was in serious trouble now. She'd gone beyond reason. She'd not been the same since that psychotic episode when she was smoking pot.

He could only pray that she wouldn't hurt the children.

*   *   *

Jez's mobile rang as he was just finishing a piece of cake. 'Damn! I thought I'd switched that thing off.'

'Better answer it,' Sophie said.

He looked to see who it was, frowning as he saw that it was Craig.

'Where the hell are you, Jez?'

'Next door at Sophie's.'

'You should have let us know. And you'd better get back straight away. Looks like Tom's wife has kidnapped the children, and she's injured Jane, too.'

'*What?*'

Craig gave him a few more details.

'I'm on my way.' He explained quickly to Sophie what'd happened.

'That's terrible! I'm coming with you.'

On the other side of the gate they found Tom standing beside Jane, who still hadn't moved. From the distance came an ambulance siren.

Within minutes Jane had been carried away and Sophie volunteered to go to hospital with her.

Kevin arrived, looking grim. 'Tell me about your wife, Tom.' He listened, asking a couple of questions, then said, 'It's definitely a police matter. I'll ring a friend and hurry things up. Don't answer your phone until we have instructions about what they want you to do.'

'I can't do that. Gail may get angry and take it out on the kids. She's — '

Kevin turned slightly away and spoke rapidly into the phone, nodding, making noises of agreement, and giving the address. He switched it off and turned back to Tom. 'I've got some equipment over in the security room. They want us to make a recording of the call.'

The phone rang.

Tom stared at it. 'I have to answer.'

'Not yet,' Kevin said firmly.

'But — '

'She'll ring back. Now, hurry.'

★ ★ ★

Gail picked up the phone and pressed redial. The phone rang and rang, but there was no answer. The children began to fidget and she pointed a finger at them. 'Stay still, I said.'

Ryan's lips wobbled as he looked at her,

Hayley scowled. But they did as she told them.

Tom didn't pick up the call. 'You wait!' she muttered. She shoved the phone back into her bag and beckoned to the children. 'If you're good I'll buy you a packet of crisps.'

Both of them brightened.

'Vinegar?' Hayley asked. 'Jane doesn't give us crisps. She says they're not good for children.'

'Well, I'm your mother and I think they're fine — but only for good little children, who keep very quiet when they're told.'

They both sat up very straight, lips pressed together.

'I'll just try to phone your father again. We're going to surprise him.' She got out her phone.

This time he answered after one ring.

'Where were you?'

'Sorry. I was taken short.'

'Trust you. No, don't say anything. Listen to me. I've got the kids and you're not having them back till you've promised me a few things.'

'What?'

'First, you and I are getting back together. I never wanted us to split up. I still don't.'

'OK.'

'You'd do anything for those kids, wouldn't you? Well, from now on, I'm going to come first with you. Understand? You can get your rich father to pay for a nanny and buy us a nice big house, and we'll enjoy ourselves, go to posh parties and things.'

'He won't do anything if you hurt the kids. He loves them.'

'Hurt them? I'd never hurt my own kids. I'm

just not letting you have them back till we've made new arrangements and you've sworn faithfully to keep your promises.'

'What about the police? They're still looking for you.'

'Your father can get a fancy lawyer to see to that. It was a silly charge anyway. I'd only had one drink. The accident was the other person's fault and . . . Tom? You're still there, aren't you?'

'Yes. Where are you, Gail?'

'Wouldn't you like to know?'

'Let me speak to Hayley.'

'No way. I'll ring you again in a couple of hours and you can tell me how the arrangements are going. Bye.'

'Wait! Don't — '

She switched off the phone, smiling at it. 'Got you, Tom Prichard!'

19

After her next counselling session, Andi felt more at peace with herself. The counsellor was experienced in this field and easy to relate to. She was able to reassure Andi that her reactions were not only normal, but those of a strong woman who hadn't let the incident destroy her.

Their session had brought lots of tears, but Andi felt better afterwards and was happy to make another appointment.

She caught the tube back instead of taking a taxi, visiting the local shopping centre on the way to buy a bouquet of flowers for her mother. She felt guilty for not showing more pleasure in the news of the engagement.

She sighed. She couldn't imagine falling in love now or wanting a man to touch her, but the counsellor said those feelings would fade — if she let them. That was the key, not to cling on to the bad side of life.

It sounded simple. It wasn't. But . . . it was do-able. She had to believe that.

She went to the side of the supermarket to choose a bunch of flowers from a big row of buckets, smiling when she heard a child asking her mother which size of crisps she could have. Then Andi realized she knew the voice and turned round. Hayley and Ryan were nearby with a woman whose clothing was crumpled and who had panda eyes where her make-up had run.

Puzzled to see the kids out without Jane, Andi stepped behind the flowers, watching as the woman picked up two bags of crisps, put them in her plastic basket with some other stuff and took everything to the checkout, not even looking to make sure the children were following her. Poor little Ryan looked very weary and Hayley was tugging him along, watching the woman anxiously.

Tom must be allowing his wife access to the children, but he should have supervised what they did more carefully.

Then, as the trio walked out of the supermarket, Hayley said clearly, 'Isn't Daddy going to be surprised when we're not there?'

'He certainly is,' the woman said.

Andi froze. It looked as if . . . surely Gail couldn't have kidnapped the children? No, that was the sort of thing you saw on TV. It didn't happen in real life.

But then her mother had got engaged to a famous pop star and she'd been raped. In real life.

She'd better follow them to make sure things were all right. Pulling a beanie out of her bag, she crammed it on her head, pulling it right down to hide her hair, then putting on her sunglasses.

Hands in pockets, slouching along, she followed the trio to the park and when they were sitting by the swings, she moved past and out of their hearing to ring her mother. 'Come on, answer it!' she muttered as it rang several times.

Just as she'd started wondering who else to ring, someone said, 'Hello?'

'Mum! Thank goodness you're there. I've just seen Tom's children with their mother. Is — ?'

'Andi, she's kidnapped them and she's injured Jane. Where are you? I'll call the police and tell them. Don't go near them, whatever you do. She's behaving irrationally and we're terrified she'll hurt the children. I'll ring you back when I've spoken to the police, or maybe they'll ring you. Don't let them out of your sight.'

Andi shoved the phone in her bag, terrified she'd lose the kids. To her relief, Gail was still sitting on a bench and seemed to be drowsing, so she found a bench too and sprawled on it, hands in pockets.

The children were sitting near their mother, eating their crisps. They were amazingly quiet and kept looking anxiously at the dozing woman as if to make sure they hadn't disturbed her. Once Ryan started to say something and Hayley put up one finger to her lips to shush him.

Come on! Andi thought. Someone come and help them.

Her phone rang and when she answered it, a man's voice said he was from the police.

'Where are you exactly?'

'Still in the park, near the playground. They haven't moved.'

'Are the children all right?'

'Yes.'

'What's she doing?'

'Seems to be dozing.'

'Do not approach them. She's dangerous, has already hurt one person. But if you can, try to keep them in sight without her realizing? Just till

341

we get there and secure the area.'

'Yes, of course.'

★ ★ ★

Everyone waited with Kevin in the security room. Tom couldn't sit still, kept pacing up and down, trying to work out what had got into Gail to hurt poor Jane. Did she really think he'd settle down with her again? She must. She'd sounded . . . well, triumphant was the only word for it.

When the house phone rang, Kevin picked it up. 'Sophie,' he mouthed. He listened intently, then turned to explain to Tom where his children were. 'The police say we're not to go near them.'

'But that park is only a few streets away from here.'

'They don't want you to spook her. They're afraid for the children. They're going to clear the park first, to make sure no one else gets hurt.'

'No way am I staying here while she's within reach. They're *my* kids, Kevin. How would you feel if they were yours?'

He felt Jez put a hand on his shoulder and that unspoken support made emotion thicken his throat, so that he couldn't go on.

Kevin was listening to Sophie again, nodding. He turned to the others. 'Jane's recovered consciousness and she's going to be all right, but they're keeping her in hospital overnight, just in case of complications.' He passed the phone to Jez. 'Sophie wants to speak to you.'

Jez listened intently then said goodbye and looked at Kevin. 'We forgot to lock up her house.

342

She wondered if there's anyone who can go and do it for her.'

'Low priority. We'll do it later.'

Jez turned to Donna. 'Will you go to the hospital and make sure Jane has the very best room and attention possible?'

She nodded and slipped out.

Tom paced up and down, then stopped and said, 'I'm going to the park. You'll have to tie me down to keep me here.'

Kevin grimaced, then spread his hands helplessly. 'My policeman friend is going to be very angry with me, but I'd be there too if they were my kids. Craig and Jez, you man the phones here. Tom, I'm only letting you go out on condition you do as I say. No rushing in. It could make things worse. She might even hurt the kids. I've a hell of a lot more experience of this sort of thing than you do, so you'll let yourself be guided by me.'

'All right.'

'I'd rather come with you,' Jez protested.

'Then I'd have to worry about you as well. Please stay here. You know my mobile number if any messages come through.'

★ ★ ★

Jez bit back another protest as he watched Kevin and Tom leave. He paced up and down, but no phone calls came in.

Afternoon shaded on towards dusk and still no news. What were they doing? What could be taking so long?

Suddenly he remembered Sophie's house. She'd told him her security code. The least he could do was go and lock up her place. How stupid of them to have left it like that! But it had been such a shock to hear about the kids being kidnapped, they'd both forgotten everything else.

He opened his mouth to suggest to Craig that he attend to this little matter, then snapped it shut again. 'Just got to use the bathroom. Won't be long.'

He walked briskly through the lengthening evening shadows. It would only take a couple of minutes to secure Sophie's house.

*   *   *

Gail realized she'd been dozing off in the late afternoon sun and pulled herself upright. This was no time to fall asleep, though she usually had a lie down at this time of day. Maybe she should hire a hotel room and then she could have a proper rest? Why not? It'd be a good place to meet Tom.

'Come on,' she said brightly to the children. 'Mummy needs her rest. We'll find a hotel, then you can lie down too, just like we used to.' She saw by Hayley's expression that her daughter didn't like the idea. Well, too bad.

There had been a little place near the station advertising bed and breakfasts. She'd go there. She got up and walked off. Ryan had difficulty keeping up and began to cry so she gave him a shake. 'Shut up!' She wasn't having people staring at her, thinking she was a bad mother.

'Want to wee-wee.'

'Not again!'

He clutched himself and with a sigh she turned round and went back towards the public conveniences they'd just passed.

'We might as well all go,' she said brightly as they went into the Ladies'.

It was as she was pulling up Ryan's trousers that she saw Hayley go and stand in the doorway. 'Come back.' When her daughter didn't obey, she pushed Ryan aside and clouted the little girl across the ear, then clouted her again for good measure. 'Do as you're bloody well told!'

★   ★   ★

Since it had clouded over, dusk was far enough advanced now to make lights come on automatically both outside and inside the public convenience. They showed Hayley clearly when she came to the doorway and stared wistfully across the park. They also showed her mother appearing behind her, yelling.

Gail smacked the little girl across the head so hard she knocked her back against the wall with a bump, then hit her again.

Outraged, Andi began to run towards the toilets. 'Stop that! Leave the child alone.'

Her cap fell off her head and Hayley yelled, 'Andi! Andi, I want to go home to Daddy.'

Gail shoved her daughter inside again, pulled out a knife and held it threateningly.

Andi stopped dead.

'Whoever you are, stay away from her or I'll

not be answerable. Who the hell are you anyway?'

'I'm a babysitter. I've looked after the children. They — um, look tired. Do you want me to take them home for you?'

'No, I damned well don't. I'm their mother and I say what happens to them. I'm waiting for their father to come and pick us up, so you just bugger off and mind your own business.'

It was clear that she could do nothing against a knife so Andi backed away. 'Sorry. I didn't know you were their mother.'

She walked until she was out of sight then stopped to peer round the corner of a nearby building that looked like a storage shed. She was in shadow and didn't think Gail would be able to see her.

There was no sign of either Gail or the children anywhere. Had they gone back inside the toilets or had they gone in the other direction? She didn't dare try to find out. Pulling out her phone, she rang the number she'd been given and reported what had just happened.

'They won't get out of the park,' the voice told her. 'We've got people stationed at every gate. We've been clearing the public from the area. Please, Miss Carr, stay away from that woman from now on.'

'I will. But hurry, please. She's hitting them and she sounds drunk.'

Gail watched the babysitter walk away, only vaguely aware that both children were crying. She looked at her watch and decided it was time to call Tom. But first she pulled the bottle of wine she'd bought at the supermarket out of her bag and took a good long swig. That tasted much nicer than whisky. Just a couple of swigs to calm her nerves, not enough to make her do anything foolish.

She pulled out her phone and dialled Tom's number. There was no answer. What was he doing? If he'd gone to the police about this, she'd make him very sorry indeed.

She sat down on top of a rubbish bin near the entrance and leaned back against the wall, suddenly feeling exhausted. 'You kids sit on the floor.'

They went across to the far side to sit. Her daughter stared at her in silent accusation, one cheek red from the slap.

'And don't look at me like that!' she shouted at Hayley. Ryan was still crying. She was tired of the noise. 'Be quiet, you, or I'll smack you too!'

'Want a drink.'

She looked down at her bag. Damn! She'd forgotten to get them a can of pop each. 'There's a tap. Let him drink from that.'

'He can't reach it.'

'Then get some in your hand and let him lap it up.'

Hayley pulled her little brother to her feet and took him across to the sink, whispering in his ear. Gail was going to ask what she was saying, but it was too much trouble and anyway, whatever it was shut him up, thank goodness.

She leaned back against the wall, tired out after her disturbed night. She could hear the tap still running. She'd open her eyes again when it stopped and then decide what to do.

She jerked awake, realizing she was dozing

again and the tap was still running. She couldn't see the children anywhere. 'Where are you two hiding?' she called.

There was no answer, no sound of giggling or rustling. She glanced towards the row of cubicles, but couldn't see any feet underneath the doors. Not in there, then. Aghast, she rushed to the entrance. There was no one at all in sight. Where the hell could they be? She couldn't lose them now or she'd have no way of making Tom do as she wanted.

'Ryan! Hayley! Where are you?' she called. But there was still no answer.

She stumbled round the building but could see no sign of them, so she had another swig of wine as she thought what to do.

How had they got so far away without her hearing them? She hadn't done more than doze for a minute or two.

⋆　⋆　⋆

Tom and Kevin ran all the way to the park and found that the police had set up barriers at the gates and were shepherding the last few people out. A group of bystanders had gathered to watch from behind some blue-and-white tape.

An officer tried to prevent Tom from entering the park, but when he told her who they were she allowed them inside, with strict orders not to move further in until she gave permission.

Kevin saw Andi standing on this side of the group of police officers and beckoned to her. 'What happened?'

'She's got the kids in the Ladies'. I blew it. I saw her slapping Hayley around really hard and ran across to stop her without thinking. She pulled a knife on me.'

He whistled softly. 'She didn't hurt you?'

'No.'

'And the kids are safe?'

'We think so. The police are moving up on the building now.'

Kevin turned to see Tom going off with an officer. He knew better than to intervene at this stage, so stayed with Andi.

'They'll feel safer with their father,' she murmured. 'Poor loves, they're all tear-stained and dirty. Beats me how Tom ever came to marry a woman like her. She's a real loser and she doesn't care two hoots for those kids. I couldn't bear it if they got hurt.'

★　★　★

Jez set the house's alarm system and locked the place up, then went back towards the gate. He saw a flash from the garden of the house behind Sophie's and stopped moving. That could only be a camera. Furious, he changed direction to find out who was spying on Sophie — or on him.

Hearing footsteps running away he took a short cut across the lawn to the small road that connected the four houses and led out to Chestnut Lane.

He wasn't surprised to see who rounded the corner.

Talbin stopped and raised his camera,

laughing as he took a photo of Jez. 'Pity I didn't manage a shot of you when your scars were more obvious, Winter. I'd have got more money for it than I will for this one. How's the lady friend? Is she good in bed? I've got some great photos of you and her saying goodnight, all lovey-dovey.'

Jez wondered why no one had seen him. The sod seemed to have the devil's own luck.

'The people in this house have kindly lent me their garden. I've been here a few times.' Talbin sniggered.

All the frustrations of the past few months, as well as fury that this man was going to start spewing out his filth about Sophie, boiled up inside Jez. Without thinking he lunged forward and snatched the camera. He was far taller and fitter too, in spite of his injuries. As he moved away, Talbin tried to grab the camera back, but missed, then gasped and stopped moving, looking beyond him.

Jez turned to see Peter Shane wink at him as he took a photo of the two of them.

Suddenly it didn't matter to Jez about his face. But as he looked down at the expensive camera, he wondered who else had been photographed recently and what other secrets were on the memory card. Whoever it was would probably be hurt by this man. And if there were one of Sophie on it, he'd delete it and hang the consequences. He took another step backwards. 'You can pick up your camera from my security staff at the front gate.'

Talbin rushed across, the camera bag still flapping on his shoulder, and as they struggled for possession of the camera, the bag slipped off and Jez picked it up, tossing it to Peter.

'Give that camera back to me this minute! It's theft if you take it.'

'You can have it once you're away from this property.'

'Well, give me the bag then. You've got the camera.'

Jez shook his head and repeated, 'You can get them both back from my front gate.'

He watched Talbin return the way he'd come, then turned to Peter. 'Fancy a coffee, Shane?'

'Sure.'

'Come over to my place.' Jez walked away, deliberately exaggerating the slight limp he still had when he was tired. He waited for Peter to follow him through the gate then closed it. Turning to the other, he whispered, 'We need to hurry.' Without any further explanation he set off, running along the grass to muffle his footsteps.

They found Craig in the security control centre. He listened to Jez's explanation, nodding as Peter was introduced. 'You shouldn't have gone out, Jez. That was stupid of you. Anything could have happened.'

'I'm not hurt. Here, see if you can download the images from this.'

Craig handled the camera with reverence. 'This is a beauty. Cost a mint, these do. Won't take me long to download the images. We've got state of the art equipment here. Why are you so keen to do this?'

Jez glanced at Peter. 'I thought if we

351

downloaded his photos we could see what he's been up to. I don't want him hurting Sophie again. And our friend here is doing an exposé of Talbin, so he's interested as well.' He opened the photographic bag. 'And I'm just going to check what's in here.'

He found the usual equipment and then a zipped compartment with carefully labelled memory cards in it. He showed it to Peter. 'Photographers don't usually carry old cards around with them, do they?'

'No. But Talbin's famous for being paranoid about his photos. He's a joke in the industry, keeps copies in the bank and who knows where else.'

Tom turned to Craig. 'Can you copy these as well?'

'Sure.'

'Keep the cards in the same order.'

Peter frowned. 'Let's hope this is worth the risk. The law won't approve of what we're doing.'

'Damn the law!' Jez said. 'I want to nail that sleaze-bag. I'm fed up of falling over him every time I turn round.'

*   *   *

Talbin went to find his car and drove round to the front of Winter's house. Someone answered when he pressed the buzzer.

'What do you want?'

'I want my camera back. *And* my bag.'

'I don't understand.'

'Go and ask your bloody employer, then. *He*

knows about it. He stole my camera and bag. He said I could collect them from you. They should be here by now.'

'Please wait there.'

'How can I do anything else?' Talbin muttered. 'The place is like Fort Knox.' He smiled suddenly at what that thought brought to his mind. This place was much more secure than Winter's old flat, the one where a man had broken in and terrorized the pop star. Pity they'd got it locked up so tightly. It'd make a good story if it happened again. Perhaps that could be arranged once Winter started going out and about more . . .

Fifteen minutes later the gate opened and a burly man stood there holding out Talbin's camera and equipment bag.

He snatched it and took the time to check that the memory cards were still there. They were in the right order, which wasn't the order of the dates on them, so he didn't think they'd been touched. They were much more important than the camera, which had been opened and viewed. But there was nothing on it that really mattered.

20

When the police closed in on Gail, she yelled
abuse and waved the knife at them. Its blade
shone in the light from the caged, fly-specked
fluorescent tube near the door. They immediately took their batons and shook them out.
Since she was waving her knife around and
staggering slightly, they soon managed to knock
it out of her hand and cuff her.

'Where are the children?' one asked her.

'How the hell should I know? They ran off.
Ouch! Let go of me.'

Another officer brought Tom over to them and
Gail looked at him pleadingly. 'Tom, don't let
them do this to me. Tom, you're my *husband*.
You've got to *help* me!'

'Where are the children, Gail?'

'I told you, they ran off. I don't know. It's dark
out there. They could be anywhere.'

'We'd better check out the Ladies' she was
hiding in first,' the officer said. 'You never know.'

'I'll come with you.'

'*Tom! Tom, come back.*'

He ignored Gail's yells and pleas, loathing her
so much for putting the children at risk that he
couldn't bear even to stand near her.

'Has she been on drugs?' the man next to him
asked. 'That's a strong reaction for just alcohol.'

'She did try smoking pot a while back, but it
didn't agree with her. She went so violent, I had

354

to take her to hospital. Psychotic incident, they called it. I threatened to throw her out of the house if she ever touched it again, but it'd frightened her so much she stopped using it.'

'It affects some people that way, for all they claim it's safe. She's not good with alcohol either, is she?'

They arrived at the public convenience. 'Let me go first.' Tom went inside, staring round, seeing no one. 'Hayley? Ryan? Are you there?'

A voice quavered from one of the cubicles. 'Daddy? Please don't be mad at us.'

With a sob of sheer relief, Tom flung open the cubicle door and found two tear-stained children standing on top of the toilet seat so that their feet didn't show, arms round one another. Scooping them up in his arms, he covered them with kisses. 'Of course I'm not mad at you. I love you both to pieces. You know that.'

The officer slipped outside to let people know the children were found, then came back and tapped Tom on the shoulder. 'I'll carry one if you carry the other. They look like they need some TLC, and we'd better get them checked out by a doctor.'

Tom wiped one arm across his eyes and nodded. 'Look, my little hobbits, we need to get you home as quickly as we can. I bet you're hungry, eh? I can't carry two of you, so the policeman is going to carry you, Hayley. Will you let him do that, darling?'

She looked at him pleadingly, but Ryan was still sobbing against his father's chest.

'You're my big, clever girl to hide like that,'

Tom said softly. 'But I think Ryan is too upset to let a stranger carry him.'

'You're not mad at me?'

'I'm proud of you.'

She gave him a watery smile.

The officer knelt down beside her. 'I'll stay near your daddy all the time.' He held his arms out and she went to him.

When they walked outside, everyone nearby gave a cheer. As they moved through the darkness lit by occasional lamps and floodlights, towards the police car that had driven across the lawn, Andi persuaded an officer to let her through.

Hayley yelled, 'Andi, come and carry me.'

With a quick smile at the police officer, she took the child into her arms.

Tom watched his daughter lay her head on Andi's shoulder and remembered Gail's distorted face, her shrill voice, her lack of care for the children. He didn't even ask what had happened to his wife. He never wanted to see her again as long as he lived. 'Thanks,' he told Andi.

She smiled at him. 'I love your children.' She looked down at Hayley, whose head was close to hers. 'I'm looking forward to hearing about all your adventures, darling, but first let's get you a warm bath.'

'And something to drink? We're thirsty and hungry too.'

'As much as you want to eat and drink,' Tom said, trying to hide a new surge of anger at his ex, who couldn't even bother to feed the children. How hard was it to buy a sandwich?

'Now, let's get you home.'

'We really ought to have them checked by a doctor,' the officer said again.

'I want to go home,' Hayley said, cuddling Andi even more tightly and starting to cry. 'Daddy, take me ho-ome.'

'If that's what you want, that's what we'll do,' Tom told her. If a doctor was needed, then one could come to the house.

★ ★ ★

The three men began to go through the downloaded photos. Jez chose a memory card whose date was close to when he'd been attacked. Perhaps Talbin knew something about the incident that the police didn't.

'Stop! Go back.' Jez leaned closer to study the photo, unable to believe what he was seeing. 'That's my bedroom — and the guy is holding a knife to my throat. How the hell did Talbin get a photo of that?'

Silence seemed to throb around them for a few moments.

'Only way Talbin could have taken that shot,' Craig said at last, 'was if he was there too.'

'I never saw him,' Jez said.

'Were you in any state to see him, with a knife at your throat?'

'I was pretty focused on that knife and I closed my eyes a couple of times. You do when you're terrified.'

'That could explain why the man suddenly left,' Peter said. 'Talbin had got the photos he

357

wanted. It's crazy. He couldn't use them, so why did he do it?'

'Perhaps the photos gave him a sense of power,' Craig said. 'Or perhaps he just hates you.'

'I'd go for that,' Peter agreed. 'He loves getting back at people. I've got photos for my exposé of his face when he's making some poor sod squirm. It's one of the reasons I detest him.'

Again no one spoke then Peter said slowly, as if thinking aloud, 'People have wondered how Talbin gets some of his scoops. Usually a whisper goes round if something's happening. I've been tracking a group of paparazzi for some time now for my article, and a rumour usually comes from several directions. But Talbin is notorious for his uncanny knack of being the only one to find out about some of the prime stories. Legendary, in fact. What if he . . . ? No, he couldn't have . . . Surely, no one would . . . ' He looked from one to the other.

'He must have set up the attack on me,' Jez said, his voice sounding harsh in his own ears. 'All these months since my face was slashed I've been having panic attacks during the night. I've had to have my security with me wherever I go. *All these months!*'

Craig looked at him sympathetically. 'We guessed you weren't sleeping properly. Some mornings your face was — ravaged.'

'I thought I'd kept that to myself.' Anger churned his stomach into acid.

'We'll have to take this to the police,' Peter said. 'Much as I'd like to scoop the news, this is too serious.'

'How do we explain how we got hold of the photos?' Craig asked.

'We tell the truth,' Jez said grimly. 'We'll check with my lawyers, but I doubt the police will do more than reprimand us. I can say I was upset and wanted to delete the photo he'd taken of my scars.' Strange, he realized suddenly. He'd stopped thinking about the scars lately, except when he shaved. Why?

The answer was easy. Sophie. She didn't care whether he was scarred or not, so they'd become unimportant.

'Get Kev on to it,' Craig said. 'He's got friends in the force still. He'll know who to contact. We can leave Talbin to the police.'

Jez nodded. The relief he was feeling made him feel almost light-headed. It was over. Over.

Then there was the sound of a car and the buzzer went.

Craig peered out. 'It's the police.' He pressed the enter button.

As the gates beeped their way open and the car drove into the courtyard, the three men hurried out to see why the police were there. A second police car came slowly inside.

Tom and Andi emerged from the rear of the first car, each carrying a child.

'Thank goodness!' Jez muttered. 'Oh, thank bloody goodness!' He ran to cuddle each child in turn, feeling near to tears with this second lifting of a burden of worry.

Kevin got out of the second car and went to open the door of Tom's house.

'I think I'd better come and help you till Jane's

359

better,' Andi said to Tom. She smiled down at Hayley. 'Would you let me look after you?'

Hayley nodded, exhausted now.

'I'll carry her,' Kevin said. 'She must be heavy.'

But Hayley clung to Andi, so she continued towards the house, talking softly to the child.

Two hours later, with the children fed, washed and in bed, Tom and Andi went to sit down for a rest.

'I can't thank you enough,' he said.

'It's good to be of use.'

'You all right?' He gave her a searching look.

She knew exactly what he meant. 'I'm getting there. In a strange way, it helped today, that I could do something useful, I mean.'

'I can never thank you enough.'

She grinned. 'You could try offering me a cup of coffee. That'd be a start.'

He chuckled, something he hadn't expected to do for a while.

★ ★ ★

Jez went to fetch Sophie from the hospital and check for himself that Jane was all right. She was, but annoyed that they were keeping her in overnight.

As they sat in the back of the taxi, separated from the driver by a glass partition, he brought Sophie up to date on what they'd found out about Talbin.

'So we have a happy ending on all fronts,' she said.

'Yes.'

'What about Gail?'

He shrugged. 'I can't pretend to much interest in her. The sooner Tom's rid of her the better. Sounds like she needs medical treatment. She'll be charged for attacking Jane, as well as for kidnapping. It'll be up to the courts to decide what happens to her.'

'Are the kids all right?'

'Yes. Thanks to your daughter. She's staying at Tom's to help.'

She cuddled up to him with a sigh. 'That's good. Your place or mine?'

'Better go to my place, if you don't mind. Everyone else is there and we have a few loose ends to tie up yet. I'm not sure if Tom has rung his mother. She won't be easy to deal with. And until it's proven that Talbin arranged my damned intruder, my security staff are insisting on maximum care still.'

'That's OK. But I warn you, I'm tired and I won't be much good for anything but sleeping.'

He smiled. 'As long as we're sleeping together.' Then his smile faded. 'I can't believe how quickly you and I have got together. I'm a bit afraid of the bubble bursting.'

She looked up at him from the shelter of his arm. 'It happened to me like this the first time. I met Bill, fell in love, no hassles, no quarrels — well, only little ones — and we were together in every way. Trust me, Jez. It can happen. And it feels the same this time.'

'Do we need to pick up some clothes for you?' he asked.

'We'd better. I feel like I'm wearing a dishrag.'

He leaned forward to speak to the driver then leaned back again to hold her close.

★ ★ ★

As Jez had predicted, the following day was busy with police interviews, not only with questions about the kidnapping, but about Talbin's activities.

Jane insisted on coming home from hospital because she was worried about the children, but found Andi coping brilliantly, so consented to go to bed because her head was very sore and aching.

★ ★ ★

The following day Sophie's son phoned while she and Andi were at her house, getting some more clean clothes. She beckoned Andi and whispered to her to get on the other phone if she wanted to listen in.

'Just a minute, William.' She watched her daughter come to sit nearby, eyes gleaming with mischief. It wasn't fair to William, really, but it was so wonderful to see Andi with that expression on her face that Sophie quashed her own feeling of guilt.

'What's been going on, Mother? Every time I look in the papers there's a photo of you — or of *him*.'

'We've had a bit of excitement.'

'*Excitement!* Danger, you mean. At your age, and with your medical history, you need to live

362

quietly. Kerry and I are really worried about you.'

Why did he always make her feel about ninety and ready to succumb to cancer again? 'I have something to tell you, William.'

'What? You're not ill again?'

'No. This is good news. I'm going to marry Jez Winter.'

Silence, then, 'You can't be serious!'

'Why can't I?'

'A man like that. It'll not last. You're only setting yourself up for misery — and embarrassment. I don't wish to be rude, but does he know you only have one breast? He'll not stick with you, you know.'

'Yes, he will!' Andi said suddenly. 'You're a sorry little rat, William, talking to Mum like that. I can't believe you're my brother. I wish you weren't. And for your information, Jez loves Mum and she loves him. They're really happy together.'

'Andi, it's all right,' Sophie said.

'Sorry, Mum, but I couldn't bear to hear him saying things like that to you.'

'Was she listening in?' William asked in tones of outrage.

'Yes. She deserved a treat. We knew you'd react in a ridiculous way, William.'

He was almost gobbling with anger, unable to speak for a moment or two, so she took the opportunity to add, 'Don't talk to me again till you can be civil about Jez.'

She and Andi ended the call, then fell into each other's arms, hugging and laughing.

'What a plonker! He'll come and apologize,'

Andi said, mopping her eyes. 'He's too afraid of being cut out of your will.'

Sophie gave her daughter another hug. It was almost worth quarrelling with William to feel so close to Andi. She held her at arm's length. 'You're all right about me and Jez now?'

'Yes. He's not like the papers say, is he? He makes a lovely granddad. And those tunes he's written for the kids are great. I wouldn't be surprised if he didn't get hits out of them.' She looked at her mother. 'You're crying? Is something wrong?'

'No. I'm just so happy.'

'Me, too,' Andi said in tones of surprise, blinking her eyes furiously.

And then Sophie knew that her daughter really had turned the corner. There would be days when Andi felt down but she was finding herself at last, even though the police had been unable to prove who had attacked her.

Andi shoved a tissue at her. 'Wipe your face and stop crying, Mum. We're happy, remember?'

★   ★   ★

In the cottage that same evening Tom sat staring at the TV, not seeing anything. His ex had been committed to a secure institution for violent offenders and had been deemed to be unfit to plead. That made him feel very sad. He hoped they could sort her out. She was still the children's mother, after all.

The phone rang and he hesitated, then picked it up. 'Hi, Mum.'

364

'How are you?'

'I'm all right. So are the children.'

'And Gail?'

He explained.

'That's sad.'

'Yeah.'

'Brian and I were wondering if we could come down to visit you and the children this weekend?'

'Of course you can. And look, you can have my bedroom and I'll sleep on the couch. It's too far to drive here and back in one day.'

'Well, I'll see what Brian says. I'll get him to ring you with the details in a day or two.'

He was glad she was no longer badgering him about Gail, glad she was coming to see the children. He'd have to make sure she didn't bump into Jez, though. He turned to see Jane standing there.

'Not bad news?'

'No. How about a cup of tea?'

'Lovely. I'll make it.'

'You're looking a lot better.'

'Oh, I'm back to normal now. I'm just glad it's all over.'

It'd never quite be over, with Gail locked away, he thought, because she'd always be the children's mother. But you had to get on with your life, and he had Hayley and Ryan, who didn't seem to have suffered any harm from the incident. He had a job too, and Jez, as well as Mum and Dad. That was enough for now.

Jane came back with two steaming mugs and a plate of biscuits on a tray. It felt comfortable. He needed some peace and quiet, and was grateful to his father for providing it.

Well, in the evenings he had peace and quiet. In the daytime he and Jez were spending a lot of time in the studio. He was learning so much.

Epilogue

Two weeks later, Jez invited everyone to take tea with him. 'It's a special occasion,' he said, but refused to tell them why.

He waited till everyone was gathered then picked up his guitar and struck a loud chord. They looked at him expectantly but it was a moment or two before he could speak, because he'd suddenly realized that these people were more than employees or acquaintances. They were friends, every single one of them.

'I have an announcement to make,' he said, 'a very important one. You all know that Sophie and I intend to get married . . . well, we've booked the day and you're all invited. It's next week. We're not making a big thing of it, just the family, because there's less chance of the press finding out that way.' He looked across at Peter. 'We have our own official press rep, who will do what's necessary and report on the wedding.'

Peter nodded.

'Tom is going to be best man, and Andi — '

'Is going to be best woman,' she said, with one of her cheeky grins. 'Equal treatment for women, please.'

Everyone laughed.

Andi leaned towards her mother. 'Pity Willi and Co have to come. They're bound to be wearing sour faces.'

'Shh. He can't help it.' But she agreed with

her daughter. Poor William. He'd apologized, but would never be happy about her second marriage, or about anything really. Some people didn't seem capable of enjoying life. But he was still her son and she loved him.

'The second thing, not quite as important but still good news, is that I've decided to record an album for little children.'

'Told you so,' Andi whispered to Tom.

'Hayley, come and sing our first song for everyone.'

She walked out, very self-important, and stood next to her grandfather. When he nodded and played a note, she began to sing. He and her father provided soft support for the tune and harmonies to go with it.

One Little Birdie . . .

Sophie watched them with happy tears in her eyes, turned to Andi and exchanged smiles.

She almost didn't dare tempt fate by thinking it, but all was right with her world.

And she was quite sure she and Jez would be happy together. She caught his eye and they smiled across the room at one another.

She was so glad she'd come to live in Chestnut Lane.

We do hope that you have enjoyed reading this large print book.

Did you know that all of our titles are available for purchase?

We publish a wide range of high quality large print books including:
Romances, Mysteries, Classics
General Fiction
Non Fiction and Westerns

Special interest titles available in large print are:
The Little Oxford Dictionary
Music Book
Song Book
Hymn Book
Service Book

Also available from us courtesy of Oxford University Press:
Young Readers' Dictionary
(large print edition)
Young Readers' Thesaurus
(large print edition)

For further information or a free brochure, please contact us at:
Ulverscroft Large Print Books Ltd.,
The Green, Bradgate Road, Anstey,
Leicester, LE7 7FU, England.
Tel: (00 44) 0116 236 4325
Fax: (00 44) 0116 234 0205

YESTERDAY'S GIRL

Anna Jacobs

The Great War opened up an exciting new career for Vi in London. But that was yesterday. Now, the war is over, her husband is dead and she needs to pick up the pieces of her life. On her way home she meets a man who needs her help. Recently demobbed, Joss Bentley has no job or home, and with his wife dead, there's a new baby to care for — and it's not his. As he searches grimly for its real father, he runs up against people who will use any means necessary to conceal dark secrets . . . and Vi finds herself faced with conflicting loyalties. Whichever way she moves it seems she'll hurt someone — or they'll hurt her . . .